CHILD OF THE ALLIANCE

PALACE OF THE ORNAMENTS

BOOK THREE

KYLIE QUILLINAN

First published in Australia in 2023.

ABN 34 112 708 734

kyliequillinan.com

A catalogue record for this book is available from the National Library of Australia

Ebook ISBN: 9781922852267

Paperback ISBN: 9781922852274

Large print ISBN: 9781922852281

Hardcover ISBN: 9781922852298

Audiobook ISBN: 9781922852458

This is a work of fiction. Any similarity between the characters and situations within its pages and places or persons, living or dead, is unintentional and coincidental.

Cover art by 100 Covers.

Edited by MS Novak.

Proudly independent. Please support indie authors by legally purchasing their work.

This work uses Australian spelling and grammar.

LP16012025

CHAPTER 1

My first evening with Pharaoh had been nothing like I expected. I hadn't even departed for his palace before learning Half had been stabbed, and that he and Tall were hidden in the grounds of the Palace of the Ornaments.

The banquet with Pharaoh and his queen was, quite frankly, boring, with little to distract me from my worries about whether Half still lived. My mind shied away from remembering what happened after the banquet and the mortification of waiting, naked, for Pharaoh's arrival. I had cried all the way back to the Palace.

Now I was back within its walls and in just a few minutes, I would learn whether Half was still alive. Whether my maids had managed to get him and Tall into my chambers without anyone discovering them. If they had been caught, there was probably nothing I could do for them. Or for myself, for that matter. We would likely all be executed for breaking what seemed to be the Palace's most fundamental rule: no unmodified men permitted inside.

I took a deep breath to steady myself as I made my way up to the main entrance. As much as I wanted to race along the path, I forced myself to walk steadily and tried not to look like I hurried in case anyone was watching. The door guards admitted me without question.

I encountered only a servant woman on the way to my chambers. Her face was familiar — perhaps she served the Ornaments in the dining chamber where I sometimes broke my fast. She kept her gaze on the floor as we passed each other.

I reached my chambers to find the door barred from the inside. Of course, they wouldn't want to risk any unexpected visitors coming in. I knocked.

"It's me," I said quietly.

Merytre let me in and was quick to bar the door again behind me.

"Oh, my lady," she whispered. "It is terrible."

"Khaemmalu said he was alive."

But he knew only as much as had happened while they were outside and his information was from several hours ago. The situation might have changed since then.

"He is, although he is mortally injured," Merytre said. "He needs a physician, but even if we could bring one, Ahmose can't say he will definitely live."

I supposed the decision they had been trying to make was whether it was worth the risk to bring in a physician, or if Half would likely die anyway. What a terrible thing to have to decide.

I went straight to the spare bedchamber. Ishtar had slept in here before Pharaoh made her an Ornament and she received chambers of her own. Before that, I had thought we would use this bedchamber for Tall and Half if they had reason to flee Pharaoh's palace. I hadn't expected that might be so soon.

The coppery scent of blood hit me as I entered the chamber. Half lay on the bed, still and pale. They had removed his shirt and Ettu held a bundle of linen cloths to his belly, but they were already soaked through. Blood coated her arms to her elbows and was splattered over her gown. Ahmose crouched on the floor, sorting through a pile of the little linen packets I recognised as her herb supplies. She held her broken arm to her chest, but having only one hand available didn't seem to slow her down, even if she left bloody fingerprints on everything she touched. Tall stood in the corner, shoulders hunched as he flapped his hands near his face and muttered. I could only make out bits of what he said. Men. Danger. Flee. Belly.

As I stood frozen in the doorway, Ettu looked up.

"He lives," she said brokenly, "although perhaps not for much longer."

"What can I do?" I asked.

Merytre came to stand beside me. The warmth of her body was reassuring and I found myself leaning against her. She didn't move away.

"He needs a physician," Ahmose said from the floor. "I have done what I can, but it's not enough. The blade missed his organs, as far as I can tell, but there is too much blood."

"Where can we locate a physician?" I asked.

She frowned and fidgeted with one of the herb packets. "We cannot call for the Palace physician. Not to treat a man who shouldn't even be here."

"What about a priestess?" I asked. "Would praying over him help?"

"He needs more than prayers at this point," Ahmose said. "He needs someone to stitch wherever the blood is coming from. I have packed the wound with honey and grease, but it's not enough."

"Someone must know a physician we can trust." Surely I wasn't the first Ornament to need a discreet physician. But who could I entrust with such a secret? Tiye? Maybe, but could I be certain she wouldn't take the opportunity to remove a competitor and report me to the administrators? Maybe Henut-mire. Ettu had smuggled the letter for Nebtu's family out of the

Palace for her. If she knew it was Half who had seen her letter to a courier, she might feel obliged to help.

My mind whirled furiously and I barely noticed Ahmose tipping little packets into two bottles. She got to her feet with a groan and filled the bottles from a water jug which sat on a nearby shelf, before stoppering them and giving them a quick shake.

"Somebody needs to go for a physician." She pressed the bottles into my hands. "Or even a healer. I know a little, but not enough to treat a wound like this. Someone must go out and get help. He has no chance of survival otherwise."

My fingers were slow to clasp the bottles and I almost dropped them.

"Me?" I asked.

"You or Merytre." Her gaze darted between us. "There is nobody else. Both Ettu and I would raise too many questions if anyone saw us covered in blood like this, and we cannot spare the time it would take to fetch bathing water and make one of us presentable. Either you or Merytre must find someone who can treat Half. Quickly now. There is no time to waste."

She gestured for me to leave and my feet obeyed, carrying me back out to the main sitting chamber. Merytre followed, her face pale and tense. We looked at each other and I suppose each of us wondered who should go.

"I can do it," she said. "But I don't know where to find a physician. I might not be back in time to…"

Her voice trailed away.

"I will go," I said.

"You know no more than I do," she said. "And you have never even been outside the gates since the night you arrived. I should do it."

Half wouldn't be here if it wasn't for me. He would still be safe at Dur-Kurigalzu, my father's palace in Babylon. If anyone was to risk going out to find a physician, it should be me.

CHAPTER 2

As I hurried through the Palace, clutching Ahmose's bottles, I tried to compose myself. I would be of no use to Half if I panicked and couldn't think clearly. The first step was to get out of the Palace grounds. Then find someone who could direct me to a physician. I would simply go to the nearest house, knock on the door, and ask. If they didn't know where to find a physician, I would go to the next house. So I had a plan, no matter how simple. That calmed me a little.

At the Palace's main entrance, the guards seemed surprised to see me leaving the building again so soon. I braced myself for questions, ready to tell them my purpose was none of their concern, but they didn't ask.

I hurried along the path to the gates. I would wait to make sure the guards there were the same ones as earlier before I drank the potion. I couldn't afford the time it would take to return for another dose if the guards had already changed. Please Marduk, let them have reason to open the gates very soon.

I had almost forgotten Khaemmalu would still be on duty until I heard his voice.

"My lady," he said softly. "There is a sheltered spot just ahead on your left."

I gave no indication I heard him in case anyone was watching, but when I reached the place where a row of shrubs provided a convenient screen, I left the path and slipped behind them. Khaemmalu was already there.

"I am going to fetch a physician," I said. "The wounds need to be stitched."

There was no point in not telling him. I could hardly avoid him seeing me leave now.

"How do you intend to get past the guards?" He made a point of looking down to the bottles in my hands, although I doubted he hadn't already seen them. Hopefully the darkness hid the blood smears from Ahmose. "A spell, I presume?"

I clutched the bottles more tightly, suddenly fearing he might take them from me.

"It would be best if you don't know any details," I said. "If something goes wrong, you can still say you know nothing about how anyone was getting out."

"I am already involved." He spoke very quietly. "If I was going to turn you in, I would have done it hours ago. I certainly wouldn't have helped your women smuggle two men into the Palace."

I had become so accustomed to not trusting anyone that it was hard to acknowledge he had given me no reason for distrust.

"The potion will allow me to walk past the guards," I admitted.

"How long does it last?" If he doubted me, his face gave no sign of it.

"Maybe twelve hours, but I need to be back before the day guards start their shift." Half wouldn't last that long anyway from what Ahmose had said.

"I assume the second bottle is for the physician," he said, with a nod towards my hands.

"It is."

"And you know where to find a physician?"

"Not yet," I admitted.

"I will go. I know where he lives."

I hesitated, desperately wanting to say yes, yet still fearing he might betray us. But he already knew I was planning to leave and he knew how I would do it. If he had any intention of betrayal, he already had more than enough information, not to mention the two unmodified men he knew were hidden in my chambers.

"It will be faster for me to go," he said. "Even if I were to give you directions, you might forget them or take a wrong turn. Give me the potion. The guards know I shouldn't be leaving at this hour and they will likely report me if they see me."

"What will you do if the physician isn't at home?" I wanted to trust him, but I couldn't make myself hand him the bottles.

"I will find a healer. My sister and her husband live not far from here. They will know where to locate one."

"I don't want anyone else involved." The more people who knew, the greater the risk.

I searched his face, wishing the darkness didn't conceal so much. How could I tell whether he was lying if I couldn't even see his eyes properly?

"You can trust them," he said. "They won't ask any questions and I won't tell them any more than I must."

There really was no other option. Half's life was at stake and it seemed trusting Khaemmalu was his best chance. I thrust the bottles at him.

"Go," I said. "As fast as you can."

"Do I just drink it?"

"Picture the guards' faces as you do. It won't shield you against anyone you don't think of as you drink it, and it will only work as long as they don't look too hard, so you must be quiet as you pass them."

"Wait here," he said. "Stay in the shadows and don't move lest someone sees you. If anyone finds you, pretend you don't know how you got out here. They will think you must have walked in your sleep and are unlikely to question you further. I will return as quickly as I can."

Then he was gone, slipping silently away in the darkness.

A couple of paces ahead of me stood a dom palm. I leaned against its trunk, hoping it would shield me from view. We would be merely one shadow, not two. The cool night air made me shiver and insects bit my arms and face. I didn't dare slap them away.

At one point, I heard the whisper of footsteps pass not far from me. I held my breath and didn't even so much as blink. The footsteps moved on, and I could only pray whoever it was had left and wasn't merely waiting a little further past me in the shadows.

To distract myself from the cold and the insects, I planned what I would do when Khaemmalu returned. The physician would be a man and I would need to get him to my chambers without anyone seeing him. I didn't even know how they got Tall and Half in earlier, but Khaemmalu did. Hopefully we could use the same route and avoid notice again.

I had no sense of how much time had passed, hidden as I was in the shadows and without any view of the moon. Had Khaemmalu managed to get out yet? Was Half even still alive? Had Tall managed to tell someone what happened?

My feet ached and the insects found their way under my skirt, leaving stinging bites around my ankles and behind my knees. My eyes were heavy and I was thankful to have something to lean against. I dearly wanted to sit down, but feared drawing attention to myself if I moved. At least standing kept me awake.

It was surely well after midnight before the shrubs rustled and Khaemmalu appeared. Behind him was a woman carrying a basket. She wore a plain shift made of a serviceable fabric and her braids were tied neatly behind her head. Her face looked much like his.

"My sister," Khaemmalu whispered. "Gautseshen. She drank the potion and we slipped in when the guards opened the gates for a messenger."

"Where is the physician?" I asked.

"Away for some time. Gone to care for his ailing mother according to his neighbour. My sister, however, is an excellent seamstress and tells me she has some experience in stitching wounds. You can trust her."

At least it would be easier to get a woman to my chambers.

"Come then," I said to her. "We must hurry."

Gautseshen pressed her hand briefly against Khaemmalu's arm, as if to reassure him. We left him standing in the shadows.

CHAPTER 3

"*D*o not speak until we reach my chambers," I said to Gautseshen as we approached the front doors. "If any explanations are required, I will do the talking."

We reached the guards and I readied myself for their questions about Gautseshen's identity, but they said nothing, only held the doors open for us. They must have assumed any woman who was inside the gates already had approval to be here.

We hurried in and I prayed to Marduk they didn't need to report to the administrators about anyone who went in or out overnight. If someone questioned me later, I would say she was a servant I happened to encounter while I was out walking and I didn't know her name. Hopefully Gautseshen would be long gone before anyone came asking questions.

We passed two female servants, an Ornament whose face I didn't recognise, and a runner boy who was too intent on his task to spare me any more than a glance. I walked as swiftly as I dared without giving the appearance of haste.

By the time we climbed the stairs to the third floor, I was so tightly wound that I could hardly breathe. We were so close, but we might yet encounter someone who would have reason to ask who Gautseshen was. Please don't let it be Panouk, I prayed. Or Amankhau. Of anyone who might see us, the chief administrator and his second would be the worst. Someone else might assume Gautseshen was merely a lady's maid they had never seen before, or perhaps a servant I had summoned for some reason or another. Panouk and Amankhau would know she shouldn't be here.

But Marduk must have heard my prayers, for we encountered nobody else. At my chambers, Merytre stood in front of the closed door, watching for my return. The relief on her face was obvious and she didn't seem surprised to see Gautseshen, even though the woman could hardly be a physician.

"Thank the gods," Merytre said softly as she closed the door behind us. She slipped the bar into place.

"Is there any news?" I asked over my shoulder, already on my way across the chamber.

"Only that Ahmose says he grows weaker," Merytre said.

Indeed, Half's face was visibly greyer than the last time I saw him. Beads of sweat dotted his forehead. Both Ettu and Ahmose held cloths to his belly to stem the bleeding. Tall still paced and muttered to himself, flapping his hands furiously. Gautseshen took in the scene without a word, then set her basket on the end of the bed.

"Show me," she said. Her voice was calm and if she felt at all intimidated about the situation, she gave no sign of it.

There was nothing I could do to help and, indeed, I would only be in the way if I tried. Instead, I went to Tall.

If he heard me when I said his name, he didn't answer, only continued his pacing and flapping. I set my hand on his arm and he startled, quickly pulling back from me.

"Come, let's go to the sitting chamber," I said.

"Knife!" he said. "Belly!"

"Yes, I know. They are doing what they can for him. Let's get you something to drink. Are you hungry?"

"Danger!" he said. I half expected he might refuse to leave, but he allowed me to lead him down the hallway. "Flee!"

"You did very well to get him here. I don't know how you managed."

"Carry!"

He held out his arms as if to cradle a child and I finally noticed the blood which had dried on the front of his tunic. Surely he didn't carry Half all the way from Pharaoh's palace? It was a walk of at least an hour and Half would be no inconsiderable weight over such a distance, even as small as he was.

"Flee!"

"Sit down," I said. "Merytre, a drink for Tall, please, and something to eat."

As Merytre poured beer and put together a plate from our evening meal, which looked untouched from its delivery, I managed to get Tall onto the couch. I sat beside him.

"Tell me what happened," I said.

"Knife! Belly!" He flapped his hands and didn't look at me.

"Did you see who it was?"

"Man!"

"Which man? Do you know him?" I tried to keep my voice calm and not show how desperate I was for him to say something I could make sense of.

"Man!" Tall's voice rose in pitch and his hands flapped even faster. He was getting too distressed. I shouldn't push him any further, but I had to know what he knew.

"What happened?" I asked again.

"Knife!"

"What is he saying?" Merytre asked as she handed Tall a mug, then set a plate of food beside him on the couch.

I had hardly noticed he was using Babylonian. He understood Egyptian well enough, but couldn't speak it.

"Nothing more than we already knew," I said. "Knife, belly,

man. I think he saw what happened, but he doesn't know who the attacker was."

"Did he tell you that?" she asked. "And what is he doing with his hands?"

Tall had set the mug on the floor and was flapping his hands again.

"He does that when he is anxious," I said. "I think it helps him to feel calmer."

She eyed him, a wary look on her face.

"He is a little odd," I said, "but he is a good man and we can trust him."

Merytre nodded but still looked uncertain, as if Tall's strangeness disturbed her. She said nothing further, only went to sit in a nearby chair.

"Drink," I said, picking up the mug and holding it out to Tall. "Then try again to tell me what happened."

He took a sip, then seemed to realise how thirsty he was. He drained the mug and Merytre rose to fill it again for him.

"What else did you see?" I asked.

Tall's gaze met mine briefly, then darted around the chamber. I had never seen him so agitated, but then, he had probably never before witnessed an attempted murder.

"Danger!" he said. "Flee!"

"You did exactly what you were supposed to," I said. "You knew to come here if you needed to flee."

There could surely be no better demonstration of the fact that Tall understood everything around him, even if he couldn't express himself. He knew they needed to leave Pharaoh's palace and he knew to bring Half here. Despite how upset he was, he must have remembered to bring Ahmose's potions and to wait until they saw the faces of the gate guards before both he and Half drank. There were so many details he needed to get right in order to reach us and he did it all. I wasn't sure I would have had the presence of mind to do all that he had.

"What can you tell me about the danger?" I asked.

"Pharaoh!" He finished his drink and set the mug on the floor again so he could resume flapping his hands.

"Pharaoh is in danger?" Tall knew what had happened. I just had to find the right words to help him express it.

"Pharaoh! Danger!"

"What is he saying now?" Merytre asked.

"There is some danger to Pharaoh. Maybe that's why Half was stabbed. He saw something he shouldn't have."

"Guard!" Tall said.

"Which guard?"

"Man!"

"One of Pharaoh's guards?"

But if Tall knew the man's identity, he didn't seem to be able to tell me.

"He is talking about a guard," I said to Merytre. "But I don't know whether he means the guard is involved in the danger to Pharaoh, or that it was a guard who stabbed Half."

"That would certainly suggest Half saw something he wasn't meant to," she said.

"Or heard something."

No matter how I asked, Tall didn't seem able to tell me anything else.

"You should eat," I said finally. As frustrated as I was, Tall surely felt it more. How terrible it must be for him to know what had happened but be unable to say what he needed to.

It was a long time before Gautseshen emerged. She was drenched in blood to halfway up her arms. A bloody smear across one cheek was evidence she had wiped her hand across her face at some point.

"I have done what I can for him," she said. "Whether he lives is up to the gods now. The bleeding has stopped, but he lost a fearsome amount of blood and the wound might yet turn putrid. If it does, I fear there is nothing anyone will be able to do for him."

"Is he awake?" I asked.

"Unconscious," she said. "He had been dosed with something before I arrived. It was fortunate for him he wasn't awake while I stitched him back together."

"Will you stay until he wakes?" She looked exhausted and I felt bad about asking, but we needed her. "There might be something more you can do for him."

"I need to go home," she said. "I have a babe who is still nursing and I must be back before he gets hungry."

She glanced towards the table laden with food and seemed to hesitate. The food here was surely finer than whatever she had at home and likely more plentiful as well.

"At least stay long enough to eat something," I said. "And fill your basket too. They will bring more food for us if we ask, so take as much as you want."

Merytre had brought a bucket of washing water and a linen cloth from the bathing chamber. She must have sent for the water after I left. Gautseshen hesitated only a moment before she went to wash her arms. Merytre helped her clean the blood from her face.

While Gautseshen ate, I tried to figure out what to say to her. Khaemmalu had said we could trust her, and he surely wouldn't have brought her if he thought otherwise, but I felt I needed to impress on her the seriousness of our situation. She must have figured out what I was thinking.

"You don't need to say it," she said. "I know unmodified men aren't permitted inside the Palace. Whatever happened tonight was dire indeed, but he must be important for you to go to so much effort to save him. I will tell nobody what I have seen here."

"He wouldn't even be in Egypt if it weren't for me," I said.

"Khaemmalu says we can trust you," she replied.

I blinked in surprise. What an odd thing to say. It should be me wondering whether I could trust her.

"Things are always changing," she said, setting her empty plate aside. She must have been hungry indeed to have eaten so fast. "Even when it seems they don't. Those who do evil will be punished eventually and the gods will reward the just."

I supposed she must be talking about the man who stabbed Half.

"If I find out who he is, I will make certain he is punished," I said.

"Send Khaemmalu to fetch me if you need me again," she said as she rose. I started to get up, but she waved me away. "You don't need to come. I can find my way out."

At the door, Gautseshen turned back to me.

"You are wise to keep your door barred," she said and slipped out before I could ask her why.

Merytre quickly barred the door again.

"What did she mean?" I asked.

"It is common knowledge that women have disappeared from here," she said, making her way back to the table where our meal waited. She eyed the remaining food, but apparently decided she didn't want any after all. She came to sit with me instead.

"You think people outside the Palace know?" I asked.

"Of course they do. Not every servant who works in the Palace also lives here. Some return to their own homes after their shift is over. They talk to their families and their friends. Some of those who have disappeared have family here in Thebes. They tell folk about how they never heard from the woman again, regardless of what the administrators say."

"I suppose you are right," I said. "It's hardly a secret."

I had almost forgotten about Tall while we were speaking and only now noticed he was asleep on the couch, curled up like a child. His mug and empty plate sat neatly on the floor.

"Should we move him to one of the chambers?" Merytre asked. "He could use mine for tonight and I can sleep on a couch."

"I suppose it's safe for him to be out here as long as we keep the door barred," I said. "Tomorrow will be soon enough to figure out where everyone is going to sleep."

CHAPTER 4

Shortly after Gautseshen left, Ahmose came out to the sitting chamber. She had always looked old to my eyes, withered and stooped as she was, but she seemed to have aged even more tonight. Blood splattered her chest and arms.

"I should have sent a runner for more water." Merytre quickly got to her feet. "I will go right now."

She slipped out into the hallway to find a runner boy, closing the door swiftly behind her lest anyone pass by and spot Tall asleep on the couch or Ahmose covered in blood. Ahmose leaned against the wall and closed her eyes. I supposed she didn't want to sit down and get blood all over a chair. That would be hard to explain if we had to ask for it to be cleaned.

"He is resting," she said before I could ask. "And he seems peaceful enough."

"Will he live?" I couldn't stop myself from asking, despite what Gautseshen had already said. Ahmose knew Half, after all. Perhaps she had seen some sign a stranger would miss.

"I don't know and that is the truth," she said without opening her eyes. "If his body is stronger than it looks, he might."

I had never thought about whether Half looked strong. He

might only be half as tall as a man, but his mind worked no less well than anyone else's. I had assumed his body would be just as strong too.

"I suppose all we can do for him now is pray," I said.

"Amun preserve him," Ahmose muttered.

Merytre returned to say a runner boy was bringing the water.

"I will wait in the hallway," she said, her gaze darting between Ahmose and Tall. "We can hardly have him bring the buckets inside."

She slipped back out again and I got up to pour Ahmose some beer. She took the mug with a nod and seemed too exhausted to speak further. When the water arrived, Merytre brought the buckets in and carried them down to the bathing chamber. While Ahmose went to clean herself, I kicked off my sandals and tucked my feet beneath me on the couch.

"I could sit up with him," Merytre offered with a nod at Tall when she returned. "We cannot communicate since we speak no language in common, but at least there would be someone here if he were to wake."

"No, go to bed. I will stay with him."

He might be confused about waking in a strange place, or he might be distressed about Half. I didn't let myself hope he would wake with the words to explain whatever he saw. Merytre shrugged and headed off to her bedchamber.

"I don't think any of us remembered to ask." She stopped in the doorway and turned back to me. "How was the banquet?"

I had almost forgotten everything that happened before I returned. Had almost forgotten I even left the Palace grounds tonight or the banquet Pharaoh invited me to as a thank you for saving his life in the boating accident. It had been an uncomfortable event, seated as I was on the dais with Pharaoh and his queen, Lady Isis, neither of whom were interested in conversing with me.

But it was what happened afterwards that caused me to leave

the palace in tears. The way I was taken to a chamber and told to undress. The way Pharaoh merely lay himself down on top of me, then left when he was finished. The way he said not a word to me, either before or after. I wasn't yet ready to tell anyone about how awful it had been.

"I will tell you in the morning," I said instead.

Merytre gave me a knowing look, as if she understood why it had taken me so long to find a response. She went off to bed without saying anything else.

Had Ishtar's experience with Pharaoh been the same as mine? She had spent the night with him more than once and he had wooed her from what I saw. Maybe they chatted first. Perhaps he even kissed her. What would that be like? I had never been kissed by a man. I supposed I never would be now unless Pharaoh thought to do such a thing.

I woke with a start when Tall rose from the couch. He gave me an apologetic look, as if he had been trying not to disturb me. I didn't even remember lying down and had no sense of how long I had slept. The chamber was still dark, although I sensed that dawn was close.

In the spare bedchamber, Half was asleep and seemed to breathe more easily than before, although his skin still looked clammy. Ettu slept too, her chair pulled up beside him and her head on the bed. Her hand was on Half's wrist, as if she wanted to feel whether his pulse still beat. She stirred and sat up when Tall and I came in. Her wig was crooked and she had blood smeared down the side of her neck, although she had washed her hands and changed her gown since I last saw her.

"He lives," I said. "That is a good thing."

"Yes," she said. "It is maybe more than I expected by now."

"His face isn't quite as pale," I added.

She studied him.

"Hmm," was all she said and I figured that meant she disagreed.

"Has he said anything?" I asked.

If Tall saw the person who attacked him, surely Half did too.

"Not a word, but Ahmose dosed him well to make sure he wouldn't know he was being stitched back together. She said her potion would take a few hours to wear off." Ettu got to her feet with a groan. "Oh, my back."

"I can sit with him for a while," I said. "You go get some sleep."

"I slept a bit. It was enough."

"At least get yourself something to drink. You don't need to be here every moment."

"I want to, though."

"He is important to you," I said, feeling rather clumsy. We had never discussed her feelings for Half, although I had seen enough to be certain she cared for him.

"He is a good man." Her voice was a little defensive as if she expected criticism. "I know he looks different, but what does that matter?"

"Different!" Tall said.

He had been so quiet, I had forgotten he followed me down the hallway.

"Yes, you are both different," I said. "You are a good man too, though. To carry Half all the way here."

"Buddy!"

A sob choked my throat and I could only nod. We all needed a friend like Tall.

Ettu finally left once I promised to fetch her if Half even so much as stirred. She took Tall with her, saying he needed something else to wear. I had become so used to seeing blood all over everyone, I had forgotten the dried stains on his clothes. It was also the first time I realised both Tall and Half still wore tunics. Had nobody in Pharaoh's palace offered them a *shendyt* like other men wore, or had they chosen to continue dressing like Babylonians?

I sat in the chair Ettu had vacated. Half breathed shallowly but steadily. With a blanket drawn up to his shoulders concealing his injury, anyone who saw him now might think he was gravely unwell but not mortally injured.

Some time later, he stirred, then opened his eyes. He gazed blearily around the chamber before he saw me. He studied me as if trying to remember who I was.

"Princess." His mouth shaped the words, but I could barely hear him.

"You are safe. We brought a healer to treat you and Ahmose helped as well. You need to rest now. Rest and recover."

"Tall?"

"He's here too. He carried you all the way from Pharaoh's palace."

Half's eyes closed and it seemed he had fallen asleep again. I leaned back in the chair, prepared to wait for him to wake. As soon as he had the strength to talk, we needed to find out what had happened.

CHAPTER 5

Half woke again just moments before Ettu returned. She shot me a look and I knew she was remembering my promise to fetch her if he stirred. I gave her an apologetic shrug, but she only turned her attention to Half. She knew her place too well to comment on my remissness.

She fussed over him, wiping the blood splatters from his arms with a wet cloth and straightening his blanket. Ahmose came to check his injury with what looked to me like a practiced eye, even if she claimed to have little experience with such wounds. She made him drink a herbal concoction she had mixed with some beer. Half groaned and spluttered, muttering about its evil taste, but he sipped enough of it to satisfy her.

I had forgotten about my lady's maids who came every morning to bathe and dress me until Merytre said she had sent them away.

"I told them you were unwell and had not yet risen from your bed," she said.

"Is there any chance someone might send a physician?" I asked.

The last thing we needed was a stranger trying to force his

way in to examine me. We would have to keep my maids away while Half recovered, and I suppose claiming I was ill myself was as good an excuse as any.

"We will keep the door barred at all times," Merytre said. "We cannot claim you are sick for long without raising concern, but it buys us a couple of days at least. If anyone comes, we will say you have told us to refuse all visitors."

I supposed in that time he would either start to recover… or he would die.

There was nothing I could do for Half and he was clearly too weak for questions. I felt like I was taking up space in the chamber, so I left him with Ettu and Ahmose. Before I even reached the door, Ettu was once again in the chair beside his bed, leaning over to whisper to him.

Merytre insisted on helping me bathe and dress, although I told her I was perfectly capable of doing it myself. The kitchen servants brought breakfast and she made them leave it in the hallway, telling them she wanted no disturbance while I was unwell. She brought the dishes in herself only once the servants were gone.

When I went out to the sitting chamber, Tall was perched on a couch, his shoulders slumped and his mouth downturned. He looked sad and lost.

"Tall, are you hungry?" I asked, trying to sound cheery.

He gave me a startled look and flapped his hands. I went to sit beside him and took his hand, meaning to reassure him, but he gave a startled squawk and leaned away from me so abruptly that he fell off the couch. It was only then I noticed the woman's shift he wore. Someone had shortened it to knee-length for him, although the hem wasn't stitched. Either Ettu or Merytre must have done it so he at least had something clean to wear until we could get other clothes for him.

"Tall, it's all right."

I reached to help him, but he shrank away from me. He curled himself into a ball where he had fallen and hugged his knees to his chest.

"What is wrong with him?" Merytre asked.

"I think I startled him."

She studied him and I expected her to make some comment about his strangeness.

"Perhaps he doesn't like to be touched," she said instead, her voice thoughtful. "There was this girl when I was a child. The daughter of a neighbour. He reminds me of her. She used to flap her hands in the same way and she would scream as if she had been grievously wounded if someone touched her. She didn't like wearing clothes either. They made her skin hurt and she often took them off and wandered around completely naked."

"What happened to her?"

"I don't remember. Strange, I haven't thought about her in years. In my memory, she was there one day and then just gone. I'm sure I must have known where she went, but I don't remember it now."

Tall continued to rock and hold himself. His breath came in shudders. Was this all because I touched his hands? I had never seen him react like this before. When we sailed along the Great River, he had offered me his hand to help me down from the boat. Why didn't he react the same way when I touched him then?

"Tall, I'm sorry," I said softly. "I only meant to reassure you. I didn't realise it would upset you so much."

He closed his eyes and seemed to hold himself more tightly.

"Would you like something to eat?" I forced a brightness I didn't feel into my voice. "We have food sent to us at breakfast and dinner so we don't have to eat in a dining chamber with everyone else. There is fresh bread and warm gruel, plenty of fruit, and there's always at least two kinds of cheese."

I didn't think Tall was listening, but eventually he looked at me.

"Cheese!"

"Would you like some? I will show you where it is. They always send far too much food."

He looked away and rocked for another few moments. Then he uncurled and got to his feet.

"Cheese!" He sounded more cheerful now.

"Come on," I said. "It's over here."

I pointed out the cheese and showed him the crockery, then stepped away. Perhaps I should leave him alone for a bit. Give him time to come back to himself.

Merytre busied herself with taking food to Ahmose and Ettu.

"Does Half want anything?" I asked when she returned.

"Ahmose said it's best if he doesn't try to eat yet, but he can have some soup tonight," she said. "I will tell the kitchen you are unwell and have asked for soup."

I picked at my gruel but found I had little appetite. I suppose Khaemmalu really couldn't have betrayed us or the administrators would have already been in my chambers demanding answers. And Gautseshen must have gotten out safely. Likely anyone who saw her in the hallways would think she was just another servant. There were thousands of servants here after all.

Ettu brought the bowls out, one of which was empty and the other still mostly full. I guessed it was Ettu who hadn't eaten. She met my eyes and gave me a wobbly smile.

"How is he?" I asked.

"Determined to live," she said. "Past that, I don't know. Ahmose said if he survived the night, he had at least a chance. He is weak and confused, which apparently is a sign of blood loss. Ahmose and Gautseshen were worried he had lost too much blood, but Ahmose seems to think if that was going to kill him, he would already be dead."

"If Half has decided he will live, then I think he will," I said.

Ettu set the bowls down abruptly. She covered her face with her hands and her shoulders shook. I went to her.

"Ettu?" I asked. I reached for her, then pulled back, uncertain whether I had meant to pat her shoulder or put my arm around her.

She took a few deep breaths and wiped her eyes before lowering her hands.

"It was just such a shock," she said. "Here I was, thinking he was safe in Pharaoh's palace, only for him to turn up here and in such a condition..." She paused to wipe her eyes again. "I truly don't know how he made it through the night."

"He has much to live for, it would seem," I said. "In situations like this, a man needs a reason to live. You can give him that."

She gave me a funny little twisted smile.

"He has not had an easy life," she said. "And it would be unsurprising if he was bitter and resentful about the lot the gods gave him. But he is not. He is kind and thoughtful, and probably the most intelligent man I have ever met."

"Does he feel the same about you?"

"I doubt he thinks I am the most intelligent man he has ever met." Her tone was wry.

"You know what I mean. Does he care for you?"

"I don't know." She looked away, casting her gaze around the chamber as if she wanted to look at anything except me in that moment. I held my tongue as I waited to see if she would volunteer anything else. "He is not the kind of man I ever thought I might love," she said at last. "I'm not sure I ever expected to love anyone. But he is a good man."

"I promised to release you from my service once I bore Pharaoh a son."

"You did." She finally returned her gaze to me.

"Would you want Half to be released at the same time? So you can leave together?"

She looked away and swallowed hard. When she spoke again, her voice was small.

"I don't know," she said. "That was not what I had planned. I wanted to make a new life for myself. I didn't intend to follow a man."

"You don't need to follow him. Couldn't you… I don't see why you couldn't be partners. Decide together where you will go."

A tear slipped down her cheek and she quickly wiped it away.

"I don't know," she said again, sounding more like herself now. "I would need to think about it. It's not something I ever considered."

I had thought she must be planning a future where they would be together. It never occurred to me she might love him, but choose to leave him behind when I released her.

"Think about it," I said. "There are no decisions that need to be made right now."

After all, we didn't even know whether Half would live.

CHAPTER 6

When someone knocked a little while later, Merytre went to stand at the door but made no move to raise the bar. Tall and I sat in silence. It was just the three of us in the sitting chamber at present, as Ettu and Ahmose were in with Half.

"Who is it?" Merytre called.

"It is me," came a familiar voice. "Belet-ili. My lady sent me to ask after her sister. She heard Lady Kassaya was unwell."

"I will tell my lady you called," Merytre said. "You may tell Lady Ishtar she feels unwell but expects to recover within the next couple of days."

"My lady asked me to look at her sister with my own eyes," Belet-ili said through the closed door.

"My lady is not seeing visitors today," Merytre replied. "But thank you for the message."

She waited, but there was nothing further from Belet-ili. She must have left without any other protest.

"It was kind of Lady Ishtar to send her to ask after you," Merytre said to me.

I didn't want to disagree with her, but Ishtar never did

anything for the sake of being kind. There was some other reason she sent Belet-ili. Had she heard something that made her suspect my "illness" was not what it seemed? Why else would she tell Belet-ili to make sure she saw me if not to confirm whether I actually looked unwell?

It was Ishtar herself who came to knock on my door next.

"As I have already told Belet-ili, my lady is not seeing visitors today," Merytre said firmly through the closed door. "I will tell her you came and I'm sure she will want to see you when she feels better."

"She is my sister." Ishtar pounded on the door. "I demand to see her."

"I'm sorry," Merytre said. "There is nothing else I can tell you. My lady is sleeping at present and asked not to be disturbed."

"But she is never ill," Ishtar said. "I want to see her."

She continued to argue with Merytre for some time before finally leaving, although not without a threat to return with the administrators. I could hardly see Panouk breaking down the door to view me with his own eyes, though.

"Do you think she suspects something?" I asked after she had finally left.

Merytre shrugged.

"She is worried about you," she said. "You are the only family she has here, and she surely has few other people she can trust."

"She has Belet-ili and I'm sure she has other maids. Pharaoh would have seen to that." I could hear the bitterness in my voice, but I was too tired to try to hide it.

"As do you," Merytre said. "But you only trust a few."

I let myself sink further back into the couch. I didn't want to argue with her and wasn't even sure why I was making such a fuss. Merytre was probably right. Ishtar might be concerned for me and nothing more. After the abuse she had suffered at Pharaoh's hands, perhaps she was concerned I might have experienced the same. Still, I couldn't risk allowing her into my chambers while Tall and Half were here. It was too much of a peril for all of us if she told Pharaoh about them.

Henutmire sent one of her maids with a small posy of flowers from the gardens. Merytre put them in a mug of water and set it on a table. It gave me a warm feeling to see them there, as if I had a friend. A real friend, not a servant. Ettu spotted them straight away when she next emerged from Half's chamber.

"Who are they from?" she asked with a nod towards the flowers as she poured herself some beer.

"Henutmire," I said. "Isn't that nice of her?"

Ettu settled herself on the couch beside Tall and frowned at me.

"Merytre said Ishtar was here earlier asking after you," she said. "Does it not concern you that so many people seem to have already heard you are supposedly unwell?"

"Only Ishtar and Henutmire." Belet-ili didn't count since she only came because Ishtar sent her.

"But how did the news even reach either of them?" Ettu asked. "And how many others have heard?"

"Why does that bother you?" I asked. "We know gossip spreads fast here."

"I did tell the kitchen servants when I went to ask for soup," Merytre said. "They have probably passed it on."

Ettu sipped her beer.

"I don't know," she said at last. "It just bothers me. I suppose it makes me worry about what else they are saying."

"You fear someone knows about Tall and Half?" I asked.

She sighed and shrugged.

"I don't know," she said. "I'm too exhausted to think clearly at the moment. I'm probably not making any sense."

"How did you get them inside anyway?" I asked. "Nobody has told me yet."

"We put a scarf over Tall's head like that priestess we saw," Ettu said. "The one with the scales on her face. We positioned it so it draped down and covered his face. We wrapped blankets around his shoulders to hide his form. He carried Half and we wrapped him in a blanket too so that nothing could be seen of him. Ettu and I wore scarves as well, so anyone who saw us wouldn't identify us. Then we walked all the way around to one of the back entrances. I thought we would have trouble getting inside, but the guards didn't even ask who we were."

"There are a number of servants who wear scarves over their hair," I said. "Perhaps the guards are used to seeing such a thing."

"That was what gave me the idea," Ettu said. "We must have looked quite ridiculous, but they never questioned us. It was quite late by then and we saw only two people once we were inside. They paid us no attention, so maybe we didn't look as odd as I thought. We made sure there was nobody around before we turned down the final hallway. As far as I know, we got into our suite without anyone else seeing us in that last stretch."

Tall was silent while she spoke and I wondered how he felt about being smuggled inside in such a way.

"We would have heard by now if anyone had suspicions about what you were doing," I said. "The administrators would have come to demand an explanation."

Ettu only nodded. She rubbed her eyes and seemed too tired to say anything else.

"I think I need to recover from my 'illness' quickly," I said. "I will eat in the dining chamber tomorrow morning so I can ask if there's any news."

"I agree we need to know what's happening, but tomorrow might be too soon since we have made you sound so unwell." Ettu sat up straighter and blinked a few times, seemingly trying to look more alert.

"I agree," Merytre added. "Too fast a recovery might only make folk talk even more. I will go to the kitchen again this afternoon. It's always the best place for the most recent news. I will tell them you are starting to feel better, but are still too weak to rise from your bed. No doubt they will pass that on quickly enough. I can ask what news there is while I am there."

There was no point arguing with them if they were both in agreement.

"In the meantime," Ettu said. "We need to make some plans. Figure out how we will conceal Half and Tall on a more permanent basis."

"I suppose my maids are the biggest problem," I said. "Maybe I can say I no longer want them to dress me each morning? That you two will manage it from now on."

"No Ornament would do that," Merytre said quickly. "Most of them delight in having so many women attend to them."

"I agree it would seem suspicious," Ettu said. "We need to make everything appear as normal as possible."

I sighed. For a moment I thought I had found a way to avoid being stripped naked and bathed by ten women every morning.

"The men will need to hide in the spare bedchamber whenever someone comes," Ettu said.

"Maybe we could move your jewels into that chamber and put a lock on the door," Merytre suggested. "After the business with Lady Tiye's stolen jewels, it would not seem unreasonable that you would want to ensure yours are secure."

"Oh, that's a good idea," Ettu said.

"We would need to have someone in to install the lock, though," I said. "And how would we hide Tall and Half while they are here?"

"Lock!" Tall said, surprising me. I had been so absorbed in our conversation I had forgotten he was even in the chamber.

"Yes, buddy," Ettu said. "We need to put a lock on the door so nobody finds you and Half in there."

"Lock!" He frowned at Ettu and flapped his hands.

"What is he saying?" Merytre asked.

"I think he means he can install it," I said. "Merytre, can you get us a lock and some tools?"

"Of course, but how will I explain that you don't want someone to come and install it for you?"

I hadn't thought of that. The administrators would be able to provide what we needed, but they would also expect to send someone to do the job. One of their modified men, who would be quick to report back to them on any suspected anomaly in my chambers.

"What about asking Khaemmalu to get what we need?" Ettu suggested. "We know we can trust him, even if he asks how you will install it."

"I wanted to thank him anyway," I said. "I could go speak with him tonight."

"You are supposed to be unwell and confining yourself to your chambers while you recover," Ettu pointed out.

"Maybe I need some fresh air after spending the day in bed," I retorted. "However we explain it, we need to get a lock on that door as soon as possible. I will have to pretend to be ill until we can secure the door, so the sooner I go out to find Khaemmalu, the better."

"I could go for you," Merytre said.

"No, I will go myself. I owe him a great debt for his help last night."

They nodded and if they thought anything of my insistence on seeing Khaemmalu myself, they didn't say it.

CHAPTER 7

Merytre went to the kitchen again on the pretext of checking they had remembered I wanted soup, and returned with confirmation that nobody seemed to be talking about strange people wandering the hallways last night. On her way back, she encountered Tiye, who asked after me. Merytre told her I was feeling somewhat better after a day of rest and might even go out for some fresh air tonight. She said Tiye nodded and seemed satisfied with her response.

When the servants brought our evening meal, including the soup I supposedly wanted so badly, it took both Ettu and Ahmose to get some into Half who insisted he wasn't hungry. Once Ahmose was finally satisfied he had eaten enough, she left Ettu to watch him and came out to the sitting chamber for her own meal.

"I think he is in more pain than he admits," she said in response to my questioning look. "The confusion seems to have abated, although he is still weaker than I would like. There's nothing else I can do for him, though. I have given him as much poppy seed as I dare."

"Should I ask Khaemmalu to bring Gautseshen again?" I was planning to seek him out tonight anyway.

Ahmose sighed and set her plate aside, the food mostly untouched.

"I don't think anyone can do more for him at this point," she said. "All we can do now is pray. The gods will either heal him or they won't."

It didn't seem enough for us to pray for Half. I wished we could bring a priestess in. There were priestesses here at the Palace, but I didn't know any of them and had no idea whether we could trust them.

"What about that priestess Ettu and I saw in the grounds?" I suggested. "Could we ask her to come and pray for Half?"

"The one with the scaled face? What do you know of her?"

"Nothing really. Tiye said she was a seer, but that her words were unreliable."

"You have only spoken with her the once," Ahmose said. "You don't know whether you can trust her."

"I thought someone who is considered unreliable might not be taken seriously if she claimed I was hiding men in my chambers."

"Are you willing to take the risk, though? You have only Tiye's word as to her reputation. For all you know, the priestess might take one look at Half and Tall, and go straight to the administrators. If she made enough of a fuss, they would surely come to see what it was all about, even if they didn't believe her claims. And when they found the door barred and we refused to admit them, they would know you were hiding something. They would not leave without finding out what it was."

"True." I slumped back into my couch. For a few moments, it had seemed like a good idea.

I waited until after dark before going in search of Khaemmalu. Merytre came with me and we were silent as we made our way through the Palace. There was nothing that could be said where someone might overhear us. We had almost reached the front doors when I spotted a familiar figure.

Nammu seemed to be looking everywhere except at me as we approached each other. We hadn't spoken since she stole Tiye's jewels and told Panouk she had found them in my chambers.

"Good evening, Nammu," Merytre said in a pleasant tone. She, at least, was pretending no ill will existed between us all.

Nammu's gaze slid over her and then, finally, to me. She sneered.

"Why did you do it?" The words came out of my mouth before I realised what I was going to say.

We stopped a few hands widths apart and eyed each other.

"Do what?" Nammu's mouth puckered, as if having to talk to me made the words taste bad.

"Lie about me stealing Tiye's jewels. Try to frame me."

She huffed.

"You think you're better than everyone else," she said.

"That's ridiculous."

"It's true." Her eyes flashed and she took a step towards me. I moved back, a little uneasy now. "You were oh-so-grand and mighty. Coming here thinking you would be Queen of Egypt. The joke's on you, isn't it? You're just one of his women. You're nobody important. Nobody special."

"That doesn't even make any sense." I tried to keep my tone even. She mightn't sound reasonable, but I was determined that I would. "If you are angry about being sent here, remember that was my father's decision. *Your king's* decision. Not mine. I had no more say about coming here than you did."

"That's a lie and you know it," she spat. "Ishtar told me the truth. She said you specifically asked for me and Belet-ili and Ettu to come with you."

"I did not." Exasperation leaked into my voice, despite my intentions. Was this another of Nammu's lies or had Ishtar really said such a thing? "My father decided. Ishtar was there when he said it. She cried when he told us the three of you would still go, regardless of which sister you went with."

"You're a liar," she said. "Ishtar told me you would probably deny it if I ever asked you about it."

"If Ishtar's so good to you, why aren't you serving her?" I asked, then immediately regretted it. It would only antagonise Nammu even more if Ishtar hadn't so much as asked for her.

"Because I serve the Top Ornament," she said with a sneer. "If anyone in this wretched place has a chance of being queen one day, it's her. Not you and not Ishtar. And when Lady Tiye becomes queen, she'll take all her maids with her."

"She might take some of them," I said. "The loyal ones. But you can be certain she won't take you. You've already shown her what kind of person you are. One who lies and steals. Why would she honour you in such a way?"

"She rewarded me. I told her you stole her jewels and she gave me a position with her. She thinks *very highly* of me."

The laugh burst out of me. Nammu actually sounded like she believed her own words. Tiye knew she had lied — one of her maids saw Nammu leaving her chambers when they were unattended — and she only gave Nammu a position to try to find out what her game was.

"I pity you, Nammu," I said, then continued walking.

"It's yourself you should pity," she called after me. "You'll get what you deserve eventually. People like you always do."

I restrained my urge to say anything else and kept walking. Merytre hurried after me.

"What a horrible woman," she said once we were far enough away. "I never had much to do with her while she served you. I didn't know she was so awful."

"I didn't realise she hated me so much. I don't know why."

"Do you think she's telling the truth about Lady Ishtar saying you asked for her to be sent here?"

"Of course not."

Was Ishtar really that cruel? Getting herself with child to avoid being sent to Egypt was about protecting herself and her way of life. It was inconsiderate, but she wasn't trying to be unkind to me, only to save herself from a life she didn't want. But ensuring one of the three women who were being sent all the way to Egypt with me would hate me was mean and spiteful. I didn't like to think that of her.

We had reached the front doors by then, so Merytre said nothing further. The guards held open the doors and wished me a pleasant evening. They didn't seem surprised to see me. Maybe it wasn't uncommon for various women to go walking at night. It was certainly cooler than during the day.

Outside, the moon was midway to its peak and I took a deep breath of the night air before realising it was fragrant with flowers. My nose immediately tingled and I sneezed.

"Oh, it is lovely out here at night," Merytre said. "I wish I could…"

"You wish what?" I asked when her voice trailed away.

"It's nothing."

"Tell me."

She sighed. "I was going to say I wished I could walk in the gardens whenever I wanted, but I don't really mean it. I have a good position with you and I would much rather serve you than any other Ornament."

"There is no reason you can't come out for a walk every day."

"But I'm supposed to attend to you."

"I don't need you at my side every minute. I have Ettu, and eight other maids as well. More maids than I know what to do with. I wouldn't object if you wanted to spend time in the gardens. Although," I added slyly. "Perhaps you would prefer to do it during the day so you might see a certain guard."

Even in the moonlight I saw how she blushed.

"Come, Merytre," I said loudly in case anyone was listening. "The fresh air is making me feel much better. Let's walk this way."

We made our way along the path to the grove where Khaemmalu had hidden Tall and Half. My skin pimpled in the cool air and I rubbed my arms to warm them.

"Wait here," I murmured to Merytre. "Watch for anyone nearby."

I slipped around behind the shrubs, certain that Khaemmalu would be there. He surely knew I would come looking for him tonight. But the grove was empty. No matter, I would wait. He had probably seen us from across the grounds and even now made his way towards me. But although I waited for a long time, Khaemmalu never came.

"My lady," Merytre whispered. "We should go. The longer we are here, the more likely it is that someone else will find us."

I wanted to say we should wait for just a little longer. Maybe Khaemmalu had been delayed. But maybe he wasn't working tonight, or maybe he knew I was here and didn't want to speak with me. Perhaps he had decided he had already risked enough for me.

Merytre and I didn't speak as we returned to my chambers. I was glad she didn't ask why Khaemmalu didn't come. I didn't think I would be able to keep my disappointment to myself if I had to talk about it.

CHAPTER 8

The next morning, I sent Merytre to find Sutem. We needed a lock from someone who wouldn't ask too many questions or insist on installing it themselves. If Khaemmalu was avoiding me, Sutem seemed like our best chance. I didn't miss the fact that Merytre changed her gown before she left. She was gone for much longer than I expected it would take to find Sutem and ask him for a lock.

"He will get one after he finishes work," she said when she finally returned. "I will meet him again tomorrow morning to get it."

I pretended I didn't notice how she blushed or that her hair wasn't quite as tidy as it was before she left.

"Excellent," I said. "Once Tall installs it, we won't have to worry quite so much about them being found. Surely nobody would break down the door to that chamber once we explained my jewels were locked away in there."

Half seemed a little better today, although he was still very weak. His face was a more normal colour, his skin was no longer clammy, and he looked like he breathed with less effort. Ettu insisted on feeding him soup every few hours, even though he said he didn't want any. Ahmose was keeping him well dosed with poppy and checked his injury twice a day. She seemed to be going through a prodigious amount of honey in an attempt to stop the wound from festering. I worried someone might ask why I suddenly needed so much honey.

"We will say it was because you were unwell," Ahmose said when I asked her. "Honey is beneficial for many things and as we have given no reason for your illness, nobody can say we weren't treating you with it."

"But what do I say if someone asks me?"

"You had a very sore throat, like knives stabbing you every time you swallowed, and the honey eased the pain."

I felt better at knowing I had a ready response and could only pray my cheeks wouldn't go red and give me away.

Merytre went off to meet Sutem again the following morning, and returned with a bag containing the lock and the tools to install it.

"Did he ask any questions?" I asked her.

Merytre blushed furiously and stammered.

"About the lock," I clarified, wondering what they had discussed to make her react like that.

"Oh, no," she said. "I told him I needed his help and that he wasn't to ask me anything about it."

"It was good of him to help."

"He seems to think I intend to install it myself." Merytre laughed. "He gave me a lengthy explanation about how to do it, but I confess I didn't listen to most of it. I wouldn't have understood it anyway. But I nodded and pretended I was listening."

Ettu came out to the sitting chamber while Merytre was talking, and Tall slipped away to see Half.

"Nonsense," Ettu said briskly. "I'm sure we could manage it ourselves if we had to. I don't know why folk always assume men are more capable than we women."

"It sounded very complicated," Merytre said. "Or at least, it took him a very long time to explain. I'm sure I couldn't do it myself."

"We have four women here," Ettu said. "And I would say we are all reasonably intelligent. Are you telling me the four of us together can't do what one man can?"

Merytre fumbled for a response.

"We are fortunate Tall is here to do it for us," I said before they could argue any further. "I'm sure I wouldn't want to try to figure it out myself."

Where did Ettu's sudden confidence come from? She had never struck me as the kind of woman who thought she could do anything a man could. She watched over Tall's shoulder as he installed the lock and I wondered whether she was ensuring she would know how to do it herself if we ever needed such a thing done again.

Tall proudly presented me with the key and I tucked it into my pouch, although not without wondering whether the administrators might find some reason to search my chambers again. We would have to be very careful we did nothing to raise any suspicion.

My maids returned the following morning to resume their usual bathing and shaving activities, and I had to endure much fussing about how unwell I had been. Abar was the only one who didn't comment, preferring instead to hang back from the others as she usually did.

She had been here some weeks now but still seemed unsure about her place amongst my maids. Indeed they mostly seemed to ignore her, although I caught a few muttered comments that might have been about her. Ettu always gave her some small tasks, but Abar showed no inclination to do anything that somebody didn't specifically ask her to. Surely she must realise that was causing my other maids to resent her.

"Abar, how do you like the Palace?" I asked as she handed Merytre the bangles and finger rings I would wear today. I spoke slowly, figuring she probably didn't have a very good grasp of Egyptian yet.

"I do not care for it," Abar said haltingly. "It is very big and you have not yet found my sister."

Her sister. With everything that had happened of late, I had almost forgotten my promise to look for her. The two girls had been taken from Kush as prisoners of war.

"I did ask Pharaoh how I would find a particular... girl." I almost called her sister a prisoner. Abar had made it clear that was how she thought of herself, but to call her such a thing to her face seemed rude. We were all prisoners here, to an extent. Did she realise that?

"So, where is she?" Abar asked.

"He wasn't able to tell me."

Already I regretted saying I had asked. It wasn't like I could give her any information and I could hardly tell her how dismissive Pharaoh had been. He had people to take care of such things, he had told me. The location of a prisoner was of no importance to him.

"You have done nothing to find her." Abar's voice was cool.

"Abar," Ettu said. "That is no way to talk to my lady."

"She promised to find my sister," Abar retorted. "But she has not."

"Actually, she told me to ask around for your sister and I have," Ettu said. "I have asked all the maids I know, but nobody has seen her. They are watching for her, though, and will tell me if they see her."

"I haven't given up either," I said. "I will keep trying."

"See that you do," Abar said.

"That is enough." Ettu's voice was sharper now. "You are fortunate my lady is so forgiving. Any other mistress would turn you out of the Palace for speaking to her like that."

"That would be acceptable to me," Abar said. "I am a prisoner.

I do not choose to be here. Your people stole me from my home country."

"You can wait in the hallway," Ettu said. "I will speak with you once we have finished dressing my lady."

Abar stomped out, slamming the door behind her. Her defiance made me wonder what her life before had been like. Perhaps in her homeland, she was the one who had servants. Perhaps she never expected to find herself in such a position. I couldn't imagine what it would be like if I were to suddenly become a servant rather than a mistress. Abar was obviously unhappy and she missed her sister. Surely we could be more gentle with her while she adjusted to her new circumstances.

I caught Ettu's eye and gave her a disapproving look, although I was reluctant to reprimand her in front of the other maids. She was supposed to be in charge of them, after all.

"She needs to learn that such talk is not acceptable," Ettu said and I figured she spoke more for the benefit of the other women than for me.

CHAPTER 9

When I rose the next morning, Ettu was wearing a *shendyt* with the top half of a gown which she had cut off at the waist. A pretty strip of embroidered linen had been sewn around the hem to make it look like it had been a shirt all along. I raised my eyebrows at her and she shrugged.

"What will we do when their clothes need to be washed?" she asked. "We can hardly send men's clothing off to the laundry. But if I have started dressing like this myself, the washers will assume they are my own. Merytre and I will make Half and Tall each a *shendyt* and a shirt."

I hadn't thought about how we would procure clothing for them. We could hardly ask for men's clothing to be sent to my chambers.

"It's a clever idea," I said. "But are you allowed to dress like that?"

"Who is going to say I can't? If my mistress has allowed me to wear such a thing, nobody else here is in a position to tell me I can't."

I supposed she was right, although I worried she would be mocked for her clothing.

"But why a *shendyt*?" I asked. "Wouldn't it be easier to make tunics for them? There is no reason they can't continue to dress like Babylonian men do."

"Because that is not what the men here wear," Ettu said. "They already look so different from other men, both of them, that I thought they would prefer to dress the way everyone else does. What does it matter if nobody but us sees them? They will look more like the men of Egypt and they will know it within themselves."

"Perhaps they ought to start shaving their heads and chins then," I said. I intended it as a joke, but Ettu huffed and stomped away down the hallway, presumably off to check on Half.

I decided to break my fast in the dining chamber, mostly so I could find out what the Ornaments were talking about. Although we had heard nothing to suggest anyone suspected there were men hidden in my chambers, I was still uneasy about the possibility that someone might have seen something.

Everyone Ettu and I passed on the way to the dining chamber studied her with curiosity. Some smothered giggles, others laughed outright. One servant woman stared with her mouth agape as she passed us and even turned to look again from further along the hallway. When she saw me watching her, she hurried away.

"No more than I expected," Ettu said, her gaze fixed firmly ahead.

When we entered the dining chamber, the chatter quickly died as the women stopped to stare. Ettu said nothing as she waited for me to choose a table. Once I was seated, she went to stand alone against the wall. I wondered why she didn't wait, as she usually did, with one of the other lady's maids. Henutmire's maid was already there and the two of them seemed friendly enough.

The serving women were quick to bring their platters and I busied myself with choosing what I wanted to eat. It was only once I had enough that I looked up and caught Henutmire's eye.

"Good morning," I said to her.

She nodded at me as she sipped from her mug.

"Whatever is your lady's maid wearing?" she asked.

I gave my best attempt at a casual shrug.

"She has decided to try dressing as a man," I said. "She says women's clothing is too fussy."

Henutmire studied Ettu again.

"Perhaps she will start a new fashion," she said.

"Perhaps." I busied myself with spreading honey on my bread and hoped that would be the end of the conversation.

"I heard you were invited to Pharaoh's palace recently," Henutmire said.

"It was supposed to be a reward."

"Supposed to be? You didn't enjoy yourself? I'm sure the food was excellent."

"It was, and Pharaoh honoured me by seating me on the dais with him and Lady Isis."

"Oh, you met the queen? What did you think?"

"She wasn't terribly friendly," I admitted, "but then I suppose I could hardly expect she would be."

How strange to sit here and speak of such a normal thing. So much had happened since then that the banquet felt like weeks ago, rather than just a few days.

"I'm not sure how I would feel if I was in her position," Henutmire said. "Having my husband parade his other women in front of me all the time. Knowing he goes off to visit them on a regular basis and does his best to get them with child."

My cheeks heated and I quickly drank from my mug, hoping it would conceal my blush. Henutmire noticed, of course.

"Why are you blushing?" she asked. "Does that mean you have…"

Her voice trailed away and she raised her eyebrows expectantly. I fumbled with my mug, almost knocking it over as I set it down.

"Well, I suppose it is too soon to know whether you are with child," she said, clearly taking my silence for confirmation. "Ishtar either. How is she faring, by the way? New chambers, new lady's maids. I've heard talk she might edge Tiye out of the Top position."

The thought that anyone was spreading such gossip was alarming. Tiye herself had told me how she overthrew the woman who was previously the Top Ornament. Despite the resentment I still felt towards Ishtar, I had no desire to see such a thing happen to her if she decided to challenge Tiye. Not that I knew how one would even go about such a thing. I supposed that was irrelevant anyway. The only thing that mattered was whether Tiye felt like she had been challenged.

"I hardly think Ishtar is any threat," I said. "Tiye has been Pharaoh's Favourite for a long time. Ishtar is no more than the newest Ornament. Of course, he would have a particular interest in her. I suppose it will fade soon enough, or someone else will arrive and gain his attention."

Henutmire shrugged.

"I suppose that's what I would be telling myself if she was my sister," she said. "But I've never seen Pharaoh so fascinated with an Ornament before. Ishtar needs to be careful. It puts her in a dangerous position. Tiye isn't the only one watching her."

"Do you mean the queen?"

In the privacy of my chambers, we had speculated about whether Lady Isis had anything to do with the missing women. Having met the queen, I felt no malice from her, but then, I was hardly a threat. Pharaoh had wanted nothing to do with me the first time we met. Lady Isis was probably well familiar with what kind of woman attracted her husband's attention.

"Not necessarily," Henutmire said, "although she is not someone I would want to make an enemy of. I was thinking about the other Ornaments. There are many, many women here who would do almost anything to get Pharaoh's attention. I have heard a lot of bitter comments about how Ishtar arrived and he noticed her immediately even though she was a servant. She hasn't won herself a lot of friends."

None of us had come here to make friends, but did that really mean Ishtar was in danger?

I crammed some bread in my mouth to avoid answering and Henutmire seemed to guess I wasn't in the mood for conversation. She said nothing more than a few pleasantries after that, although she gave me a cheery farewell when I left. I was pleased she didn't seem offended at my reluctance to chat.

It had been a few days since I'd visited with Tiye, so I went there next. If folk were gossiping about Ishtar, it would have reached Tiye's ears and I wanted to see how she was reacting. We were almost there when we encountered Ishtar herself. Belet-ili trailed behind her, the bored look on her face quickly changing to surprise when she saw Ettu's new clothes.

"Good morning," I said, resolving to be civil. Ishtar had, after all, asked after me while I was supposedly unwell.

"Sister." Ishtar's face was pale and her smile looked more like a grimace. "Are you recovered? I came to see you while you were unwell, but your maids wouldn't let me in."

She shot a disapproving look at Ettu, then raised her eyebrows, presumingly having only just noticed Ettu's attire. Belet-ili's mouth was hanging open. Ettu seemed to studiously avoid looking at either of them.

"I am quite well, thank you," I said. "I did hear you came to enquire and also that you sent Belet-ili as well."

Ishtar nodded and we stared at each other for a few moments. Was that it? Was that really all either of us had to say to the other? Nammu's words echoed through my mind and I made a quick decision to ask Ishtar about what she said.

"I ran into Nammu recently," I started, then hesitated, unsure how to frame what I wanted to ask.

"I have things to do," Ishtar said and started to move past me.

I let her go. She obviously didn't want to speak with me.

"Goodbye then," I said.

She was gone before I could say anything else. Ettu and I looked at each other.

"Did she seem odd to you?" I asked.

"She looked rather pale. She can be moody, though. And if she has just finished cleaning Lady Tiye's bathing chamber, perhaps she was in a hurry to return to her own chambers and bathe."

We paused at the end of the hallway. Tiye didn't allow anyone else's servants down the hallway that led only to her chambers, or so I had been told. I didn't see how she could stop anyone from walking there, but I also didn't want to antagonise her.

"Please go straight back to my chambers," I said.

"I will wait here for you. Nobody other than Lady Tiye's own maids come this far, so I'm sure it is safe enough."

"We don't know that anywhere is safe."

"If I scream, you will surely hear me. It is no more than two dozen paces to Lady Tiye's door."

She had that stubborn look that said she wasn't going to change her mind no matter what I said, so I left her there. In Tiye's chamber, I sat down without waiting to be asked. Tiye was standing at a window, looking out at the gardens, while her maids cleared away the breakfast things.

"I saw one of your lady's maids out there the other day," Tiye said in the off-hand tone that always indicated trouble.

"Oh?" I kept my voice deliberately casual.

"She met with one of the guards and he gave her a small sack."

"You surely didn't see such a thing from your windows." I studied her back, trying to figure out whether she was bluffing.

"What were they doing?"

"I have no idea," I said. "I allow my maids to take a walk

through the grounds if they wish and I don't necessarily ask what they did out there. Perhaps it was a gift. There is a guard who seems to have a particular interest in a certain one of my maids."

Tiye chuckled.

"You keep surprising me, Kassaya," she said.

"I suppose that's a good thing."

She turned to eye me briefly, before turning back to the window.

"It might be, or it mightn't," she said. "Your sister, on the other hand, is as boring and predictable as they come."

"I ran into her on the way here. I assume she's still cleaning your bathing chamber."

"She comes every morning like a good little Ornament. I bet she's torn between praying some other new woman comes along to take over from her and hoping nobody does because it means she has a chance of keeping Pharaoh's attention all to herself."

"I hardly think she has all his attention," I said. "You've been his Favourite for too long."

"Favourites can be replaced. They get boring."

With her back to me, it was hard to read her words, but she seemed to hold herself stiffly. Perhaps she was more upset about Ishtar than she seemed.

"You told me yourself your future is assured, since you've given him six sons," I said.

"Yes. My boys."

"Do you see them often? You've never told me anything about them. I don't even know whether they live here or somewhere else." Maybe if I could get her talking about her sons, she would forget about Ishtar.

"They live in Pharaoh's palace, of course, as do all the royal children."

"How old are they?"

"My oldest, Pentaweret, is fourteen." Tiye left the window and came to sit opposite me. She seemed to take a long time to smooth her gown over her knees and I wondered whether she did it to avoid making eye contact. "The others are ten, nine, seven, four and three."

So it had been three years since her last babe. Did that indicate Pharaoh was no longer as interested in her as he used to be? Or was it merely that she was no longer a young woman and couldn't conceive as easily?

"The last birth was difficult," she said, as if she knew what I was thinking. "I almost went to the West, but I prayed to the goddess Isis the whole time and she saved me."

I waited for her to continue, but it seemed she had said all she meant to. Maybe she had been unable to conceive again since that last birth, or maybe she had taken precautions to prevent it. There must be herbs or a potion for such a thing. She had given Pharaoh enough sons that nobody would blame her for avoiding another pregnancy.

"Wouldn't you rather they lived here with you?" I asked.

"Of course." Tiye's eyes glittered as she shot me an annoyed look. "What mother wouldn't? But they are the sons of Pharaoh and they live with him as they should. They receive the best education. Tutors from all over the world, acknowledged experts in their fields. And they are raised with many other boys of their ages. When Pentaweret was born, Pharaoh sent officials throughout the country to collect every boy child born on the same day. They were all brought back to the palace so they could grow up with Pentaweret. It was a very great honour Pharaoh gave my son."

And the mothers of those boys would probably never see their sons again. Did she think about that?

"And yet he's only the second oldest boy?" I asked.

I immediately wished I had worded it differently, thinking my question might anger her, but Tiye's reply was unexpectedly cool.

"Pharaoh's oldest living son, Ramses, resides in Memphis," she said. "That's a long way from here and they don't see each other often. My Pentaweret is very well placed since he lives in Pharaoh's own palace. He sees Pharaoh almost every day and has many opportunities to show why he would be a better heir than Ramses."

"You said Ramses was his oldest living son. There was another?"

"A boy of Isis. He went to the West a couple of years ago."

Her tone was nonchalant. The death of a competitor to the position of heir was obviously something that didn't bother her. After all, it elevated her son from third in line to second.

"Tell me about Pentaweret," I said. "What is he like?"

"He is very clever." Tiye leaned back against the couch and seemed more relaxed now. "He reads and writes in both Egyptian and Akkadian, and now he is learning Greek. He studies history, geography, politics and religion. He has tutors from all our ally countries and he is already so knowledgable that Pharaoh sometimes asks his advice on diplomatic matters. He writes to me every month to tell me about his studies."

"He sounds very intelligent."

"He is nothing like Ramses," she said fiercely, glaring at me as if I had suggested otherwise. "Ramses is a lazy, self-indulgent brat. He has never even lived in Thebes. How can he expect to rule if he has never lived in the capital?"

"Why doesn't he? Wouldn't it make more sense for him to be near his father?"

"Pharaoh thinks he will be better prepared to take the throne if he manages the affairs in Memphis himself. What Pharaoh doesn't see, or rather what he refuses to see, is that Ramses does absolutely nothing. He spends all day drinking and hunting and carousing, and leaves the work to his administrators and officials. How does that prepare him to rule? Meanwhile, my son dedicates his days to learning. Pharaoh has promised to send him on a military expedition soon. He will be in charge of the troops.

Tell me he isn't a better candidate to be heir than that sloth, Ramses!"

It was the closest I had ever heard her come to criticising Pharaoh. Wasn't she afraid of her son being sent off to battle? Didn't she fear he might be killed? Tiye surely would have thought of such a thing, but if she was pretending it didn't bother her, she wouldn't thank me for bringing it up.

"So why doesn't Pharaoh make Pentaweret his heir then?" I asked instead.

"Because Ramses is the oldest and the son of his queen, whereas Pentaweret is merely the son of a courtesan." Her voice was bitter now and I realised she truly believed her son was the better candidate. "But it will be the gods who determine which son inherits the throne when Pharaoh becomes a hawk and flies off to the west. And the gods are watching, even if Pharaoh isn't."

CHAPTER 10

When I emerged from Tiye's chamber, Ettu was waiting in the hallway as she had promised. Her *shendyt* didn't look quite so odd to me now. Strange how quickly I had become accustomed to seeing her in it. How would it feel to wear such a thing? Were her legs cold? Did it feel odd to stride freely without a skirt wrapping around them? Perhaps one day, I would try it for myself.

"It isn't safe for you to wait here," I said, even though I had known she would.

"It is no less safe than for you to walk back alone," she retorted.

Back in my chambers, everything was quiet. Half was resting, with Tall at his side, and seemed a little more comfortable. He and Ettu took turns sitting in the chair beside his bed, so he had someone with him at every moment. In the sitting chamber, Merytre was busy working on a shirt for Tall. If he felt ridiculous in the shift he wore in the meantime, he gave no sign of it. I supposed it wasn't all that much different from wearing a tunic.

Ahmose sat with the distant expression that meant she was mentally compiling a list of herbs or some such thing. I sat with them for a while, but felt restless and I didn't want to risk Ettu or Merytre offering me some stitching if I looked too bored. I went to look out the window, hoping I might see something interesting.

"Is Sutem out there?" Merytre's voice was studiously casual and when I glanced over at her, her gaze was fixedly on her stitching.

"I can't see him," I said. "Maybe I should go out for a walk. I'd like to thank him for the lock and we need to return his tools."

I felt the way Merytre restrained herself from asking if she could come with me.

"I will stay here," Ettu said quickly. "Merytre, give me that shirt and I will keep working on it. You can accompany my lady on her walk."

Merytre handed over the shirt with a grateful smile and went off to her bedchamber to fetch Sutem's tools. Before we were even out the door, Ettu was already stitching furiously, as if each stitch she made held her anger about Half's injury.

It was only when we reached the grounds that I realised it was really too hot to be out walking so close to midday. Sweat already trickled down my neck, but Merytre was eagerly looking around for Sutem and I didn't want to disappoint her. I genuinely wanted to thank him anyway. He had aided me twice now. When he helped me climb down from Tiye's window on my first day, he said I owed him a debt. I supposed he was tallying up my debts.

To Merytre's disappointment, we saw no sign of Sutem, although at times it felt like someone watched us. Another of the guards, I supposed. If it was Sutem, he surely would have come to speak with us, especially since he seemed as infatuated with Merytre as she was with him.

Back inside, we didn't even reach the first set of stairs before a voice called out from behind us. I restrained a sigh. That was someone I really didn't feel like dealing with today, especially not when I was so hot and sweaty from our walk.

"Lady Kassaya." Amankhau bustled up, all officiousness with his voice dripping with condescension. "There is a letter for you."

"Thank you."

I held out my hand to take it, but Amankhau didn't pass it to me. Instead, he tapped the rolled scroll against his palm as he studied me. I tried to conceal my irritation, aware the heat was likely making my temper shorter than it should be, despite how I despised the man.

"It's from your father," he added.

"Do you have some problem with my father writing to me?"

"Not at all." He continued to study me and I felt like he was enjoying my annoyance. "But Pentau tells me you haven't sent your father any letters since you arrived."

Only I had. We had smuggled it out in order to be sure the letter that reached my father would be exactly as I intended and not altered by Pentau, the Palace scribe.

"Are you suggesting my father isn't allowed to write to me unless I have written to him first?" I asked.

"That's the interesting thing." Tap, tap, tap of the scroll against his palm. "Your father seems to imply he is responding to a letter from you."

"You read my father's letter? You have no right to do that."

"All correspondence in and out of the Palace is monitored by the scribe to ensure the safety and security of the residents." He gave me an oily smile. "As I'm sure you are already aware. But you haven't answered my question."

"You didn't ask a question." I focussed on breathing steadily, trying to conceal my irritation.

"I want to know why your father implies he is replying to a letter you never sent."

"You would have to ask my father that. I can't presume to

speak for him. Now if you would kindly hand me my letter, I have other things to do today."

He only continued to smile and tap the scroll against his palm. The longer he did that, the more my irritation built until I was almost ready to snatch the scroll from his hand. I might have tried except that he might move faster than me and leave me looking like a fool.

"Must I go to Panouk and tell him you refuse to give me my father's letter?" I asked.

"I think Panouk would be very interested in the matter of why Pentau was unaware you wrote to your father."

"For Marduk's sake." My voice came out louder than I intended, but my temper was well and truly on edge. I was hot and sweaty, and I intensely disliked this man and the game he was playing. "I didn't. You are misinterpreting whatever my father said. Now give me my letter or I will go straight to Panouk. And when I am finished with him, I will complain to Pharaoh that communication from one of his best allies is being withheld from me."

"Always so dramatic." He rolled his eyes. "There really is nothing worse than an hysterical woman."

He held the scroll out to me and I snatched it from his hand, then turned and strode away up the stairs before anything else could come out of my mouth.

"He is a most unpleasant man," Merytre observed once we were far enough away that he wouldn't hear.

"Odious," I said. "And contemptible."

"Are you not worried he knows about your letter?"

"He can't prove anything."

"I wonder why he is here at this time of day," Merytre said. "Isn't he supposed to work the night shift?"

I didn't answer. I had no more information than she did. Maybe Amankhau was waiting to personally hand me the letter just so he could make his point about it. I couldn't guess why he wouldn't have brought it to my chambers, though, if that was the case, unless he went there after Merytre and I had left.

Back in the sitting chamber, Ettu was still working on the shirt for Tall. Her gaze went immediately to the scroll in my hand.

"From your father?" she asked.

I told her about my conversation with Amankhau as Merytre fetched us each a mug of melon juice. The liquid was sweet and cool against my parched throat and it was only once I had satisfied my thirst, that I let myself look at the letter. I unrolled the scroll and immediately realised how Amankhau knew I had written to my father.

My Daughter, the letter read.

It pleases us to hear of your safe arrival in Egypt. I trust Pharaoh was well pleased with the gifts which accompanied you. As a Princess of Babylon, it is your duty to do as your father bids you. Do as is expected of you and be grateful we sent you to such a worthy ally.

Your father

Marduk-apla-iddina

Disappointment surged through me. That was all the reply my father deigned to send? A reminder to do my duty? There was no warmth in the letter. No well wishes for either of his daughters. No message from my mother.

"What does it say?" Merytre asked.

I read it out to her, translating as I did.

"So he writes in Egyptian?" Ettu asked.

"No, Babylonian, but Merytre wouldn't understand if I read it as it is written."

"I'm surprised Amankhau can read Babylonian," she said. "So how did he know what the letter said? Or even that it was from your father?"

"I suppose a courier brought it and told him who it was from," I said. "But as for what it says, I found it quite easy to learn Akkadian because it's so similar to Babylonian. I cannot read Akkadian fluently, but I can parse it well enough to make sense of it. Perhaps Pentau can likewise figure out what a letter written in Babylonian says, even if he can't read every word."

"But we don't know for certain that Amankhau actually knows what the letter says," Ettu said.

I sighed and tossed the scroll onto the couch beside me.

"Even if Pentau couldn't make any sense of it, Amankhau might have been guessing," I said. "Perhaps he was suspicious I somehow sent a letter without Pentau knowing and wanted to see if I gave myself away."

"You didn't," Merytre said. "I thought you did a very good job of pretending you had no idea what he was talking about."

"I hope so." I picked up the scroll and studied it again with a frown. "I should have warned Father not to mention my letter. It didn't occur to me he might make it obvious he was replying to me. Actually, I didn't really expect him to respond."

"Of course he would," Ettu said. "You're his daughter."

I shrugged, unwilling to explain that Father's only care was for the alliance.

"If anyone asks again, you could say you sent a messenger to your father as soon as we arrived in Egypt," she said. "Nobody needs to know your letter wasn't sent until later."

I gave her a grateful smile. It was a good idea and I wished I had thought of it when I was speaking with Amankhau.

"He doesn't mention Lady Ishtar," Merytre said. "I wonder if this was sent before she was?"

"From what Ishtar said, she was only a couple of weeks behind me," I said. "My letter couldn't have arrived that quickly. But maybe he wrote to her as well."

"I wonder whether Amankhau has had the same conversation with her?" she asked.

"Given it's well known Pharaoh favours her, I think it unlikely," I said. "I'm sure he's treating her much better than he treats me."

"I can ask Belet-ili next time I see her," Ettu offered. "If he has written to Lady Ishtar as well, she will surely say so."

"Yes, do that if you can," I said.

When I went to look in on Half, both Tall and Ahmose were there with him. Half's eyes were closed, so I spoke quietly, assuming he was asleep.

"How is he?" I asked.

"Alive," Half said.

"And awake," I said.

He opened his eyes and squinted at me. "It's good to see you, Princess."

"It's very good to see you alive. We weren't sure you would make it."

"Teacher says there's no certainty yet." His gaze flicked to Ahmose. "But I suppose it's looking better than it did a few days ago."

"Can you tell me what happened?"

Tall got up from the chair beside the bed and gestured for me to take his place. I gave him a nod of thanks as I sat down.

"I assume you want to know who stabbed me," Half said. "And that, I'm afraid, I don't know. It happened so fast and I was too busy staring at the dagger in my belly to think to look at his face."

"Why did he do it?"

Half glanced over at Tall and they shared a knowing look.

"Princess, what we know is dangerous," he said. "I'm not sure I should tell you."

"Tell me. We are in no danger here in my chambers."

He and Tall looked at each other again.

"Woman!" Tall said. "Quarry!"

CHAPTER 11

"Tall thinks we should tell you," Half said. "He said that right from when I told him what I had heard, which was before this happened." He raised one hand to gesture towards his belly. "I still disagree, but if you insist…"

"I do," I said.

"As Tall says, a woman's body was recently found dumped in the quarry a couple of leagues out of Thebes."

My heart sank. I hadn't believed the administrators, but until a body was found, there was still hope she would be found safe and well.

"Nebtu?" I asked.

"I don't know and that is the truth. She is not the only one to have gone missing of late. I heard only that it was a woman."

"So where is the danger? Why does it matter if you know such a thing?"

"Because the discovery was being covered up. Nobody knows about the body."

"Why?" I couldn't fathom why anyone would hide such a thing. Folk knew we were waiting for news of Nebtu. If she had been found, it would be better for her family to know, rather than to always be waiting and wondering.

"Because someone in the Palace was responsible for her death," Half said. "Or, at the very least, covering it up."

Although it was no more than we had suspected, his words still shook me.

"Who?" I asked.

"That is the thing I don't know."

"Could it be the queen?"

Half shook his head. "Honestly, Princess, I cannot say. If the queen is involved, she can't have been the one to…"

His voice trailed away, but I guessed what it was he didn't want to say. The queen surely couldn't have overpowered a woman and killed her, nor could she have been the one to hide the body away.

"How did she die?" I couldn't bring myself to call her by her name, but surely it was Nebtu.

"I didn't hear any specifics, only that a body was found at the bottom of the quarry."

I hadn't realised Ettu and Merytre were listening from the doorway until Ettu spoke.

"Could she have jumped?" she asked. "Or fallen?"

Half seemed to take Ettu's suggestion seriously, which told me he really didn't know and wasn't just trying to protect us from the details.

"I have heard nothing that suggests that isn't a possibility," he said. "Or indeed, anything that suggests it is."

"So what else do you know?" I asked. "And how?"

"I overheard a man reporting to one of the administrators. He said only *she has been found*. The administrator asked if he meant the one at the quarry, and the guard said yes."

"The one at the quarry?" Merytre repeated. "Dear Amun."

"That suggests there are others," I said.

"We know there is at least one other," Ettu said. "Lady Nebtu and the servant woman."

"Half, are you sure it was one of the missing women they were talking about?" I asked. "If they only called her *she*, surely there are other matters they could have been discussing."

"With the greatest respect, Princess, there is no doubt in my mind that they spoke of a missing woman. It was all done very quietly and secretly. They met in the gardens, well away from anyone else."

"How did you overhear them?" Ahmose asked from her position by the window.

"I had been out for a walk and was taking a rest beneath a tree," Half said. "They happened to stop just behind the tree I sat beneath."

"And they didn't see you?" I asked.

"I thought not at the time, but it seems someone did."

"What else did they say?" I asked. What a terrible situation he had found himself in. Stabbed in the belly and all because he was in the wrong place at the wrong time.

"One man reported the discovery and the other told him to take care of it. Take her somewhere she won't be found again, he said. That, Princess, is not merely covering up a murder. If I understand what the folk here believe, it is far more serious."

"That's true," Merytre said. "If her body is not properly looked after, she can't be resurrected in the afterlife."

"So by hiding her body away," I said, "they are... what?"

"Condemning her to eternal death." Ahmose's voice was grim.

As ridiculous as the concept sounded to me, I held my tongue. This was what the Egyptians believed and mocking their belief would serve no purpose other than to offend Merytre and Ahmose.

"Somebody very high up in the palace must be involved if the administrator is giving such instructions," I said.

"Something I found particularly interesting," Half said, "is that both men knew what was being discussed without either of them explaining or asking questions."

"You mean they already knew a body was likely to be found?" I asked.

He nodded.

"Who were they?"

"That, Princess, I can't be sure of. I think one was an administrator. I'm sure I recognised his voice. But the other? It could have been another official, or a guard or a servant."

"You never saw their faces?"

"Marduk, no. I stayed right where I was and didn't dare even to breathe until I was sure they were gone."

"So how did anyone know you heard them?"

"Someone knew I was there, or they saw me when I left and realised I must have overheard. There are guards constantly patrolling the grounds. It's not unreasonable to assume somebody saw me, even if I didn't see them."

"Just like here," I said. "There is always somebody watching."

"Indeed," he said.

"How long ago was this conversation?" Ahmose's tone was thoughtful, as if she was putting together the pieces of a puzzle I hadn't yet noticed.

"The same day I was stabbed. That morning."

"And where did that happen?" I hadn't yet heard the whole story. This was the first time Half had been able to speak so much.

"Inside. We had eaten in one of the dining chambers and were returning to our bedchamber. Tall decided he was still thirsty and went back to get another drink. I kept going, planning to return to our bedchamber rather than wait for him in the hallway. As I came around a corner, a dagger suddenly appeared in my belly."

"He was waiting for you?" I asked.

"It would seem so."

"Could it have been a random attack?" Merytre asked. "Maybe you just happened to be walking down the wrong hallway at the wrong time."

"No," Half said. "He spoke to me after he stabbed me. Something like, it seems another body will be found tomorrow. That might not be precise. I wasn't exactly expecting a conversation and, at the time, I didn't even comprehend his words. It was only later that I remembered."

"Definitely a targeted attack," Ettu said grimly.

"And Tall saw it?" Merytre asked. She seemed to avoid looking at Tall and I wondered if she was still discomfited by his strangeness.

"From what I understand, he heard me cry out and came running back. He saw the man standing over me as I lay on the ground."

"Chase!" Tall said sadly.

"No." Half's voice was growing weaker. "If you had chased him, he would have stabbed you too and I would have died waiting for you to return."

Tall only shook his head. I guessed he felt guilty for not trying to apprehend the attacker, but Half was right. He had been injured so badly that there was no time to waste in chasing after whoever it was.

"Tall," I said. "Was it a guard who stabbed Half?"

"Guard!" Tall's mouth twisted, as if it was something else he wanted to say, but he couldn't find the words.

"Do you know the man who stabbed him?" I asked.

"Man!"

Perhaps if I could ask in just the right way, Tall would be able to answer.

"What is the name of the man who stabbed Half?" I asked.

"Userhet!"

"Userhet?" I repeated. "Half, do you know who that is?"

Half only shook his head. He was looking rather pale now. Perhaps he was too tired to keep talking.

"You should rest," I said. "If there is more to the story, you can tell us later."

His eyes were already closed.

"I'll sit with him." Ettu waited beside me, the half-finished shirt for Tall in her hand. I vacated the chair and she pushed it a little closer to the bed before she sat down.

Ahmose, Merytre and I tiptoed out, leaving Ettu and Tall with Half. Back in the sitting chamber, I paced as I thought about what we had learned. Ahmose sat down, her broken arm propped up on a cushion. Like Half, she too looked rather pale. We mustn't forget she was an old woman and still healing from her own injury. Spending so much time caring for Half might be too much for her.

"You should rest this afternoon," I said to her. "Maybe take a nap."

"I will survive, my lady. Half is in a much worse way than I am."

"He is also much younger than you."

She shrugged and didn't seem inclined to argue with me, but I also sensed she wasn't likely to do as I said in this instance. I continued to pace, still too restless to sit still. Something about this new information seemed odd, but I couldn't quite figure out what.

"How far away is the quarry?" I asked.

"A few leagues, I think," Merytre said. "Although I have never been there myself, so I could be wrong."

"Why would they take her body that far?" I asked. "Is there nowhere closer they could have hidden her? Buried her in the sand somewhere? Or burned her body?"

Merytre only looked at me blankly, so I turned to Ahmose. Her face was thoughtful as she considered my question.

"I suppose burying her in the desert might not be a reliable means of disposal," she said. "One good sandstorm and she would be revealed. As for burning the body, that would take a large fire and much time. It's not something that can be done without drawing attention."

"So why the quarry?" I asked. "Why go to all that effort to transport a body that far away?"

There was something significant in this information. If we could just figure out the *why*, maybe we would also know who. There was silence in the chamber as we thought. I continued to pace, pausing only briefly at the window to see if anything was happening out in the grounds.

"Maybe the man who was originally tasked with hiding the body works at the quarry?" Merytre suggested eventually. Her voice was tentative, as if she wasn't sure she offered a valuable suggestion, but Ahmose was already nodding.

"A supervisor," she said. "Or an overseer. Perhaps he had to go to the quarry for some reason and it made sense to take the body with him."

"But wouldn't he expect someone to find her?" I asked. "Surely a supervisor would only be there if his workers were too."

Ahmose shrugged. "Perhaps he left the body in an area that isn't currently in use. Or perhaps there is no work happening there at present and he had to go for some other reason. We cannot say."

"But surely that information lets us narrow down who he is," I said. "There can't be that many men who are supervisors or overseers at the quarry."

"I know Ahmose suggested he might be a supervisor," Merytre said. "But he could just be someone who went to an isolated place with which he is familiar."

Ahmose acknowledged her words with a nod.

"A fair point," she said. "I'm afraid this doesn't help us to narrow the possibilities at all. It could be anyone in Thebes who knows of the quarry and has some means of transport."

"And any man could borrow a beast from some farmer he knows," Merytre added.

"Also, we are talking only about the man who hid the body," Ahmose said. "Not the poor woman's killer. If these crimes are being concealed at the level we suspect, he is hardly going to tell us who told him to hide her body, even if we could identify him."

"Why not take her straight to the House of Life then?" I asked. "Didn't you say a body would be immersed in natron for weeks? Surely nobody would be able to identify her once she is covered in natron."

"But whoever took her there would have to identify her to the priests," Ahmose replied. "They need to know who the deceased person is so they can ensure her name is written on the amulets that will be placed on her body when it is wrapped."

I sank onto a couch, suddenly gloomy. What had seemed like the tantalising possibility of solid information had turned out to be nothing.

"How do we get this Userhet arrested then?" At least that was something we could do. "Do we go to the police chief?"

"And tell him what exactly?" Ahmose asked.

"Tall saw the attack," I said. "He can identify the man. The police chief would have to arrest Userhet. It was attempted murder, after all."

"You think he would be arrested on Tall's word?" Ahmose's voice was measured with no hint of skepticism.

"He saw what happened. He could testify."

"Tall is… limited in how he communicates," Ahmose said. "And I'm sure you are well aware that folk judge him for that."

"He also can't speak in Egyptian," Merytre said. "So he wouldn't be able to tell the police chief what he saw."

"We could have someone translate for him," I said. "Ahmose could do it."

"A friend of the witness?" Ahmose asked. "How reliable do you think I would be considered?"

"You think they would believe you were lying just because you're a friend to Tall?" I asked.

"Not lying perhaps," she said. "But mistranslating to make it seem that Tall knows more than he does."

"But you wouldn't do that," I said.

She shrugged. "I am merely an old woman. Nobody believes someone like me."

"I believe you. We all do."

"We can't go to the police chief," she said. "Neither Tall nor I would be considered credible witnesses."

"But the men Half overheard know exactly what happened to the woman they found," I said. "Whether that was Nebtu or the servant, her killer should be punished. She deserves to have her body prepared for the afterlife, if that is what she believed. And Userhet needs to be punished for attempted murder. We know too much to keep quiet."

"You will make your own decisions, my lady," Ahmose said. "But if you want my counsel, I would suggest we know too much to speak up."

"That doesn't make any sense."

"I agree with Ahmose," Merytre said. "It puts you in too much danger if you say anything."

"And how would we explain the presence of Tall and Half in your chambers?" Ahmose asked. "There is no way for you to tell anyone what you know without revealing your sources, and if you do that, the first question will be how you are communicating with them. Do you intend everyone to know there are two men hidden in your chambers?"

"Unmodified men," Merytre added.

I could see the sense in their words, but I didn't like it.

"It doesn't seem right to keep quiet about this," I said.

"We need more evidence," Ahmose said.

"We need to know exactly what happened to the woman who was found," Merytre added.

"And her identity," Ahmose said. "Her body would have been hidden away by now, so your only evidence is the words of two men who would not be thought to be reliable witnesses and whose location you can't reveal."

"Even if we say nothing about the body, surely we can report the attack on Half," I said.

"And the first question anyone would ask is how you know," Ahmose said. "How will you answer that?"

They were right. We couldn't tell anyone what we knew. Not until we had more evidence. Evidence that would outweigh the presence of the unmodified men in my chambers.

CHAPTER 12

We rarely left my chambers over the next few weeks. I never asked the other women why they didn't go out, but for me it was because of the secrets we kept. There were too many and I feared I would give myself away. Half grew stronger each day and soon he was able to get out of bed and join us in the sitting chamber for an hour or so at a time.

My lady's maids came every morning to bathe and shave me, spending an excessive amount of time dressing me to sit around in my chambers. Servants continued to bring meals for us morning and evening. There had been no need to ask for extra food as they always brought far more than we could eat anyway. I wondered whether anyone commented on the fact that suddenly less was returned to the kitchen each day. Although Half still ate little, Tall's appetite was as hearty as ever.

The men went to their bedchamber when anyone was expected. We would lock the door and hide the key in the pouch I wore around my waist. Tall and Half would have to be still and silent so as not to give anyone cause to wonder if the locked door hid something other than the jewels we claimed to have hidden away. Panouk didn't question my request for an additional bed and had it set in the spot I showed him against the wall in the sitting chamber. Tall moved it into the men's bedchamber as soon as he left.

Ettu had told my maids our agreed story: that after the incident with Tiye's stolen jewels, I trusted nobody near mine but her. My jewels would remain behind a locked door, she said, and only she was permitted to fetch the items I would wear each day and return them to their chests at night. If my maids thought anything odd of the situation, they didn't comment, not where I could hear them anyway.

I ate in the dining chamber only twice, both times at the insistence of Ettu and Merytre who said I needed to be seen out in the Palace. Folk would start to wonder why I locked myself away, they said, and the last thing we needed was any new rumours. So I went to the dining chamber and sat in my usual seat next to Henutmire.

I tried to speak to her as little as possible, though, and hardly even let myself look at her, too afraid she would see I knew something. She had been closer to Nebtu than any of the other Ornaments. If there was a possibility it was Nebtu's body that had been found, Henutmire would want to know. The guilt at not telling her ate away at me. She must have noticed my strangeness and she became cooler towards me. No longer did she smile and chat when I sat down. Instead she only nodded and continued with her meal. She surely wondered at the change in me, but never asked.

We were well into *akhet* by now and the days were noticeably hotter as Merytre had warned they would be. One morning, we were all in the sitting chamber with every window flung open to catch the breeze when an unexpected knock came at the door. We froze. Half gestured towards the bedchambers, as if asking whether they should try to sneak out quietly, and I held up my hand for them to wait. Ettu went to the door, although she didn't raise the bar to unlock it.

"Who is it?" she called.

"Benerib," came a female voice I didn't recognise. "I am lady's maid to Lady Tiye."

"Do you bring a message for my lady?" Ettu asked.

"My lady asks why Lady Kassaya hasn't come to visit her for several weeks now."

"My lady has been very busy of late," Ettu said. She shot me a questioning look and I nodded. "However, she is planning to visit Lady Tiye tomorrow if that suits."

"I will tell my lady."

Ettu put her ear to the door, listening.

"She has left," she said. "I heard her walking away."

"I probably should have gone to sit with Tiye sooner," I said. "Of course she will be wondering where I've been."

"You could say you have had a slow recovery from your illness," Merytre said.

"What if she wants to know what I was so ill with that took weeks to recover from?" I asked.

"Fevers," Ahmose said promptly. "You have had terrible fevers that left you weak and sweating. You have been fatigued ever since and still don't quite feel like yourself yet. And, of course, there was the sore throat that necessitated you taking all that honey."

"That's very good," I said.

I was envious of Ahmose's knowledge. She had promised a number of times to teach me things, but the opportunity never seemed to come. I would ask her again when I found a private moment.

When I woke the next morning, my stomach churned ferociously as soon as I moved. I barely made it to my bathing chamber before I vomited.

"My lady?" Ettu rushed in after me. "Are you unwell?"

"I suppose this is Marduk's way of punishing me for feigning illness," I said, wiping my mouth. My legs suddenly felt weak and I leaned against the wall.

"Could it be something you ate?" Ettu asked.

"I have eaten nothing different from you." I hadn't even been to the dining chamber since the day before yesterday.

"Do you think..." Ettu's voice trailed away.

I peeled myself off the wall, but the movement made the chamber tilt and I vomited again. There was nothing left in my belly now, although it still shuddered as if the vomiting was not yet finished.

"When did you last bleed?" Ettu asked.

I leaned back against the wall, my legs weak once again, although for a different reason this time.

"Not since..." I couldn't say it.

We looked at each other and she nodded.

"Congratulations, my lady," she said. "It would seem you are with child."

I set my hands on my belly, searching for some sign of the life growing inside me. My belly was as flat as ever. If a child was in there, shouldn't I be able to sense it?

Please Marduk, if it is indeed a child, let it be a boy. Let me give Pharaoh a son like Father ordered me to.

CHAPTER 13

I went back to bed while Merytre delivered my apologies to Tiye. Ettu sent my lady's maids away, telling them only that I needed no assistance with dressing today.

"Won't that make them wonder why?" I asked. My stomach rolled as I inhaled the scent of the melon juice she brought me. "Oh, please take that away. The smell is making me ill."

Ettu returned the mug to the sitting chamber without comment.

"That's exactly my point," she said when she returned. "Everyone knows you went to Pharaoh's palace a few weeks ago. It won't take long before the rumours start."

"We should wait and make sure I really am with child before we start any rumours," I said, although it was too late to change what she had done.

"Even if you aren't," she said, "it will remind folk that you have spent time privately with Pharaoh."

"I don't particularly want anyone gossiping about whether or not I might be with child. Maybe you should have said I was ill again."

"I don't think you have a choice. Not in your situation. You need to remind people you are intimate with Pharaoh. It makes you an important person in a place like this."

I groaned and hugged my belly as it started churning again.

"Will I feel like this until the child is born?" I asked.

"I will fetch Ahmose. She knows more than I do about matters like this."

To my immense relief, Ahmose said the illness would likely only persist for the first few weeks, and probably not even all day.

"How do I know if it is a boy?" I asked.

I didn't explain why I needed to know. She would understand I had to give Pharaoh a son.

"I will procure some barley and emmer," Ahmose said. "You urinate on the seeds. If it is the barley that sprouts, the child will be a boy. If the emmer sprouts, it is a girl."

"What if neither sprouts?"

"Then there will be no child."

"Have you ever borne a babe?" It suddenly occurred to me I had never asked. She was married for several years before her husband died.

"Just one," she said, her voice wistful now. "A daughter."

"What happened to her?"

"I don't know. She was taken from me when I was given to my husband's creditor. They didn't tell me where she would go."

"So she could still be alive?"

"I pray to Amun every day that she is."

"Why haven't you mentioned her before?" I rolled onto my side, trying to find a more comfortable position. My stomach churned no matter how I lay.

"What good does it do to speak of her? I will never see her again, not in this life anyway. I pray I will meet her in the after-life. If the gods are good to me, I will be reunited with my husband and our daughter."

"Do you still miss your husband?" He had been dead for such a long time that it had never occurred to me she might.

"Sometimes," she said. "Our fathers negotiated the marriage contract, as is usual with our people. I had never spoken with my husband before the day I moved into his house, although I knew who he was. We grew up in the same village, but he was a few years older than me and there was no reason for us to ever meet, let alone spend any time together."

Ahmose undoubtedly knew better than I had realised how I felt at being sent halfway around the world to a man I had never met. Of all those who came with me from Babylon, she was probably the one who understood the best. And, of course, she was the one who gave me the potion I had put in Pharaoh's wine the night of the banquet.

"Thank you," I said. "For giving me a way of ensuring I conceived so soon. I would not want to—"

I stopped, realising it might be unwise to tell anyone, even Ahmose, that I didn't want to suffer Pharaoh lying with me again. But if anyone understood what such a situation was like, it was her, and she probably guessed what I didn't say.

"I will leave you to rest," Ahmose said. "That is what will be best for you. Later once the nausea settles, you should eat, whether you want to or not. You must keep up your strength. You will need it as the babe grows."

Her quiet footsteps left the chamber and I burrowed down into my bed. The morning was still cool enough that I wasn't too uncomfortable under the linen sheet and I soon drifted off to sleep. When I next woke, the air was stifling and sweat drenched the sheets. I sat up with a groan, which Ettu must have heard. She came in, took one look at me, and rushed to open the shutters.

"Oh my," she said. "Let's get you bathed. There is fresh water waiting for you. It will be cold by now, but I doubt you want a hot bath anyway."

I let her help me up and staggered down the hallway. I had

never before appreciated the stool in the bathing stall, but today I was pleased to sit there and have Ettu pour cool water over me. Merytre came to help and between them they scrubbed me with natron, then rinsed me off. Dressed and wearing a wig, I felt a little more normal. Merytre wanted to make up my face, but I waved her away.

"I won't be leaving the chambers today," I said. "There is really no point."

"What if somebody comes to visit you?" she asked. "Surely you wouldn't want to be seen without your face done."

"I don't care, to be honest." I gave her a small smile so the words would seem less harsh than they sounded. "I feel too weak to be bothered with visitors anyway. If someone comes, send them away."

But when someone did come, it was Ishtar and I agreed to see her, remembering how aggrieved she had been last time when she wasn't allowed in. Ettu waited until Tall and Half were safely locked away in their chamber, before she opened the door. If Ishtar wondered at the delay, she didn't comment.

"Oh, Sister," she said, coming to sit beside me on the couch. She patted my hand with a solicitousness that surprised me. "You look atrocious. What ails you?"

Did I really look that bad or was it just that she had caught me without any makeup on? I didn't want to tell Ishtar. Not yet. I wanted to keep it to myself for just a little longer.

"I am still fatigued from my recent illness," I said instead and hoped she wouldn't be able to tell the lie from my voice.

"Well, I have marvellous news," she said brightly. She set her hand on her belly and smiled at me.

"You are with child?" I hoped my face didn't show my dismay. Of course she would be. She had been with Pharaoh several times, compared to my once.

"I pray to Marduk every day that it will be a boy." She leaned close to whisper conspiratorially to me. "I haven't told Pharaoh yet, not until my belly starts to swell. I want him to see that when I tell him."

I nodded, unable to find anything that seemed like a suitable response.

"Have you been ill with it?" I asked eventually, realising I had to say something.

"Oh no, not for a moment," she said brightly.

Too brightly. Why would she lie about something like that? I hesitated, wondering whether I should tell her I knew she was lying, but decided not to. Ishtar always liked to be viewed as the perfect daughter. I supposed she wouldn't want anyone to know the babe had made her unwell. It made her seem a little less perfect.

"Good," I said instead.

"Do you think I should write to Father?" she asked. "Wouldn't he be pleased to know one of his daughters is—"

She stopped abruptly and I wondered what she had just remembered. That she wasn't supposed to be an Ornament? That it wasn't she who was sent to fulfil the alliance? That it was me Father had bid bear sons for Pharaoh, not her?

"Maybe you should wait until you are certain." Had she already forgotten the babe she had lost? "You wouldn't want to tell Father something like that and then have to say it was a mistake."

Ishtar patted my hand again, before she rose.

"I will leave you to your recovery," she said and swept out.

She was gone before I remembered I still hadn't asked about what Nammu said. Ettu slid the bar into place, then turned to raise her eyebrows at me.

"Well, that was interesting news," she said.

"She didn't really come to see how I was, did she? She only came to tell me she had managed to get herself with child before I did."

"You think she sees it as a competition?"

"You know her better than me," I said bitterly. "What do you think?"

Ettu only gave me a funny little smile and didn't answer. I assumed that meant she agreed with me, but didn't want to say it.

CHAPTER 14

nother week passed before a morning came when I felt well enough to visit with Tiye. My stomach still churned, but perhaps not quite as badly as the day before. It was Nammu who answered the door when I knocked. She sneered, although she said nothing, and I knew that she, like me, was remembering our last encounter. Tiye was elegantly arranged on a couch, looking as if she had expected my arrival.

"Well," she said. "You finally return."

I sat and smoothed my gown over my knees.

"I have been unwell," I said. "I have hardly left my chambers for several weeks."

"You look remarkably well for someone who has been indisposed for so long."

She gave me an arch look. I shrugged and pretended I didn't know what she was hinting at.

"My tutor, Ahmose, has cared for me well," I said. "She is very knowledgable and it's most useful to have someone like her around."

"Hmm." It seemed to be what she said when she knew I wasn't

telling the whole truth. "I hear our newest Ornament is with child."

How did she already know about Ishtar? When I met her gaze, she looked briefly over to Nammu who sat on the other side of the chamber, suggesting it was from her that the information came. Nammu had her hands clasped in her lap and seemed to be doing nothing. It was hard not to compare her to Ettu and Mery-tre, who were always busying themselves with stitching or something when I didn't need them. But if Ishtar had seen Nammu recently, she undoubtedly would have told her, or maybe it was Belet-ili who shared her mistresses's news. I could hardly ask with Nammu there to hear me.

"Yes, Ishtar came to tell me." It took me far too long to reply and Tiye had noticed. She narrowed her eyes, but didn't comment. Maybe she too was cautious about what she said in front of Nammu.

"I hear your two companions have left the palace," she said instead.

Her comment both startled and confused me, and my face probably gave far too much away before I composed myself.

"What do you mean?" I asked.

"Pharaoh tells me the little funny man hasn't been seen for weeks, and nor has his companion. A rather odd, tall fellow."

So she meant Pharaoh's palace. My limbs went weak with relief. For a moment, I had thought she was hinting she knew Tall and Half were hidden in my chambers.

"So where are they?" Please Marduk, don't let me blush and give myself away.

Tiye eyed me.

"That's the thing," she said. "Nobody seems to know. They simply vanished."

I shrugged and feigned nonchalance.

"I suppose they might have returned to Babylon," I said. "After all, they travelled here expecting to be with me. As they weren't allowed into the Palace, there is no reason for them to stay in Thebes."

"Hmm."

"Since you seem to be the first to hear the news, is there any word on Nebtu?"

I hoped she would tell me if she had heard about a woman's body being found, but Tiye leaned back against her couch in an exaggerated display of disinterest.

"Nothing past the messenger who confirmed she had returned to her father's house." She raised one hand and snapped her fingers. "Nammu, go get more melon juice. And fetch it from the kitchen yourself this time so you can make sure it's fresh. Don't let me hear you merely stood in the hallway and sent a runner again."

"Of course, my lady." Nammu hurried out.

Tiye waited until the door had closed behind her before she leaned towards me.

"You need to smarten up if you are to survive in this place," she said.

"I don't know what you mean."

"You ask too many questions and you do it too publicly. The administrators have said quite clearly that Nebtu went back to her family."

"I'm sure you don't believe that any more than I do."

"The difference, my dear, is that I don't go around being heard to ask questions."

"I was hardly asking in public. I asked you in the privacy of your chambers."

"In front of Nammu." She arched her eyebrows at me. "You surely know that woman cannot hold her tongue."

"Who could she tell that would cause a problem for me?"

"It doesn't matter *who* she tells. She will tell someone, who will tell someone else. Sooner or later, everyone knows you're still asking questions. Still mistrusting the word of the administrators."

"But they're lying," I said. "Nobody believes she went home."

Tiye sighed and shook her head.

"Kassaya, there are many secrets in a place like this. Plans are being laid, plots developed. There are people you can trust and those you can't."

"And which are you? Are you someone I can trust or not?"

"That you will have to decide for yourself." She gave me a steady look.

"What of me then? Have you decided whether I can be trusted?" I hadn't yet forgotten Henutmire saying she thought they had decided to trust me.

Tiye looked at me very hard, as if she was trying to see right through my flesh and into my heart.

"I think you are trustworthy enough," she said, "but you are too naive to be trusted."

"That doesn't make any sense. I'm trustworthy, but can't be trusted?"

"If you want people to trust you, you need to show you know when to keep your mouth shut."

"You mean I should stop asking about Nebtu?"

She only looked at me and didn't reply.

"What if I told you I had information about her?" My heart pounded. I hadn't meant to tell her anything, but the words slipped out. Maybe I wanted to prove she could trust me.

"What information?" Tiye asked.

I only shrugged at her.

"As you pointed out, we have yet to decide whether to trust each other," I said.

She looked down at her hands as if surprised to find she was clenching them. I took note of the careful way she relaxed her fingers and set her hands on her thighs. She took a deep breath and seemed to be trying to compose herself. Something I said had obviously rattled her, but I wasn't sure what.

"Kassaya, if you know something, you'd be advised to keep it to yourself," she said, meeting my eyes at last. "No good can come of that knowledge, and it would be dangerous for anyone to think you might know something."

CHAPTER 15

"My lady, there is news," Merytre said when I returned after visiting Tiye. They were all in the sitting chamber, even Half who was now strong enough to spend a few hours at a time out of bed.

I poured a drink, more to have something to do with my hands than because I was thirsty. Something in Merytre's voice said I wouldn't like this news.

"Go on then," I said.

"First of all, a messenger came to say Pharaoh is visiting the Palace next week and you have been invited to meet with him."

"Invited or summoned?"

Ettu cleared her throat pointedly.

"Do we know whether he is meeting with anyone else?" I asked.

"I asked the messenger boy, but he said that was all he had been told to tell you," Merytre said.

"I assume that means yes." I took a seat on the other end of the couch where Tall sat.

"I think so," Merytre said. "The boy looked decidedly uncomfortable when I asked."

"And you said I would be attending?"

"Of course," she said. "You cannot reject an invitation from Pharaoh."

I sighed. I was feeling particularly fatigued today and the prospect of an afternoon listening to Pharaoh talk about himself was less than desirable.

"Will you tell him about the babe?" Ettu asked.

"I'm not sure," I said. "Maybe I should wait until I'm more certain. What if there is no babe and I have already told him?"

All eyes went to Ahmose who shrugged.

"It appears you are indeed with child," she said. "But there is no certainty until your belly swells."

"I would rather wait a little longer," I said.

I leaned back against the couch and closed my eyes. I was too weary to bother going all the way to my bedchamber. I could rest here if the others weren't too noisy.

"There is more," Merytre said.

"More news?" I opened my eyes, although my head felt too heavy to bother raising it.

Merytre went to stand at the window. She tapped her fingers on the windowsill and seemed to be debating whether to say anything more.

"What is it?" Alarm seeped through me. Whatever this other news was, it could hardly be pleasant. She wouldn't spend so long trying to figure out how to tell me otherwise.

"My lady." She started, but stopped again and went back to staring out the window and tapping her fingers.

"Merytre, just say it whatever it is," I said. "It can't be that bad."

Merytre sighed.

"I heard something this morning when I went to fetch some more lotion for you. Remember how we ran out yesterday? I meant to get some then, but forgot."

She stopped again.

"Go on," I said.

"The servant woman who gave me the lotion told me something I think you need to know. It's about Lady Tiye."

I was more intrigued now than concerned. Tiye gave away little information about herself. It made it difficult for me to really understand her. Whatever this was, it would be one more piece to her puzzle.

"There is a rumour," Merytre said. "Some folk say…"

Her voice trailed away and I restrained my sigh. Marduk, surely it couldn't be that bad. I had never known Merytre to take so long to say something before.

"They say Lady Tiye is involved in the matter of the women who go missing." Merytre finished in a rush, as if she suddenly couldn't wait to get the words out.

"That's ludicrous," I said. "Tiye is as concerned as anyone else. She has actually warned me on several occasions to be careful."

"It wouldn't be the first time she has been responsible for a woman's death," Ettu said.

Indeed, it was well known that Tiye had engineered the downfall — and execution — of the woman who was Top Ornament and Pharaoh's Favourite before her.

"Tiye told me about that herself," I said. "It's not something she tries to hide."

"But if we know she has done such a thing before," Ettu said, "doesn't that make it more likely she is still doing it?"

"Tiye is not the type to be so underhanded," I said. "If she was involved, she would tell people. She would be proud of destroying a woman she sees as a competitor. She wouldn't keep it a secret."

"Maybe she only tells folk about that woman because it was already known that she was responsible," Ettu said. "It might not have been possible to cover it up. But she is older and smarter now. More savvy. She might have realised it would be wiser to do such things covertly."

"I have been in her chambers numerous times," I said. "And never have I felt like I was in any danger."

"I hardly think she would do anything there," Ettu said. "It would be too obvious."

"There would be no way for her to claim ignorance if a woman died in her chambers," Merytre added. "Lady Tiye is smarter than that."

"You both sound like you believe this nonsense," I said. "What about you, Ahmose? Do you believe it too?"

Ahmose gave me a steady look as she contemplated my question. She was never quick to give an opinion, and when she did, it was always well considered.

"I cannot say, my lady," she said at last. "I have never met Lady Tiye in person, so I know only what I have heard around the Palace, none of which is terribly complimentary, but that is to be expected in a place like this and with a woman of her status."

"Do you think she could really be a murderer?" I asked. "And not just once, but many times over?"

I wanted her to say yes or no. I could trust her opinion, whereas Ettu and Merytre might be more inclined to be swayed by gossip. But Ahmose only shrugged.

"She could be involved," she said. "But we must keep in mind that the Palace of the Ornaments is not the only place women have gone missing. We know it happens in Pharaoh's palace too. How would Lady Tiye, confined as she is here, impact on anyone there?"

"Allies," Ettu said quickly. "Alliances. We know she spends a lot of time with Pharaoh. He would have certain guards who are always with him. Particular servants who attend him."

"When Lady Tiye goes to his palace, she probably sees a certain administrator or official," Merytre added. She returned to her seat and seemed more at ease now. I assumed that meant she had revealed all her news.

"There would be people she sees on a regular basis," Ettu said.

"People who she has formed relationships with over the years. How long did you say she has been here?"

"Sixteen years," I said. "Since she was ten."

"And didn't you tell us her mother was a lady's maid to Queen Isis?" she asked. "So Lady Tiye probably grew up in Pharaoh's palace. There would be children she knew back then who are grown up now and have important positions there."

"This still all sounds like nonsense," I said. "I really can't believe Tiye would be involved."

"You were quick to think the queen might be," Ahmose said. "Why are you so fast to think it might be one woman but not another?"

"So you do think Tiye is responsible," I said.

Ahmose shook her head. "I am merely pointing out that your beliefs are not consistent. I have no opinion on whether she is or isn't involved."

I leaned back against the couch again with a weary sigh. Tall and Half had been silent while we spoke. They didn't know Tiye, but they had been immersed in Pharaoh's palace, so perhaps they had learned something useful about her.

"What do you two think?" I asked them. "What do folk in Pharaoh's palace say about the missing women?"

"Danger!" Tall said immediately. "Pharaoh!"

Half's response was a little slower.

"I myself have heard little speculation on the matter, my lady," he said. "There was much gossip when the servant woman disappeared — Kawit was her name — and folk spoke of how it wasn't the first time such a thing had happened, but nobody seemed willing to discuss who might be responsible. If they even know women disappear from here as well, I heard nobody say it."

Kawit. I hadn't heard her name before. Anyone who mentioned her had only described her as the servant woman. I felt a rush of sadness at her anonymity and resolved to remember to call her by her name in future.

"Speaking of gossip," I said. "Ettu said you would listen for rumours about the matter of Tiye's stolen jewels. Did you hear anything?"

Half shook his head. "Not even a whisper, I'm afraid."

That surprised me. It had been such a big event here, and my maids said everyone was talking about it. So, matters at the Palace of the Ornaments weren't always of consequence for those at Pharaoh's palace.

"I am going to tell Tiye," I said. "If folk are spreading mistruths about her, she needs to know."

"Are you sure that is wise?" Ettu asked. "If she is involved, telling her you know might be dangerous."

"What is she going to do? Stab me while I sit on her couch? No, the agreement we made was of friendship. That I would tell her if I heard gossip about her. This is my chance to act on that and show her I truly mean to be in alliance with her."

And maybe it would finally convince Tiye she could trust me with whatever "business" the women felt they couldn't discuss in front of me. There was some plan afoot amongst them and I sensed it might be big. Perhaps it was even something to do with the missing women. But until they brought me into their confidence, I would always feel like an outsider amongst them.

CHAPTER 16

$\mathcal{I}$ went to visit Tiye the very next morning, even though it wasn't usual for me to go two days in a row, not lately anyway. She was sitting in front of a little table which bore a rectangular box. The uppermost side was marked with a grid and had playing pieces positioned on various squares. A game of some sort. One of her maids sat opposite her, but quickly left when I arrived.

"Kassaya," Tiye said. "What a surprise."

She followed my gaze to the box.

"*Senet*," she said. "Do you play?"

I shook my head. "I have never even heard of it."

"You should learn," she said. "It is all about strategy. I suspect it will suit you."

I studied her as I took my usual seat, wondering what her comment meant. I had decided that if there was any sign she was in a particularly unpleasant temper today, I wouldn't tell her what Merytre heard. Not yet anyway. But Tiye actually seemed pleased to see me and her smile was as welcoming as it ever got. There were two maids in her sitting chamber, one of whom was

Nammu, and Tiye certainly wouldn't thank me if I said what I needed to in front of them. I leaned forward to whisper to her.

"I need to speak privately with you," I said.

"Nammu," Tiye said abruptly with a click of her fingers. "Melon juice. Benerib, is my laundry from yesterday ready to be collected yet?"

Nammu was already on her way to the door, but the other woman didn't rise from the chair she had just sat in. It was she who had been playing against Tiye.

"You already told Henuttawy to check this afternoon," she said.

"Go check it now," Tiye said.

"But—" the woman started. Tiye shot her a fierce glare and she quickly got to her feet.

It surprised me to hear her maid arguing. I didn't expect Tiye to be the kind of mistress who inspired loyalty, but I had thought she would be ruthless and her maids would be in fear of her. It seemed their relationship was combative, which showed me a different side to Tiye than I had known before. The door closed behind the two maids and we were alone in the chamber.

"Well then," Tiye said cheerfully. "This is all very mysterious."

"I promised to be a friend to you," I said. "That I would tell you if there was gossip being spread about you."

"You did." She eyed me, seeming a little more cautious now.

"One of my lady's maids heard something yesterday which I think you need to know about."

She said nothing, only nodded for me to continue. I felt rather daft now the moment had come. How could I tell her people thought she was responsible for murder?

"Apparently folk are connecting you with Nebtu's disappearance." I could hardly breathe as I said the words.

Tiye cocked her head to the side and studied me.

"How so?" she asked.

"There is talk that you are responsible for arranging for her to..." My voice trailed away. It was too ridiculous to say.

Tiye let out an exhalation that might have been either a laugh or a scoff.

"Oh my," she said. "Is that what concerns you? You looked so serious, I thought it must be something truly terrible."

"You don't think it's terrible people believe you responsible for women who disappear from their chambers in the middle of the night?"

"Folk will talk no matter what I do."

How could she be so unconcerned? Maybe it's because she really is involved, a voice inside me whispered. No, she couldn't be. She wouldn't sit here and look me right in the eyes if she was. She wouldn't dismiss such gossip. She would be horrified at being found out. She would demand details — where did my information come from, what exactly was said, who else have I told. Regardless of what was being whispered about her, there was no possibility of Tiye's involvement.

"That you came to tell me says much about your character," she said. "I confess I didn't believe you when you said you'd tell me if you heard gossip about me."

"I always keep my word," I said, a little stiffly. "If I can."

"That's unusual in a place like this."

I shrugged. "I said you could trust me and I wanted to prove it."

Tiye crossed her legs and leaned back against the couch, still studying me.

"I, too, have news," she said. "And I think it might particularly interest you."

I waited for her to continue, but I wasn't expecting what she said next.

"A woman's body was found yesterday," she said.

I was so busy trying to make sure I didn't reveal my guilty knowledge that it took me a little too long to respond. Tiye watched me closely and I was sure she didn't miss the emotions that must have played over my face.

"Nebtu?" I asked. It couldn't be, though. Tall and Half had known about her for several weeks. Unless it wasn't her body that was found at the quarry.

"Maybe. My source couldn't confirm." She didn't take her gaze from me.

"Where?"

"On the riverbank. Not far from the docks. It seems she washed up from the water."

So this wasn't the same body Half heard of. Two missing women and now two bodies. One of them must be Nebtu.

"What will happen to her?" I asked.

"She will be taken to the House of Life to be prepared for burial, of course. What standard of treatment she will receive depends on whether her identity is known and her family can be located to pay for it."

"And if nobody knows who she is?"

Tiye shrugged. "Her body will still be preserved, but she won't receive all the other treatments and blessings. I suppose she will be interred in a tomb for the poor."

"Where exactly is the House of Life?" I noticed how tightly I was clasping my hands and I relaxed them, hoping Tiye hadn't noticed. I didn't want to seem too interested.

"On the outskirts of the city."

Other questions longed to burst from my lips, but I kept my mouth closed. Too many might make her suspicious. Nammu returned with the melon juice and I made my excuses to leave. There was nothing more we could say in front of her, and I couldn't sit there and pretend to make pleasant conversation after Tiye's news.

Back in my own chambers, Ettu and Merytre were stitching away at projects of their own. They had finished two sets of clothes for each of the men. Half had been pleased enough to receive a new shirt and *shendyt*, but Tall was delighted. It seemed Ettu was correct that he wanted to seem less different to other men. He was in the men's bedchamber, but came out to the sitting chamber when I returned.

Ahmose sat nearby, immersed in conversation with Half. Her broken arm was less painful now and I rarely saw her with it propped up on a cushion anymore. I shared Tiye's information, careful to relay only what she had said herself, and not add any speculation of my own. Ettu gave me a sideways look.

"I fear I know what you're thinking," she said.

"We need to know whether it's Nebtu," I said. "If the body in the House of Life isn't, then the woman from the quarry must be. Either way, we will have confirmation of her death."

"Not necessarily," Ahmose said. "The body may not be in any condition that allows identification by now, especially if it is Nebtu, who disappeared some weeks ago. Whoever this woman is, let's say she was in the water for at least a few days. Her body will be bloated and some river inhabitant or other has probably taken a limb, at the least. It may not be possible to tell who she was. And separate to that, the priests might have rushed the preparation process and could already have the body immersed in natron."

"And surely other women have disappeared of late," Merytre said. "Neither body is necessarily Lady Nebtu."

"We only know of two women who have disappeared recently," I said. "Surely one of the bodies must be her."

We all looked to Ahmose, although I couldn't have said why I felt like she was the only one who might have an answer for this.

"It could be," she said, "and equally, it might not be. Women die for all sorts of reasons. Childbirth, ill health, misadventure."

"And murder," Merytre added darkly.

"Thebes is a large city," Ahmose said. "There would be deaths every day. However this woman died, we cannot assume the circumstances were suspicious, despite where her body was found. She may be from a very poor family who can't afford even the most basic embalming. Or she might be from an immigrant family who don't have the same beliefs about the afterlife as we Egyptians do and have no need for the preservation of bodies. Disposal in a river might even be something sacred according to their beliefs."

"I suppose you intend to try to see the body," Ettu said. She picked at a loose thread on her sleeve.

I was a little confused about her lack of interest. Weren't we all anxious to know whether the woman could be Nebtu?

"I will go to the House of Life," I said.

I hadn't intended to do it until that moment. Hadn't even considered it, in truth. But Ettu's assumption that I would do something made me want to be that kind of person. Someone who would grasp the opportunity to resolve the matter of a woman's death. Someone who would help the dead to rest easy by ensuring justice for her murder. I had never been expected to amount to anything more than the wife of one of my father's allies. Even I had never expected anything more for myself, but I had changed since I arrived in Egypt. I wanted to do something important. I wanted to *be* someone.

"So you intend to sneak out of the Palace, walk all the way across the city, and break into the House of Life to view a body?" Ettu shook her head. "Marduk, I can't imagine Lady Ishtar ever doing such a thing."

"I am not my sister." My tone was a little defensive. "And I want to know if this is Nebtu."

"Why is it so important to you?" she countered. "You spoke to her, what, once or twice? You barely knew her. Yet you are so desperate to know her fate that you're willing to put yourself in a lot of danger to do it."

"Because that could be any of us." I couldn't have articulated it before, but my tangled thoughts seemed to straighten as I spoke. "Ornament or servant, what difference does it make? We are all human. We are all women, and we are vulnerable. If it can happen to one woman, it can happen to anyone. If nobody will protect us, we must protect ourselves, and we can't do that without more information."

"But even if you see the body and verify it's Lady Nebtu, you can't tell anyone," Ettu said. "Not even Lady Henutmire. You will have to keep it a secret from the person who was her closest friend. Did you think about that?"

I hadn't, but it didn't make the matter feel any less urgent.

"If I can confirm it's Nebtu, I will find a way to let Henutmire know," I said. "Maybe I can say one of my servants heard something from someone else who heard about it."

Ettu sighed and shook her head.

"I suppose that's it then," she said. "When do we go?"

"You don't need to come with me."

"Of course I do. You can hardly go alone. Do you really intend to walk all the way across Thebes in the middle of the night by yourself? And how would you find this House of Life unless you take someone who knows where it is?"

"That wouldn't be you then," I said.

She shot a look towards Merytre.

"Oh no," Merytre said quickly. "Not me."

"Do you know where the House of Life is?" Ettu asked.

"Well…" Merytre looked away, studying first the floor, then the ceiling.

"Do you?"

"Not precisely."

"But you know roughly where?" Ettu pressed.

"Yes," Merytre admitted with a sigh. "More or less."

"That's settled then," Ettu said. "Merytre and I will go with you."

"Go!" Tall said.

"No," I replied.

"What did he say?" Merytre asked.

I kept forgetting she couldn't understand him.

"He wants to come too," I said.

"I think he should," Ettu said, and Merytre was quick to agree. "It will be safer if we have him with us."

"But then only Ahmose and Half will be here," I said.

"And neither of us will be alone," Ahmose said.

Half nodded in agreement. "I admit I would be of little help in any kind of scuffle just yet, but surely my mere presence would provide some security for Teacher, if only in the way of reassurance."

I would have preferred Tall stay with them, but I had to admit I would feel safer with him.

"You must promise to bar the door behind us," I said. "And don't open it for anyone until we return."

CHAPTER 17

We decided to leave as soon as it was dark. Ahmose prepared the potions to get us out of the Palace grounds and an extra dose for each of us in case we were delayed coming back. Merytre went to tell the kitchen to bring our evening meal early and that I wanted extra bread and cheese due to having a particular longing for them at present. We would take the bread and cheese with us.

"Maybe you should stay with Ahmose and Half," I said to Ettu. "There is really no need for so many of us to go."

The more who went, the higher the risk of someone being seen when they shouldn't. Ettu shot me a fierce look.

"I'm going with you," she said.

"I have Merytre to show me the way and Tall for protection. Wouldn't it be better for you to stay here?"

I thought it was a reasonable argument, but Ettu shook her head and the stubborn look on her face told me she wouldn't be persuaded. I supposed I could order her to stay, but then she would be upset with me and probably offended as well. It wasn't worth the hassle that would cause.

We watched from the window as darkness fell, and only once the last of the light was gone from the sky did we leave. Tall was swathed in blankets and scarves, and I figured the only other thing we could do was pray nobody would look too hard at him.

"Bar the door," I reminded Ahmose. "If anyone comes, tell them I have fallen ill again and have given orders that nobody is to be admitted."

"I will wait right here by the door," she said. "May Isis spread her wings of protection over you."

Tall brought her favourite chair and set it beside the door for her. It was a bulky, heavy thing, but he carried it with ease. Ahmose sank into the chair with a grateful sigh. I supposed she had intended to sit on the floor while she waited for us, which surely wouldn't have been comfortable at her age. As we hurried through the Palace, I thought about Ahmose's blessing. There was something comforting in the idea of a goddess wrapping wings of protection around us, like a giant blanket.

We took hallways which were less well used and departed through a back entrance. There was no way to avoid the door guards seeing Tall — we would have to open the door for him to see them before he drank the potion — so I could only pray they didn't ask any questions we couldn't answer. So far, they hadn't seemed particularly curious about the identity of any of the scarf-wrapped persons suddenly going in and out of the Palace.

We kept close to the wall that surrounded the grounds in the hope we would be less noticeable in the darkest shadows. Halfway to the gates, someone nearby cleared their throat. We froze.

My heart pounded so loud, I could hardly hear anything else. All we could do now was pretend we were merely out for an evening stroll and pray whoever had found us didn't want to see Tall with the scarves removed.

"Lady Kassaya." Khaemmalu stepped out from behind a tree.

Relief flooded my body so swiftly, my knees went weak. Thank Marduk it was Khaemmalu who found us. He was the only one of the night guards we knew we could trust.

"Good evening." My voice was steady, although I could already feel myself blushing beneath his intense stare.

Khaemmalu's gaze wandered to the sacks carried by Ettu and Merytre.

"Just a little snack in case we get hungry," I said and blushed even harder. It was a stupid thing to say, but I felt I needed to give some explanation. Khaemmalu raised his eyebrows but didn't comment.

"Where are you walking to?" he asked instead.

"Well, uh…"

I couldn't think of a reply fast enough. If anyone saw us, I had only planned to say we were taking a walk. I hadn't expected to be asked where we were going, but then Khaemmalu was the only one who would know we might plan to leave the grounds. And indeed his next words showed he had guessed our intention.

"The gates are currently closed," he said. "And I'm not aware of any visitors or messengers expected tonight. I'm afraid it's unlikely the guards will have any reason to open the gates before dawn."

"Oh." My hope of getting out fizzled. Ahmose's potion only worked as long as nobody looked too hard. If we had to knock and ask for the gates to be opened, the guards already knew we were there and the potion would be useless.

Khaemmalu sighed.

"I suppose you have some urgent reason for what you do tonight?" he asked.

"We do," I said. "It is most important."

"And do all four of you intend to leave?" he asked.

I only looked at him. He knew Ahmose's potion would get us past the guards, so there was no point in trying to deny it. Khaemmalu sighed again.

"Will all your companions be returning with you?" His gaze went to Tall, signalling he knew exactly who was under the scarves.

"Yes."

I waited for his reaction. I had thought for a moment he might help us, but would he still do it if he knew we intended to sneak Tall back in again afterwards? Just how far would he be willing to break the rules for me?

Khaemmalu hesitated for a long moment. My heart pounded so loudly I wondered whether he could hear it.

"Let's go then," he said at last. "Keep to the shadows and wait until the guards are distracted. Not that I suppose it matters to you."

We crept through the darkness, stopping at one point when Khaemmalu gestured for us to halt. He stepped out and spoke amiably with another guard, who soon continued on his way. As we approached the gates, I saw they were indeed closed. Khaemmalu pointed out where we should stop and we huddled together as he whispered to us.

"I will go and talk to them," he said. "When will you return?"

"Before dawn. Is there a way you could have the gates opened again for us?"

"I will go out an hour before sunrise. If you are back by then, you might be able to slip inside."

"We will be as fast as we can," I said. "If we aren't back in time, we will wait until tomorrow night."

"I don't suppose you want to tell me where you're going?" he asked. "In case something goes wrong. It wouldn't hurt to have someone here who knows where you are."

"There are people who know our plans," I said.

His mouth twisted a little.

"Khaemmalu, it's not that I don't trust you," I added quickly. "It's safer if you don't know too much."

"I am already inextricably involved in whatever you are

doing," he said. "I have been involved from the moment I discovered Ettu had left the grounds."

"I know and I'm sorry. I never meant to get you involved."

He only shook his head. Maybe he meant he didn't believe me, or maybe it was that he thought his involvement was inevitable.

"I will go now," he said. "Unless you need more time?"

"No, we can get out as soon as we see the guards."

He gave me a brief bow, then strolled away to the gates. He pounded on them and they opened. I saw the way he set his hand to one gate, opening it further as he passed through and giving us a good view of the two men outside. Khaemmalu greeted them, although his voice was too soft for me to make out his words.

Merytre passed us each a bottle and we drank. The potion had a sharp, aniseed taste with the sour undertone of something I couldn't identify. My heart pounded a little harder as I waited to see whether I felt anything. This was the first time I had taken Ahmose's potion myself, and although Ettu had said she felt no ill effects from it, I was still nervous.

Merytre set the empty bottles back in the sack, careful not to make any noise. We would dispose of her sack somewhere in the city rather than leave any evidence within the Palace grounds. Ettu carried the spare doses we would need in case we didn't get back before dawn.

"Ready?" I whispered and they nodded.

We tiptoed across the open space between the trees and the gates. My legs shook so hard, I feared I'd fall right over. The only time I had left the grounds since I arrived was when Pharaoh summoned me to his palace, and he sent a palanquin to fetch me then. Tall's cold fingers briefly touched my arm.

"Here!" he whispered.

I suddenly felt like I would burst into tears if I spoke, so I only nodded at him. As we snuck through the gates, Khaemmalu was still speaking with the guards. He had his back to us and I saw the way his shoulders stiffened. What would he do if the potion failed and the guards saw us?

Then we were through the gates and hurrying down the dark street. We had done it. We had made it out of the Palace of the Ornaments.

CHAPTER 18

For a while, I didn't even think. I just concentrated on putting one foot in front of the other, careful not to trip in the dark. The savoury aroma of evening meals reached my nose and my stomach churned a little in response. I seemed to be particularly sensitive to any kind of scent at the moment, no matter how palatable.

I didn't see Merytre dispose of her sack, but the next time I looked at her, it was gone. Ahmose was confident that if anyone found the empty bottles, there would be no way to identify the previous contents other than as some herbal concoction. Tall had removed the blanket and scarves, rolled them up, and carried them tucked under his arm.

It was a long walk and my feet were sore well before we arrived. I tried not to think about how much more they would hurt when we had to walk all the way back. The House of Life was a complex of mud brick buildings, some of which were in darkness, but a few had lamplight shining around the shutters. Someone was still at work. Maybe several someones.

"How do we know where to look?" I whispered to Merytre.

"I don't know," she whispered back. "If the body was only just brought in, it might still be in one of the preparation chambers."

"I suppose all we can do is look in the windows," Ettu said. "Although I don't know how we will see anything in the dark. We didn't think this through well enough."

"Doors!" Tall added.

"Yes," I said. "We could see if any of the doors are unlocked. I'm not sure I want to go sneaking through the buildings in the dark, though, especially while someone is still working. We might trip and make too much noise."

"What if one of us went and knocked?" Ettu suggested. "Pretend we are there to ask some questions? I could say my father has just died and I want to know what the process would be to have his body prepared here."

We looked at each other, considering it. Ettu looked unsure, even though it was her suggestion.

"What if whoever you speak to knows you are from the Palace?" I asked. "Or they might want to know where you live so they can collect the body for you."

"I think it would seem unusual for someone to enquire so late," Merytre said. "Especially a woman on her own."

I looked at Tall, waiting for him to comment, but he only frowned. Perhaps he didn't have the words to express whatever he thought, but he certainly didn't look like he thought it was a good idea.

"I don't know," I said. "There are so many ways that could go wrong."

"More than sneaking out of the Palace and spying through the windows?" Ettu asked archly.

I hesitated, hoping someone would have a more solid reason why Ettu shouldn't do as she suggested. When nobody replied, she shrugged.

"I'm going to knock," she said and hurried away before anyone could object.

I let her go. Calling her back would only draw attention to us and I was too tired after the long walk to chase after her if she was determined to do such a thing.

"I'm going to look in the windows," I said, trying to sound braver than I felt. If Ettu could go right up to the door and ask questions, I could at least peek through a window.

We snuck up to the nearest building with lamplight since there seemed no point in trying to see into the darkened chambers. I waited for someone else to go first — if Ettu were with us, she would be the one to step forward boldly — but nobody moved. So I tiptoed up to the window and peered through the shutters.

A lamp hanging by the door lit the chamber. Rows of shelves lined the walls, filled with a variety of crates and baskets and canisters. A large work table in the centre of the chamber. More crates on the floor, stacked tidily against the wall. No sign of a body.

I shook my head to let the others know there was nothing useful there. We moved on to the next window. I started to step forward, but Merytre stopped me with a hand on my arm and gestured that she would go. She didn't look like she wanted to and I figured she was only doing it because I already did. She looked in through the shutters for what seemed like a long time, only to return to us with a shake of her head.

At the next window, I peered between the slats and stifled a gasp. A naked woman lay on a wooden work table, her dark-skinned body neatly arranged with her arms and legs extended. The sound must have been enough to lure Merytre to join me. She came to stand with me, close enough that I felt her body stiffen when she saw the woman.

A man with the head of a long-eared dog came into my view, or at least I thought he was a man. The scene was so strange, I could almost believe he was a god. He held a large knife aloft and chanted something I couldn't quite hear. A prayer? A curse?

Suddenly, he plunged the knife down into the woman's belly. A gasp burst out of me and I slapped my hand over my mouth.

The naked woman didn't move or scream as the knife parted her skin. She was dead, of course. I had somehow forgotten that. Had thought it was a living woman who lay there.

Beside me, Merytre gagged and fell back from the window. I hadn't realised Tall was right behind us until she crashed into him. He let out a surprised "oof".

The dog-headed man looked up, cocked his head to the side. He started towards the window.

We rushed back to the street, Tall in the lead. He dashed behind a row of houses and gestured for us to follow.

I peered around the side of the building we hid behind. Back at the House of Life, the shutters stood open and the dog-headed man peered out. He seemed to shrug, then the shutters closed.

"See!" Tall whispered.

The image was burned into my brain. I would never forget seeing the dog-headed man loom over the naked woman and plunge the knife into her belly.

"Oh my," Merytre said, one hand to her chest. "I'm so sorry. If I hadn't stepped back in such a hurry, I wouldn't have crashed against Tall. That must have been what drew his attention."

Tall's face was tight and he flapped his hands.

"It's all right," I said, restraining my urge to reach for his hand. "That was the most disturbing thing I have ever seen. I thought she was alive. I thought I was witnessing a murder."

"Anyone lying in the House of Life will already be dead," Merytre said. "I'm sorry if I didn't explain that clearly enough. I didn't think we would witness something like that. I have never seen a dead person before and the thought of watching while he pulled out her organs—" She gagged again.

"It's obvious in hindsight that she must be dead," I said. "But that wasn't what I was thinking when I saw it."

"Dagger!" Tall whispered.

Now I understood a little of what he must have felt at seeing Half get stabbed. Only he knew Half was very much alive at the time, and Half was his friend. If I felt so discomfited at seeing such a thing when the woman was a stranger and already dead, how much worse must Tall feel?

"Do you think it was Lady Nebtu?" Merytre asked. "When I saw the knife and realised what was about to happen, I forgot I was supposed to be looking for her."

I had been so disturbed, I had entirely forgotten as well.

"I cannot say," I said. "I didn't see her face properly."

So that was it? All the risk we had taken to get out of the Palace grounds and to the House of Life, and we had no more information than we started with. Hopefully Ettu would return with something at least.

"Black!" Tall said.

"What was that?" Merytre asked me.

"He said black," I told her.

"Of course." She grabbed my arm in excitement, then quickly pulled away and gave me an apologetic glance. I waved away her indiscretion. "Her skin. She was too dark to be Egyptian."

The scene played again in my mind and I tried to ignore the horror of the dagger plunging into the woman's body and focus instead on the colour of her skin. Tall and Merytre were right. Her skin was black like Abar's, or the haughty-looking woman I saw in the courtyard the day Pharaoh came to the Palace. I nodded at Tall.

"You are right," I said. "It can't be Nebtu."

"Also I got the sense she was younger than Nebtu," Merytre said.

"Could she be the servant from Pharaoh's palace?" I asked. "Kawit."

She shrugged. "I never met her. Oh, look, here comes Ettu."

We waited in silence as Ettu hurried over to us.

"Well," she said, a little breathless. "That was interesting."

"Go on," I said.

"I spoke to one of the embalming priests. He was a bit stand-offish and I felt like I was asking all the wrong questions. But when I mentioned I had a 'cousin' who disappeared a few weeks ago and I wondered whether any unidentified bodies had been brought in recently, he stopped talking and practically shoved me out the door."

Merytre gave a little gasp. I shook my head.

"Ettu, do you really think that was wise?" I asked. "What if he reports that someone came asking questions?"

"What can he say? A woman who called herself Nefertari came to ask about making arrangements for her father, and also happened to mention a cousin who disappeared."

"You didn't tell him your real name?" I should have given her more credit. Ettu was probably the most sensible person I knew.

"Of course not," Ettu said. "But from the way the priest reacted, I think a mystery woman has definitely been brought in recently."

"Even if somebody knows who she is, and knows she doesn't have a cousin called Nefertari, there is nothing to link her to us," Merytre said. "They would probably just assume Nefertari's missing cousin is some other woman who hasn't been brought to them yet."

"But tell me," Ettu said. "Did you see anything useful from the windows?"

Merytre made a noise that suggested she would start gagging again. Nausea rose within me, quick and violent, at the memory of the knife plunging into the woman's belly. I swallowed bile and tried to feign composure as I filled Ettu in.

"We know one woman was found in the quarry," Ettu said. "So I would think her body would be…"

"Damaged," Merytre supplied faintly when she hesitated.

"Yes," Ettu said. "Broken bones and cuts, or something. Did you see anything like that?"

Merytre, Tall and I shook our heads.

"The other woman was in the river," she continued. "We don't know how long she was there, but Ahmose said her body would be bloated. I should think that would be quite recognisable, even from across the chamber."

"So it probably wasn't her either," I said.

"It wasn't either woman?" Merytre asked. "The one from the quarry or the one from the river?"

"I don't think it can be," Ettu said. "The woman you saw, the one with black skin, must be someone else."

"Should we check the other buildings then?" Merytre asked. "If that wasn't Lady Nebtu, she might still be in there somewhere." The look on her face said she wanted to do anything but that.

"The man that heard you will be listening for intruders now," Ettu said.

"Police!" Tall added.

"I agree," I said. "We don't want to risk getting arrested. I think that is all we can do for tonight."

"At least now we know an unidentified woman was definitely brought in," Ettu said as we started the long walk back to the Palace. "Even if we don't know whether it is Lady Nebtu, or the servant Kawit, that's more than we knew before."

"Maybe we can try again another night," Merytre said, although she didn't sound like she wanted to.

I said nothing, reluctant to reveal how much the thought of going back to the House of Life filled me with horror. The image of the dead woman stayed in my mind all the way back to the Palace. Her dark limbs neatly arranged on the table. The way she lay so still, her face turned away from us as if she watched the doorway for the man's return. Her bald head gleaming in the lamplight with no wig to give her dignity. The dog-headed man. I knew it was a mask, just like the ones the women wore at the ritual for Isis and Nephthys, but that didn't make the image any less disturbing. There was something wrong about seeing the head of a dog on a man's body.

"Safe!" Tall's hand briefly touched my shoulder.

I could only nod my thanks to him, certain I would burst into tears if I tried to speak. Thank Marduk he came with us tonight. Even though the dog-headed man surely wasn't following us, I felt much better at knowing Tall walked beside me, strong and true.

It was still a couple of hours before dawn as we drew near the Palace. We stopped where we would be out of sight from the guards, who would surely be suspicious if they noticed our party lingering, even if they didn't recognise any of us. There was nowhere to sit other than the road and nothing to lean against. I sat down anyway, although it would surely ruin the delicate fabric of my gown. My feet ached, I had blisters under the straps of my sandals, and I still felt queasy.

Ettu retrieved the bread and cheese from her sack, and shared it around. I waved her away when she offered me some, but she frowned so hard that I took a small piece of bread. I nibbled at the edge to make her think I was eating, but my stomach rolled and I kept picturing the knife plunging into the woman's belly. I could hardly make myself swallow even a few crumbs and I didn't miss that Merytre ate nothing.

"Time!" Tall said, getting to his feet. He held out his hand to help me up and didn't flinch even when he grasped my hand. Perhaps he didn't mind being touched if he was the one to initiate it. I would have to keep that in mind. We wrapped him in the blanket and scarves and made our way back to the gates.

They stood ajar, just as Khaemmalu had promised. He leaned against a post, chatting with the guards who each held a mug. I guessed he had brought drinks to give him a reason to be there. Khaemmalu and one of the guards stood facing the direction we came from, and I saw the way he studied them both, as if wondering why they didn't see us walk right down the middle of the road.

I held my breath as we passed between the guards. For a moment, I thought my sleeve brushed a man's arm, but if it did, he must have thought it merely a swirl of wind. Then we were through the gates and hurrying around the perimeter of the grounds. We stopped in a sheltered area to confer.

"Do we go back to the rear entrance?" Ettu whispered.

"I think we should wait until the guards change shifts at dawn and then go in the front," Merytre said. "If they have only just come on shift, they won't have any reason to wonder if we've been out all night. They'll just think we are returning from an early morning walk. And the guards at the back who saw us leave earlier will assume we went back in through the front entrance."

"Khaemope and Karpusa will be on duty at dawn," I said. "I have spoken to them a couple of times. I don't think they will ask any questions."

My gaze went to Tall and I hoped I was right. As incurious as Khaemope and Karpusa seemed, would they question the identity of this very tall person shrouded with scarves? Would we be safer going around to the back? My legs were tired and my feet throbbed where they were blistered. I didn't know how I would manage to walk all the way around the Palace, but if it was what we needed to do to keep Tall safe, I would find a way.

Tall met my eyes and must have thought I was waiting for him to offer an opinion.

"Wait!" he said.

I took that as an agreement with the plan to wait until dawn. With nothing else to do in the meantime, we sat down. The grass was cool and slightly damp beneath me. My gown was probably already ruined from sitting on the road, so it hardly mattered if it also had grass stains. I didn't think I could bear to wear it again anyway. It would always remind me of the night I saw a knife plunged into a woman's belly.

The sky was only just starting to brighten when Khaemmalu found us. He came to crouch beside me.

"Did you achieve what you needed?" he asked.

I shook my head, images of the dead woman again flashing through my mind.

"You look upset," he said. "Did something happen?"

"We just… saw something I would rather not have seen," I replied.

He frowned a little, but didn't push me for details. "Will you be returning to your chambers now?"

"We are waiting for the guards to change," I said.

"Aah." His gaze went to Tall, still hidden beneath his scarves. "You had no difficulty leaving the building earlier?"

"The back door guards were the only ones who saw us," I said. "They didn't ask any questions."

Khaemmalu frowned harder.

"That is good for you, but they really should have asked who that was, at the least." He nodded towards Tall.

"Do you intend to report them?" I asked.

He sighed. "I don't know. I should. They have been derelict in their duties and that jeopardises the safety of the residents. But if I say anything, it will make it that much harder for him to leave next time. It may also raise suspicion about whether somebody in the Palace shouldn't be there. The last thing you need right now is for the administrators to start sniffing around."

"That would be very bad," I said.

"I'm sure you are aware your men will be executed if they are discovered." He gave me a steady look.

"There is no other option. This is still the safest place for them."

"The one who was stabbed," he said. "Half, is it? Has he recovered?"

"Mostly. He still tires very easily. Gautseshen did very well. Ahmose says he wouldn't have survived without her aid. I'm very appreciative that you brought her and I want to give her something to thank her. Would you pass it on to her for me?"

I should have thought to offer a gift for her sooner.

Khaemmalu nodded, his face still conflicted. I held his gaze as I waited for him to decide whether to report the door guards for neglecting their duty. At length, he looked away and shook his head.

"I won't say anything," he said. "It is against my better judgement, but I will hold my tongue. For now at least."

"Thank you," I said. "I owe you a debt several times over."

"Go," he said with a nod in the direction of the Palace. "The guards will have changed shift by now. Get your man inside. I hope I don't see you or any of your servants sneaking out the gates again any time soon. The more often you do it, the more likely someone else will notice."

We ambled along the path that led to the front doors, trying to give the appearance of a leisurely stroll. It was indeed Khaemope and Karpusa at the doors.

"Good morning," I called as we approached. "A fine day, is it not?"

"Good morning, my lady," one of them said. I could never remember which was which. "You must have left very early."

"Well before dawn," I said with what I hoped would pass for a rueful chuckle. "I couldn't sleep and was so restless I woke some of my servants and asked them to accompany me for a walk. The sunrise today is magnificent, don't you think?"

"Very," the other guard said. He held the door opened and gestured for us to enter. I saw their gazes flick over Tall's shrouded figure, but to my relief, they asked no questions.

Back at my chambers, I knocked quietly and Ahmose swiftly let us in.

"Thank the gods," she whispered, closing the door behind us. "You were gone so long, I was beginning to fear something had happened."

I had thought Half might still be in bed given how early it was, but he was in the sitting chamber and looked far more awake than Ahmose. But, of course, she would have sat up waiting for us. Somebody needed to be there to unbar the door when we returned so we didn't make too much noise trying to rouse them. Tall moved Ahmose's favourite chair back to its usual spot. She hobbled over and eased herself down into it.

Tall gave a great sigh as he sat down and even Ettu groaned a little as she dropped onto the couch beside Half. Merytre went to stand at the window. I didn't know how she could bear to stay on her feet a moment longer, but maybe she was hoping to catch a glimpse of Sutem who would have come on duty at dawn.

I sat down and eased my sandals off. The blisters were red and swollen, but still intact. Hopefully that meant they would heal quickly. I explained to Ahmose and Half how we had to wait for the door guards to change shifts before we came back inside.

"That would seem wise," Half said. "But tell us, did you establish whether it was the Lady Nebtu who was taken to the House of Life?"

I waited, hoping someone else might explain, but Ettu and

Merytre only looked to me. Tall, of course, wouldn't be the one to tell them. Haltingly, I described the scene in the House of Life. My words didn't adequately describe the horror, but Half still looked disturbed. Ahmose only nodded, as if it was no more than she had expected.

"The internal organs need to be removed," she said. "Before they putrefy. The body can't be preserved properly once it begins to rot."

I didn't let myself think about what that might mean for either of the missing women if it had been some time since they died. Ahmose's unbothered explanation didn't erase the awfulness of seeing the knife descend into the woman's body.

"There is more, though," I said and nodded towards Ettu for her to share the information she had gained.

"Well," Ahmose said when Ettu had finished. "It seems that was quite an informative visit. Even though the body you saw wasn't Lady Nebtu, we know it's quite possible she is indeed at the House of Life and probably now being rushed through the usual preparations before anyone else comes looking for her."

I opened my mouth to comment, but nausea rose up within me, sudden and vicious. I must have made some sound, because Ettu was quick to jump up and bring one of the buckets we had positioned around the suite for just such a moment. She held it for me as I vomited. I felt bad she had such a distasteful task, but she handled it as calmly and efficiently as she did everything.

"I will leave this in the hall," she said when I had finally finished. She set a clean bucket by my feet.

"Do you intend to go back to the House of Life again?" Half asked. "To search for more definitive information about the Lady Nebtu?"

We were all silent as Ettu opened the door to set the bucket outside. Neither Half nor Tall moved to leave the chamber and nobody commented on it. I supposed it was still early enough that surely nobody should be wandering the hallways, but it also worried me that we had already become so casual. We needed to be more vigilant about the possibility of someone seeing them. It was only once the door was closed that Ettu answered Half's question.

"I don't think there is anything to gain from it," she said. "From the way that priest rushed me out when I asked about my 'cousin', it is clear he won't provide any information. I had hoped he might let me see the body if someone had indeed been brought in, to confirm it wasn't my dear cousin, but that seems unlikely."

"We would have to break into the building to try to see her," Merytre added. "The priests will be suspicious if someone else comes asking about a missing relative."

"Whoever she is," Ettu said, returning to her place beside Half, "at least her body is being preserved. That seems important for those of the Egyptian faith."

"I suppose that's the end of it then," Merytre said.

Ettu nodded in agreement. "We know a woman has been taken to the House of Life," she said, "but we cannot confirm she is Lady Nebtu."

I hated not knowing and I had hoped to be able to give Henutmire some certainty. But they were right. We had gained all we could and it was highly likely that whoever the mystery woman was, her body was now buried in natron in case anyone else came asking.

"Same!" Tall said.

He looked intently at me as if expecting me to understand. I puzzled over what he might have meant.

"I don't understand," I said. "I'm sorry."

Tall held up his hands and flapped them near his face.

"Same!" he said again.

"Buddy, can you tell us more?" Half asked. "What is the same?"

"Body!"

I still had no idea what he meant, but Half was nodding.

"You could be right," he said. "We don't actually know there were two bodies found."

"But we do," I said. "You heard about the woman found at the quarry and we know a second body was found near the river."

"That's just it," Half said. "We have been assuming they are two different women. We know the woman from the quarry was being moved to somewhere else, but we don't know where. How do we know her body wasn't moved to the river?"

It made no difference, though. Whoever the woman was, we had no way of getting any further information about her. She might be Nebtu, or she might not. I had desperately wanted to solve the mystery of Nebtu's disappearance, but it seemed this was as far as we could go.

CHAPTER 20

*I*n the dining chamber a few days later, I took my usual spot next to Henutmire. Ineni and Gilukhipa were there also, their tables drawn close together as they whispered to each other. They didn't seem to notice when I entered, but Henutmire gave me a cool smile. She obviously hadn't forgotten how strange I had been with her lately.

"Good morning," she said when the serving women who swarmed as soon as I sat down had finally departed. "I haven't seen you here for a while."

"I haven't been very hungry in the mornings," I said, fixing my gaze on my table in the hope my face wouldn't give me away. I fiddled with my mug, already regretting taking my usual portion of goat's milk. My stomach churned and I wasn't sure milk would stay down.

"Are you with child?" Henutmire asked. "I heard your sister is."

Forgetting myself, I shot her a look to find her watching me with an odd expression. Happiness for me, perhaps, but mixed with something else. Wistfulness maybe. Or longing.

"You are blushing," she observed.

"I blush a lot." I was aiming for an airy tone, but knew I didn't quite manage it. "I hardly know why half the time."

"This is a difficult place in which to keep a secret." She bit into her bread and studied me as she chewed.

"It's not exactly a secret. I'm just not ready to tell anyone yet."

"Does Pharaoh know?"

"No, I wanted to be certain before I told him."

"Well, it would seem your future is assured," she said. "Both you and Ishtar."

A serving woman came to offer a tray of fruit. Henutmire took half a pomegranate and began scooping out the insides, dumping them on her plate in a tidy pile, before she ate them one by one. I shook my head when the tray was offered to me and waited until the woman left before I replied.

"Does everyone know?" I asked.

"About you? Or her?"

I shrugged. "Both."

"I'm not sure Ishtar has told anyone herself, but her maids have made it known. You, on the other hand, I've heard nothing about. It was only the look on your face that made me suspect it."

"I can't help blushing. I wish it wouldn't happen."

"Perhaps you need to care less what others think of you," she said. "You might be slower to blush then."

"You make it sound easy. Just care less." I toyed with a slice of bread, knowing I should eat something. It seemed too much effort, though, and I really wasn't hungry.

"I find there tend to be two kinds of women here," Henutmire said. Her voice was a little warmer now. Maybe she had forgiven my recent oddness. "Some find a way to live their life without caring a great deal about what anyone else thinks."

"Like Tiye."

"Exactly. Have you ever seen her blush because she suspected someone knew something about her?"

I scoffed. "Of course not."

Tiye cared desperately about maintaining her position as Pharaoh's Favourite, but as best I could tell, it was about conserving the extravagant lifestyle she had become accustomed to. She didn't seem to care about Pharaoh himself. I'd never heard her say anything that could be taken as criticism of him, other than her comments about how he couldn't see his heir for who he was, but she had also never given any indication she liked the man. However, she was ruthless when it came to the security of her position.

"She doesn't care what any of us mere mortals think of her," Henutmire said. "She only cares what Pharaoh thinks."

"I thought the two of you were friends," I said.

"We are." She gave me an amused look as she ate the last of the pomegranate. "I haven't said anything I wouldn't say in front of Tiye herself. She knows how folk see her. The point I'm trying to make is that she doesn't care. You, however, do care. Desperately."

I took a bite of bread, not because I wanted it, but to give me a reason to not answer her immediately. As I chewed, I mulled over Henutmire's words. I did care what people thought of me. Having grown up in the shadow of my older, more beautiful, and more accomplished sister, I was always painfully aware of being the lesser daughter. The one who wasn't as pretty, who couldn't sing and dance and make witty conversation.

What of Nebtu, I wondered? Had she cared what folk thought of her? Did that have anything to do with her disappearance? Maybe she had been in some kind of trouble but had hidden it, not wanting anyone else to know there was a problem. I wanted to ask Henutmire what she thought, but one of the servant women was close enough to overhear.

"I am right," Henutmire said when I didn't respond. "Aren't I?"

"I suppose. I don't know how I'm supposed to just stop caring, though."

"Tell yourself that everyone is far more concerned with themselves than with you," she advised. "That helps for me."

"So you don't care what anyone thinks of you."

She hesitated, as if trying to find the truest response.

"Not quite," she said at last. "I try. I don't always succeed, but all I can do is try."

I nodded and ate some more bread to avoid talking. We didn't say much else and she took her leave soon after. As Ettu and I walked back to my chambers, I noticed fewer of the folk we passed reacted to her *shendyt*. It seemed it was becoming commonplace to see Ettu, at least, wearing men's attire. It almost made me wonder if I could try it myself.

"Lady Ishtar's pregnancy is all anyone is talking about," Ettu said, drawing me from my musing. "Three different lady's maids mentioned it to me while you were dining."

"Henutmire says Ishtar's maids have been telling everyone."

"One of the women who told me this morning said she heard it directly from Belet-ili. I suppose Lady Ishtar must have told her to tell folk."

"I don't understand why she wants everyone to know so soon." Realising I was limping, I tried to walk more normally. The blisters I gained on our expedition to the House of Life were healing, but one on my toe was still uncomfortable when I walked. I didn't want anyone speculating on how far I had walked to develop blisters.

"She's new, and she wants to increase her status," Ettu said. "I gather it's quite unusual for a new Ornament to be with child so soon, but then Pharaoh has paid her an uncommon amount of attention."

If only Ishtar didn't keep seeking so much attention from everyone else too.

"Maybe I should speak with her," I said. "Encourage her be a little more discreet."

"Do you think that will do any good? Isn't she likely to…"

Ettu's voice trailed away, but I could guess what she was thinking. After all, she served Ishtar before she served me. She knew my sister well.

"She will probably think I am jealous," I said.

Was I? Was that why I felt so uncomfortable with the news of Ishtar's pregnancy spreading through the Palace?

<h1 style="text-align:center">CHAPTER 21</h1>

"*D*o you think you should write to your father?" Ettu asked me later that day. "Tell him you are with child?"

It was barely mid morning, but already the day was uncomfortably hot. She had opened the shutters as soon as she rose, but there wasn't even a whisper of a breeze today and the air felt heavy. I couldn't see her from where I lay on a couch, but could hear her walking and straightening things around the chamber. I had my hands on my belly, which was still as flat as it had ever been, and I was feeling far too lazy to lift my head to look at Ettu. Ahmose said it was the growing babe which made me feel so tired, but surely it was too soon for that, given my belly hadn't even started to swell yet.

"My lady?" Ettu prodded.

"I suppose I should. I was waiting until I was more certain."

"Lady Ishtar might have already written to him."

Of course she would have. She would be eager to reinstate herself as our father's favourite.

"And Henutmire might not be the only person who has

128

figured it out," she added. "It would be better for your news to come from you, not your sister."

"If Ishtar had heard, she would have come to ask me," I said. "She would want to hear it for herself. I don't think she would tell Father if she couldn't be sure it was no more than gossip, even if she was writing to tell him of her own babe."

"It is your decision, of course. I only know that I wouldn't want my father to hear such a thing from my sister, especially..."

"Especially what?"

I swung my legs down and manoeuvred myself around to sit up. My head spun a little from the sudden movement and I clutched the couch while I waited for it to stop.

"Especially since she's now an Ornament," Ettu said. "Surely she would have written to tell him that."

"I suppose so." I didn't tell her I wondered whether Father had sent Ishtar to me with the expectation of her catching Pharaoh's eye. I was all but certain it was Father's way of ensuring at least one daughter would bear a son for the alliance. I couldn't tell anyone, though. It was too humiliating. "Very well then. I will write to him today. Send for the scribe."

Pentau arrived a couple of hours later. He was a skinny little man, with a belly that sank in beneath his ribs, and a scalp that looked naturally bald rather than shaven. He glanced around the chamber, and I was sure he took note of who else was there: Ettu, Merytre and Ahmose. Tall and Half were in their bedchamber, with the key to their door secured in my pouch. They had been warned to be absolutely silent and still while the scribe was here. I had little doubt he spied for the administrators and would be swift to tell them of any suspected anomaly.

Pentau dropped to his knees and set up his wooden writing table, meticulously arranging his various reeds, inks and sheets of papyrus on it. When he was finally ready, he gave me an expectant look.

"We shall begin," he said.

"You will write to my father," I said. "His name is Marduk-apla-iddina and he is the king of Babylon."

Pentau dipped his reed in the ink and waited.

"What language will you use?" I asked.

"It doesn't matter," he said. "You tell me your letter and I will transcribe it appropriately."

"But I want to know," I said.

He sighed as if I was being unreasonable. It was exactly the same noise Amankhau often made at me.

"Akkadian," he said. "Since I assume your father is not learned in Egyptian."

It was a snide comment, almost insulting, but I let it pass without comment. It was true my Father didn't read Egyptian, or at least I thought it was. He could read and write in both his native Babylonian and the diplomatic language of Akkadian, and he could speak a little Egyptian, but if he had ever learned to write in that language, I was unaware of it.

"You should start with, to the great and mighty Marduk-apla-iddina," I said. "Father, I was very pleased to receive your letter."

I was careful not to mention that his letter was in reply to mine. Pentau would, of course, be well aware he had never before written to my father for me, and I had no doubt Amankhau would have confirmed that with him. I waited until Pentau's reed paused before I continued.

"I write to tell you that Ishtar has arrived safely. I am most appreciative to have her here with me."

I wouldn't mention that she was supposed to be my maid or her elevation to Ornament. The less said of Ishtar, the better. This letter was to remind him of his other daughter. The one who had been sent to marry Pharaoh and seal the alliance.

"I have met with Pharaoh on three occasions now," I said. "In fact, I contributed in a small way towards saving his life when the boat we were sailing on overturned in a sudden wind."

Ettu cleared her throat, which I took to be a commentary on

the way I minimised my part in saving Pharaoh. I didn't want to sound boastful though, or to describe the situation in a way that might make Father think I was exaggerating, or worse, had made it up.

"Pharaoh was swift to thank me by inviting me to a banquet at his palace," I said. "I dined with him and his queen."

A subtle reminder he hadn't told me I wouldn't be queen myself.

"He has invited me to meet with him again. I hope to have the opportunity to remind him of how Babylon is his best ally and that you, Father, are a true and worthy friend."

Another reminder of why he sent me.

"Our two countries will soon be united in another way — with a shared child. Father, I confirm I have done the duty for which you sent me here. I carry a child of Pharaoh in my belly. A child of the alliance between Babylon and Egypt."

That was what I needed to tell him, but now I didn't know what else to say. Should I ask him to pray the babe would be a son? That my child would be delivered safely? That I would survive the birth? Surely any father would pray for such things without being asked.

"I hope this news pleases you," I said instead. "I remain your dutiful daughter, Kassaya."

I waited while Pentau finished his scribbles. He seemed to take longer than necessary for what I had said and I wondered whether he was embellishing my somewhat brief letter.

"Read it back to me," I said.

Pentau was already packing up his things.

"There is no need," he replied. "You know what it says."

"I want to make sure you have written it correctly."

He got to his feet and gave me a look which seemed rather more hostile than was reasonable.

"I am the Royal Scribe of the Palace of the Ornaments." His voice was chilly and already he moved towards the door. "I am extremely experienced and Pharaoh himself appointed me to this role. Anything you ask me to write for you will be transcribed appropriately."

"I would still like…" My voice trailed away. There was no point in saying anything else as Pentau was already gone.

"Well," Ettu said as the door not-quite-slammed behind him. Merytre jumped up to slide the bar into place. "I think we can all agree he is a rather unpleasant fellow."

"He said your letter would be written appropriately," Merytre said. "Not accurately."

"I wondered whether I misunderstood," I said. "But it's probably why he reacted like that when I asked him to read it back to me. He has changed my words and doesn't want me to know."

"Do you want to send your own letter as well?" Ettu asked. "I could take it and find a courier."

"No, Father would think it strange if two letters arrived, whether they say the same things or different. If he replies, he would probably comment on it, even if I asked him not to. The administrators are already suspicious about whether I sent a letter that didn't go through Pentau and that would only confirm it."

"Of course," Ettu said. "And we don't want them looking too closely at you. Not now."

Her words reminded me that Tall and Half were still locked in their bedchamber. I fished the key from my pouch and passed it to her so she could let them out.

Ettu was right. I couldn't afford to do anything to call attention to myself while we concealed the men within the Palace. I needed to pretend to be a compliant and obedient Ornament. I needed to be more like Ishtar.

CHAPTER 22

On the morning I was to see Pharaoh, my lady's maids took an interminably long time to bathe me. Ettu had selected the gown and wig I would wear, but I heard several muttered conversations about their unsuitability and how it really should be an Egyptian who chose my attire on such an important day.

I spent far too long debating whether to remind the mutterers that Ettu was in charge of my lady's maids, but conversation turned to other matters and I decided to hold my tongue. It was Panouk who had chosen her for the job, not me, and he obviously didn't think it necessary the position went to an Egyptian. Besides, I wasn't sure it would help Ettu if I was seen to favour her. Best to let the women come to their own understandings.

When I was finally ready, both Ettu and Merytre escorted me to the chamber where I was to dine with Pharaoh.

"I wonder who else he has asked," Merytre said as we made our way through the Palace. Our destination was apparently on the far side and it was quite a walk from my chambers.

"I don't know." Please, Marduk, let him have invited someone else. Anyone. Just don't let me have to be alone with him.

"Will you tell him you are with child?" Ettu asked.

"It depends on who else is there." And whether the chamber had a bed. If it did, I would be swift to tell him in the hope I wouldn't have to suffer him trying to get me with child again.

They both lapsed into silence after that. I wished they would talk, if only to distract me from worrying about the evening, but I supposed my brief answers had done little to encourage conversation. They probably thought I preferred silence.

At length, we reached a chamber with a row of guards stationed in the hallway. I caught the eye of one who gave me a brief nod. Flustered at his unexpected acknowledgement, I looked away without responding, before belatedly realising it was he who led me back to the palanquin after Pharaoh bedded me. He had been kind, even if he didn't directly acknowledge my distress. I would have liked to thank him if it didn't mean speaking to him in front of half a dozen of his colleagues.

By the time I looked at him again, he was looking elsewhere and the opportunity had passed. A guard at the door searched me for weapons before waving me in. Ettu and Merytre followed, having similarly been searched.

The chamber was the same one I had gone to the last time Pharaoh summoned me at the Palace of the Ornaments, the one with the strange murals of the gods. The time I took Ishtar and he noticed her but not me. I was hardly surprised to find her already there.

Her gown, the colour of lapis lazuli, emphasised her dark eyes, and silver bands around her wrists and ankles drew attention to her graceful limbs. I couldn't stop my gaze from dropping to her belly, but as with me, there was no visible sign of her pregnancy yet. She looked at me, studying me as I studied her, and I was somewhat taken aback by the hostility in her gaze. Here I was, still thinking of her as my sister. Still trying to forgive her for what she had done. Yet it seemed she saw me as nothing more than a rival for Pharaoh's attention.

I don't want him, I longed to say. I am not the enemy. Ettu and Merytre were fussing around me, straightening my gown and smoothing back stray hairs, and I let my attention be diverted. Ishtar and I needed to talk. Really talk. But she wouldn't be receptive to such a conversation now while we waited for Pharaoh. Finally satisfied with my appearance, my maids went to join Belet-ili and another maid who stood with their backs to the wall. I heard them murmur quiet greetings before they all fell silent.

"Good evening, Ishtar," I said once I was sure the wrong words wouldn't burst out of my mouth. "Are you well?"

Her hand went to her belly and I would have sworn a glimmer of concern crossed her face.

"Wonderful," she said. "And you, Sister?"

I pressed my hands against the sides of my thighs, not wanting to give myself away by letting them stray to my belly as hers had.

"Well enough," I said. "Do you know whether anyone else has been invited tonight?"

"No." Her tone was rather short now. "I was under the impression I would be dining alone with Pharaoh."

A serving woman came to offer me wine, saving me from the need to reply. What did Ishtar expect me to do? Refuse Pharaoh's invitation just in case she had also been invited? She's nervous, I told myself. You know she isn't really as hostile towards you as she seems. She's just trying to find her place here, like all of us.

I wandered around the chamber as I sipped my wine, looking at the murals so I wouldn't have to come up with something to say to Ishtar. The painting of the elongated woman balancing on her hands and feet still puzzled me and I stared at it for some time, trying to make sense of it. Ishtar made no such attempt to be engaged by the art and I could feel her eyes on me as I studied the painting. I held my head high and pretended it didn't bother me.

As usual, Pharaoh kept us waiting for a long time before he finally deigned to arrive. I knew the wait was almost over when guards swept through the chamber, checking for whatever hidden threats they thought might assail Pharaoh. Finally, the man himself sauntered in.

He lowered himself to a couch with a heavy sigh, and serving women rushed to offer him wine and a footstool. Ishtar and I dropped to our bellies in front of him. I hated this moment, waiting with my face to the floor for him to condescend to let us get up. It felt like an act designed to be humiliating.

Pharaoh, however, seemed to be in a good mood tonight, because as soon as he had a goblet in his hand, he told us to rise. I was careful not to trip on my hem and acutely conscious I didn't get to my feet as elegantly as Ishtar. I should probably practice. Merytre could undoubtedly teach me how to get up without looking as awkward as I felt. I sipped my wine to give myself something to do.

Pharaoh offered a benevolent smile and waved his goblet towards us.

"Well," he said.

I waited, but it seemed that was all he had to say. I should try to make conversation. Say something clever before Ishtar spoke. Why hadn't I thought to prepare some topic we could discuss? While I was still trying to think of what I could say, Ishtar beat me to it.

"My lord, it is such a pleasure to dine with you tonight," she said in a voice that dripped with adoration. "How generous of you to invite us."

"Yes indeed," Pharaoh said. "Very generous."

He eyed us both. I looked away to the elongated woman, discomfited by his examination.

"You look enough alike that you could be sisters," he announced.

Did he really not remember he had seen us together twice before? Was I that forgettable?

"We are, my lord," I said quickly before Ishtar could respond. "Our father is Marduk-apla-iddina. He sent me in fulfilment of the alliance between Babylon and Egypt."

"Babylon, yes." Pharaoh studied us both from head to toes. Ishtar blushed charmingly while I tried not to fidget. I had always hated being stared at and it was even worse when it was him. It made me feel like a piece of meat he was about to tear into. Predictably, his examination of me was brief while his gaze lingered on Ishtar.

"Sisters." His voice was thoughtful. "How pleasant."

I didn't like the change in his tone. Hopefully he wasn't picturing himself in bed with both of us at once. How would I get out of it if that was his intention? I could feign a sudden, violent illness. If I said I had loose bowels, surely he would tell me to leave. He wouldn't want to be subjected to such a thing. I should have asked Ahmose to give me something I could take if I needed a sudden sickness.

"I hope you were pleased with the gifts our father sent you." It was only after the words were out of my mouth that I remembered asking him about this previously. He had brushed me off then and no doubt he would again. But now I had started, it would seem odd if I didn't finish what I was saying. "There was livestock, rolls of fine cloth, gold and silver, and many gems."

"I believe my scribe sent a message to Babylon to acknowledge their receipt," Pharaoh said with what I supposed was meant to be a magnanimous nod. I was surprised he gave me that much.

"Did you receive any reply?" I asked since he seemed to be in an amenable mood.

"Oh yes, something about a new trade agreement."

Pharaoh drained the last of his wine and held up the goblet to be refilled. A serving woman rushed over. She wore only a woven girdle, as was usual for the women who attended him and I realised I was becoming so accustomed to seeing nakedness that I hadn't even noticed. I waited until she left and Pharaoh had taken a gulp before I spoke again.

"I trust you were able to come to an arrangement that benefits both countries?" Father had bid me to advocate for Babylon's benefit and this was my first opportunity. But how could I do such a thing when I knew nothing of the details?

"You don't need to worry your head about it." Pharaoh gave me a smile that felt too much like a leer to be reassuring. "Come, my dears. Sit with me, one on each side. Yes, that's better."

I had moved before Ishtar could and claimed the spot on the same side as the hand he held his goblet with. My speed paid off, because we had barely sat down before he had his free hand on Ishtar's thigh. He squeezed her leg and I heard her soft inhalation. Was he hurting her?

"My lord," I said to distract him. "Perhaps you could tell us about this trade agreement with Babylon? Both my sister and I would be very interested to hear the details. Wouldn't we, Ishtar?"

"Of course," she said in a very quiet voice. Pharaoh finally released her leg.

"No, no," he said. "That is far too serious a subject for dinner conversation and it would be too much to expect you to understand. We will talk of something else."

He gave me an expectant look and I realised I was supposed to suggest an alternative topic. I searched my mind frantically.

"Will there be any kind of ceremony to farewell Kia?" I asked.

Her body would be undergoing preparations in the House of Life for some weeks yet, but that didn't mean arrangements couldn't be made in the meantime. Surely there would be some official farewell for her.

"Who?" Pharaoh gave me a blank look, his free hand once again searching Ishtar's thigh.

"Kia," I said. "The Ornament."

"I'm afraid I don't know who that might be," he said. "Let's talk about something more interesting."

"Surely you remember Kia," I said, confused by his reaction. "She was there when we went sailing on the pleasure lake behind the Palace. The three of us and Kia."

He gave me a vague shrug and took a long drink of his wine.

"The day the boat turned over," I said. "There was a sudden gust of wind. Kia and a serving woman both died."

I didn't even know the serving woman's name. How terrible that I had never thought to ask.

"The day I almost drowned," he said. "Yes, you have been rewarded for that. How does it feel to have played some small part in saving the life of a god?"

"But Kia couldn't be saved." I should stop talking. I probably wasn't thinking clearly, but I couldn't figure out why he was pretending not to know who she was. But even though I *knew* I shouldn't say anything else, my mouth kept moving. "She was too long at the bottom of the lake."

"Aah," he said, jumping to his feet. "It would seem dinner is finally served."

He headed over to the dining tables where the serving women waited with their platters. I couldn't tell whether he really knew nothing about Kia's death or if he just didn't want to remember. Could it be true that nobody told him two women died that day?

CHAPTER 23

I made my selections from the platters offered by the serving women, although my appetite had fled in the face of Pharaoh's refusal to acknowledge Kia's death. Roasted hen and goat, baked fish, a variety of vegetables and salads. I piled my plate with more than I would normally eat, since if my mouth was full, Pharaoh surely couldn't expect me to make conversation. I had already said too much.

I should be hungrier than I was, having eaten nothing but a few bites of bread this morning. The nausea I was experiencing each day made food unappealing until sometime after noon when it finally settled. Ahmose said it would pass in a few weeks and I prayed to Marduk she was right.

Ishtar ate sparingly, and I wondered whether she, too, was experiencing nausea, despite her insistence on how well she felt. She offered a few comments — observations about the recent weather and other trivialities — but Pharaoh made little response, too intent on his meal. What was his queen doing tonight? Was she relieved to have an evening away from him? Maybe she had her own lovers who were invited to visit her when Pharaoh was away. The thought amused me so much that I must have smiled without realising.

"Why do you smile?" Pharaoh asked abruptly.

I had thought him too focused on his meal to notice anything I did.

"I was merely thinking how fine the food is," I said. "It is certainly much grander than what we normally eat."

"Yes, well, one can hardly serve slop to a god," he said, before raising a goat shank to his mouth and gnawing on it.

"Of course not," I said.

His attention was already gone, though, and it probably wouldn't have mattered how I replied. Although I had dined with him before, it still amazed me how much Pharaoh could eat. The serving women brought their platters again and again. He fondled the bare buttocks of one and she hastened her step away from him. She was careful to only approach him from the front after that and to back away, giving no further opportunity for grasping fingers. So, not every woman in Pharaoh's vicinity desired his attention. It made me feel a tiny bit better to know I wasn't the only one repulsed by him.

It was only when Pharaoh had eaten his fill that Ishtar and I gave up pretending to eat. He glanced at Ishtar's barely touched meal and frowned.

"Does the food not please you?" he asked as he got to his feet.

"It is very good, my lord," she said.

"Then why didn't you eat?"

"I wasn't hungry."

He frowned at her.

"What is wrong with you then?" he asked. "Are you ill?"

Her hands went to her belly and it was only because I knew her so well that I recognised the way she hesitated. There was no babe, I realised with sudden clarity. She made it up. Perhaps she thought Pharaoh's fascination with her would mean she'd be with child shortly anyway and nobody would know of her lie.

"No, my lord," she said. "I am with child."

He didn't react.

"Your child," she said.

"Well," he said. "That pleases me greatly. You have done well."

"Thank you, my lord," she said softly.

"And what of you?" Pharaoh turned his attention to me now. "I know how sisters like to compete. Are you with child as well?"

As if he thought I could make myself conceive by merely wanting to better my sister. I glanced at Ishtar while I tried to decide how to reply. She peered at me from beneath her lowered lashes. Her smugness irritated me, especially since I had figured out her secret.

"I am." Why did I say that? I had decided I wouldn't tell him yet. But it was hard with Ishtar standing there, her hands covering her still flat belly, shooting me a look that said she had achieved something I hadn't.

"Well, well," he said.

Ishtar's face had changed. Her mouth twisted and she glared at me with steely eyes.

"Sisters," Pharaoh said. "And both carrying the child of a god at the same time. They will be sons, of course. You should take care to ensure that."

"Of course, my lord," Ishtar said.

I didn't reply. It was a nonsense thing to say anyway. No woman could control whether her babe was a boy or a girl. Unless Ahmose knew a way. If she could ensure my babe was a son, perhaps I wouldn't need to endure Pharaoh lying with me again. Provided the child lived, I would have done my duty and ensured my future of a retirement villa in the city, or at least that was what Tiye said would happen.

We returned to the couch, and this time Ishtar beat me to the spot where I sat previously. Now I was on the side of Pharaoh's free hand and it was me who suffered his fingers searching my thigh. I barely listened as he spoke — it was nothing of consequence anyway — too intent on the hand that edged higher up my leg. I managed to move it down a little by shifting as if to straighten my gown, but the hand went straight back to creeping up my thigh. I edged backwards, pressing myself against the back of the couch, but that left me with nowhere else to go.

"I shall have rewards sent to you both," Pharaoh announced suddenly. He held out his goblet to a serving woman and she departed to refill it. I had lost count of how many times he had drained his goblet tonight. "What would you like?"

He looked from Ishtar to me, his eyebrows raised as he waited for our requests.

"Whatever my lord thinks is suitable," Ishtar said, her voice so demure I had to stop myself from scoffing. "But if it pleases you, I should like a pretty necklace. I don't have anything nearly as nice as all the other women here."

"Excellent," he said.

I held my head high and tried to pretend I couldn't feel his hand on my leg. He squeezed my thigh, hard, and I bit my lip to restrain my gasp. Surely he only did such a thing to provoke a reaction. Perhaps he would stop if I gave no sign of noticing.

"And you?" he demanded of me.

A sudden feeling of recklessness tore through me. He was clearly feeling amenable and if he wanted to reward me, perhaps this was my opportunity. If someone was covering things up, he surely knew, and if not, it might provoke him to make enquiries.

"I would like information," I said. "An Ornament went missing a few weeks ago. Her name is Nebtu."

He gave me a dark look. He might have pretended not to know Kia, but he definitely knew Nebtu.

"What of her?" he asked in a tone that held none of the affability he had displayed on learning there were to be two babes.

"I would like to know whether she has been found." I held my breath as I waited for his response. Was this too much to ask?

Should I have asked for a necklace like Ishtar? I knew I had made a mistake when his face changed.

"Get out," he shouted and shoved me so hard, I fell right off the couch and sprawled on the floor. "Out. Both of you. Leave me at once."

I caught Ettu's eye. She and Merytre still stood against the wall with Ishtar's two maids, and the look on her face said she was wondering if she should come to help me. I shook my head slightly. It might only incense Pharaoh even more.

I got to my feet slowly, hissing at the pain in my shoulder. There had been no time to brace myself as I fell and I landed on my arm. I straightened my gown and walked to the door, determined not to limp or show any other sign of pain. Pharaoh would probably take pleasure in that. Ishtar followed me, her sandals whispering against the floor, and our maids hurried after us. A guard opened the door as we approached.

"Wine!" Pharaoh bellowed as the door closed behind us.

Ettu and Merytre rushed to my side.

"Oh, my lady, are you hurt?" Ettu asked. Her fingers were already reaching to straighten my wig.

"Your sleeve is quite ruined," Merytre said. "You must have scraped it on the floor as you fell."

"My shoulder hurts," I said. "But I don't think anything is broken."

"You must let Ahmose look at it," Ettu said, taking me by the arm. "Here, let me help you. Your legs are probably unsteady after such a fall."

I had forgotten Ishtar until she spoke.

"Sister," she said.

I stopped and turned back to her. She cast a glance towards the door, as if wondering whether anyone in the chamber would hear her, and came closer to me before she spoke.

"You should not mention such things to him," she said. "He doesn't like to hear of any unpleasantness."

"Unpleasantness? Ishtar, a woman is missing. Probably dead. That's more than just unpleasant. How will her spirit ever rest peacefully as long as there has been no reckoning for her death?"

"But it will not be Pharaoh." Her eyes seemed to beg me to understand something she wasn't saying. "Understand this, Sister. You don't just endanger yourself when you anger him. You endanger all of us."

She hurried away down the hallway with her maids at her heels.

"Come," Ettu said, tugging my arm. "We do not want to be loitering here if he comes out."

CHAPTER 24

It wasn't until we were back in my chambers with the door safely barred that Ettu spoke again.

"What an abhorrent man," she said.

"You shouldn't say such a thing." I sank onto a chair with a sigh of relief. Merytre was already pouring me some wine, which I accepted with a nod, although my stomach churned at its aroma.

"There is no one in here who will disagree," Ettu said.

"Did something happen?" Ahmose asked as she returned from unlocking the door to Tall and Half's chamber. She took in my appearance, which was surely dishevelled, with a frown. "Are you injured?"

"He pushed her right off the couch," Ettu said. "She fell on her shoulder. It is probably dislocated."

"Let me look." Ahmose was already at my side, her careful fingers probing my shoulder and neck. "It is not dislocated. You would be in far more pain if that was the case. I think you have wrenched it, though, and it will likely be sore for a few days. I will fetch you some willow bark to ease the pain so you can sleep."

"I don't think I can—" I started, but my stomach made a most alarming sound. I clapped my hands over it. "A bucket. Quickly."

Merytre had barely shoved a bucket in front of my face before my stomach emptied. When I finally sat back with a groan, Ahmose frowned as she inspected the bucket's contents.

"What are you doing?" I asked. "Put it in the hallway and send a runner to have it emptied."

"What did you eat?" Ahmose still examined my vomit and made no move to do as I said.

"I don't know." Fatigue suddenly washed over me and it seemed like far too much trouble to think. My stomach gurgled and growled again. "Nothing unusual."

"Be specific," she said.

"Fish. Hen. Vegetables."

"And to drink?"

"Wine."

"How much?"

"One goblet, and I didn't even finish it."

Ahmose frowned and held the bucket closer to sniff at it.

"What is it, Ahmose?" Ettu asked. "You are suspicious."

Ahmose shrugged. "It may be nothing."

"But you don't think so," Ettu said.

Ahmose took one last look at the bucket's contents and went to the door. She waited until Tall and Half disappeared back down the hallway again before she opened it and set the bucket outside.

"I will go find a runner," Merytre said and slipped out.

"Well?" Ettu asked Ahmose. "What concerns you?"

"The possibility of poison," Ahmose said.

"I have been poisoned?" I sat up, although the sudden movement made my stomach roll. I clasped my hands over it and prayed I wouldn't vomit again. Ettu fetched another bucket and set it by my feet.

"It's just a little odd," Ahmose said. "You were well when you left and you return only a couple of hours later violently ill. It is different to your pregnancy sickness."

"I didn't eat anything different to Ishtar," I said. "Or Pharaoh, and he ate far more than either of us. Do you think they have been poisoned too?"

"As soon as Merytre returns, she and I will go check on Lady Ishtar," Ettu said. "If she, too, is ill, we can assume you have all been poisoned."

"Do you think someone was trying to kill Pharaoh?" My heart felt like it was beating way too hard and I suddenly couldn't catch my breath. "Have I…"

"Without knowing what you have taken, I can't tell you anything else," Ahmose said. "If you survive the night, we can probably assume you didn't ingest a fatal dose of whatever it was."

A knock came at the door and Ettu let Merytre in.

"Ahmose thinks it was poison," she told Merytre.

They all stared at me.

"Maybe the fish was bad," I offered. "That would make me ill, wouldn't it?"

"It would," Ahmose said. "Although I'm not sure it would take effect so fast."

"We will go check on Lady Ishtar," Ettu said. "Come, Merytre."

It was only after they left that Tall and Half came back out to the sitting chamber. Tall sat beside me, patted my arm reassuringly, and didn't seem to mind that I reeked of vomit.

"Sick!" he said.

"Yes, I fear I have eaten something I shouldn't have," I said.

"Do you need anything, Princess?" Half asked. "Perhaps we could help you to your bedchamber?"

The thought of being alone and possibly poisoned filled me with terror. I shook my head, unable to voice my fear.

"I will sit up with you," Ahmose said. She probably guessed I was afraid I would die alone in my chamber. "Let me just fetch a few herbs to make you more comfortable."

"Should I try to purge it?" I asked. "In case it's poison."

She gave me a steady look. "I can give you something to make you vomit again, but if it can be purged, you have probably already done so. If not, it's likely too late."

My hands cradled my belly. The babe was too small to feel yet. I hadn't even felt it move.

"The babe?" I couldn't bear to look at her as I asked. Didn't want to know if she lied to me.

"I cannot say," she said. "If you have been poisoned, undoubtedly the babe has too."

Tears welled. I hadn't really thought of the babe before as anything other than the fulfilment of my duty to my father and my country. But I suddenly realised I wanted it to survive. I wanted it to live.

The babe would be taken from me once it was born. I knew that much from talking with Tiye. All Pharaoh's children lived in his palace. They received schooling and had companions their own age. My child, be it a son or a daughter, would grow up as the child of Pharaoh, a prince or princess, surrounded by half-siblings. My child would live in ultimate luxury with the finest tutors and instructors. If it survived to be born.

Ettu and Merytre returned, their faces grave.

"She is ill, isn't she?" I asked. They hardly needed to say it.

"Yes," Ettu said. "We didn't see her, but her lady's maid said she vomited before she even reached her chamber."

"Belet-ili?"

"No, another one. I don't know her name. I think she is new. Belet-ili was attending to Lady Ishtar."

"I'm sure she will be well looked after," I said.

A great wave of weariness washed over me and suddenly I could barely hold up my head.

"I will fetch you a blanket," Ettu said.

Ahmose had disappeared while we were talking and she returned now to press a mug into my hands. A familiar aroma — spicy and sweet at the same time — reached my nostrils. I had smelled it often while Half was recovering.

"Willow bark," Ahmose said. "And a couple of other things. Drink it all, if you can."

"I will probably just vomit it back up."

But my stomach wasn't churning the way it had before and it was only when I raised the mug that I remembered the pain in my shoulder. Compared to how ill I felt, my shoulder was nothing.

"Drink it anyway," she said. "The longer you can keep it down, the better."

It was unpleasantly bitter, although she had tried to mask the taste with honey. My stomach churned as I sipped it, but at least I didn't vomit again. By the time I finished drinking Ahmose's potion, Merytre, Tall and Half had all gone off to bed. Merytre blew out the lamps before she went, leaving just one to light the chamber.

Ettu took the mug from me and helped me lie down. She draped a blanket over me and sat on a nearby couch.

"I can sit with her," Ahmose said. She fetched a blanket from her bedchamber, then turned down the last lamp and settled herself in the chair beside it.

"I will keep you company," Ettu replied, tucking her feet beneath her.

Ahmose said nothing further, likely recognising the stubbornness in Ettu's voice the same way I did. She spread the blanket over her lap and folded her hands on top.

I watched the two of them for a while. They sat in silence and each seemed absorbed in their own thoughts. I kept finding myself in darkness and realising I had closed my eyes. Eventually I gave in and let myself drift off to sleep.

I woke when my stomach spasmed violently. The chamber

was still dim, lit only by the single lamp. Ahmose snored softly, still propped up in her chair. Ettu lay on the couch and seemed to be dozing, but she woke when I sat up.

"My lady?" she asked quietly. "Is there a problem?"

I couldn't speak. The pain was coming in waves. Ettu came to crouch beside me.

"What is it?" she asked. "Are you going to vomit again?"

I shook my head.

"Ahmose." Ettu's voice was sharp and the old woman woke with a start. She eased herself out of her chair and came to look at me. She set her hand to my forehead and leaned close to sniff my breath.

"She is not as ill as before." Ahmose picked up my hand and lay her fingers over my wrist. "Her pulse is strong and she has no fever."

"My lady, what woke you?" Ettu asked. "You must tell us so we can help you."

"Belly," I said, panting a little. "Cramps."

I didn't miss the fearful look Ettu gave Ahmose. They lay me back on the couch and Ahmose probed my belly firmly. She put her hand between my legs, perhaps checking whether I was bleeding. At last, she pulled the blanket back up over me.

"I don't think it is the babe," she said. "It is just the poison working its way through her body."

"Are you certain?" Ettu asked.

"As much as I can be without being able to see into her belly," Ahmose said.

"Should we call for a physician?" The look Ettu gave me suggested she thought I was about to die.

Another wave of cramps gripped my belly and I groaned.

"There's nothing a physician can do for her at this stage," Ahmose said. "I don't believe she is in mortal danger. Her body is resolving the poison, if that's what it was."

"She will survive?"

Ahmose nodded. "I am quite confident of it."

They stayed beside me until the cramps eased. Eventually I drifted off again, although it was a restless sleep filled with confusing dreams. The priestess with the scaled face lay in a bed in a dark chamber. Suddenly her eyes opened and she looked right at me.

You, she seemed to say, although I never saw her mouth move. *I see you. I warned you. Leave while you can.*

CHAPTER 25

By morning, the cramps had passed and the nausea had settled, although my stomach was still tender. My whole body felt fragile, as if I was a mud brick crumbling to dust. Ettu had gone off to her bedchamber at some point since I last woke, replaced by Merytre who was still curled up on a couch, fast asleep. Ahmose woke shortly after I did and got to her feet with a groan. She rubbed her wrist absently as she hobbled over to me.

"Do you still think it was poison?" I asked as she felt my forehead and wrists and belly.

"If it was, you got only a small dose," she said. "Maybe it was just some bad fish, like you thought."

But she frowned and didn't look convinced. She rubbed her wrist again.

"Does it still hurt?" I asked. She no longer kept it bandaged, but I had noticed she seemed to avoid lifting anything with that hand.

"It aches sometimes," she said. "Mostly in the mornings while the air is still cool."

Tall came stumbling out from the men's bedchamber, looking

more asleep than awake. His hair was sticking up and it struck me that even when they lived in Pharaoh's palace, neither he nor Half had taken to shaving their heads or chins as the men here did.

"Sick!" he said to me.

"I'm feeling much better," I said.

"Belly!"

"Yes, it was very sore."

"Danger!"

"You think it was poison too?"

Tall's face was serious and he seemed to think hard. He opened his mouth, then snapped it shut, as if the words he sought weren't what were about to come out.

"Danger!" he said again. "Pharaoh!"

"Pharaoh was probably ill too. If there was poison in the food or the wine, we all had it."

Only Pharaoh had consumed more of both than Ishtar and I put together. How sick was he? Was the poison strong enough to kill a living god? I supposed we would hear something very soon if he had died. I absently noted my lack of emotion at the thought, and didn't let myself think too hard on why I didn't care if he had gone to the West, as the Egyptians put it.

"Oh, you're awake," Ettu said as she came in. "You look much recovered."

"I do feel better," I said.

"I will go check on Lady Ishtar as soon as Merytre is up," she said.

"I'm awake," Merytre said, sitting up and straightening her wig. "Let me just get changed."

"Should we send a messenger to tell your lady's maids you won't need them today?" Ettu asked.

"Yes, please." It would be a relief to not have to endure their ministrations, especially while I felt so fragile.

Ettu and Merytre returned with word that Ishtar was likewise much recovered. There was no mention of her supposed babe and I didn't ask. I felt better at knowing she was well enough. I had feared she might be more gravely ill than me, that she might die while there were still things unsaid between us. I would speak to her as soon as we were both recovered. I needed to tell her how much I had resented the position she put me in by her scheme to get herself out of being sent to Egypt. But I would also tell her I had forgiven her. She and I might never be friends again, but we could at least be sisters.

I spent the day on the couch, dozing on and off, and watching the others as they made use of the daylight hours. Ahmose disappeared into her bedchamber, muttering about checking her stocks of herbs. Ettu and Merytre worked on their stitching, a task they both seemed inordinately fond of. Merytre was almost finished her wall hanging of the lion-headed goddess. I tried not to look at it because it made me feel quite odd. There suddenly seemed to be too many lions in my life. Lions everywhere I looked.

Half was carving a small chunk of wood with a knife. I couldn't quite make it out and he covered it when anyone got too close, so I assumed he didn't want us to see it just yet. Tall seemed to spend a lot of time standing beside the window. He was careful to position himself where he wouldn't be seen if someone in the grounds happened to look up. I wondered whether he was watching for something particular, but I felt too tired to bother asking.

I passed my time thinking and often caught myself with my hands pressed to my belly. Father had told me to provide Pharaoh with many sons, but I hoped he would be satisfied with just one. The thought of giving birth terrified me, but I would have Ahmose with me and there would surely be a midwife I could call for. In a place like the Palace of the Ornaments, where women giving birth must be a frequent occurrence, there would be an abundance of experienced midwives available. Pharaoh would want his children delivered as safely as possible. Especially if they were boys, I thought, remembering his admonishment that Ishtar and I should ensure we both bore sons.

"Ahmose," I said as the old woman came back out to the sitting chamber. "We need to do that test. The one that will tell me whether I carry a boy or a girl."

"I was going to wait until your belly began to swell," she said. "But perhaps we should do it now. I will get barley and emmer today."

I guessed what she didn't want to say: that if it was poison and I had lost the babe, neither the barley nor the emmer would sprout. At least I would know.

Father knew that whichever daughter he sent to Egypt wouldn't be queen. He told Ishtar, but not me. I had made my peace with the knowledge, but now I carried Pharaoh's child, everything seemed possible.

If I bore a son, he would be another boy child who might one day be heir to the throne. He wouldn't be the most likely — there were other, older boys, including Tiye's, who were ahead of him — but it was still possible. After all, many children didn't make it to adulthood. They suffered illnesses and injuries, ailments and accidents. Too many died as infants or as young children. Who other than the gods knew whether Pharaoh's heir, Ramses, would live long enough to succeed him? And Tiye's boy might not survive either. Or any of the other sons. One rampant plague could wipe out the royal children in a matter of days. If I had a son, he might yet be heir.

And that would make me the mother of the heir. Pharaoh would surely bestow great favour on such a woman. Maybe she would be the next queen if Isis died. Even a queen wasn't immune to death. Wouldn't that surprise my father if I became queen despite all the obstacles between me and that position?

I scoffed at the ridiculousness of my own thoughts. Even if I bore a son, and even if all the other sons somehow died, Ishtar would likely get herself with child sooner or later. And Ishtar being Ishtar, she too would bear a son, and he would be the most impossibly perfect child.

If we both had sons and there was nobody else to be heir, Pharaoh would surely choose her child before he chose mine. It was ridiculous to even think about such a thing.

CHAPTER 26

Several days passed before I felt fully recovered. In that time, I was unable to eat anything more than a few bites of bread without my stomach churning. Ahmose procured a tray of soil, sprinkled barley and emmer seeds on it, and I urinated over it. She set it on a table in the sitting chamber, where we would all see as soon as something started to grow.

I tried not to look at it too much, fearing my stare would make the seeds reluctant to sprout. It was probably a ridiculous thought, but I didn't want to do anything that might interfere in the process. If neither barley nor emmer sprouted, there would be no child delivered, and I wanted to know my babe would live almost as badly as I longed to know whether or not it was a son.

By the time I felt well again several days later, I was restless to get outside. To feel the muscles in my legs move as they carried me. Feel the sun on my skin and the breeze against my face. But every time I suggested leaving the chamber, someone would be quick to voice their disagreement. Ahmose would say I should rest. Merytre would comment that I still looked very pale. Ettu would urge me to think of the babe. Half would say I should do whatever Ahmose said.

Only Tall never commented. I sometimes saw him looking towards the window with an expression of longing on his face. I had only been confined to my chambers for a few days. How must he and Half feel knowing they could never leave? I couldn't expect them to stay here for the rest of their lives, scurrying away down the hall to be locked in every time we needed to open the door. It was not a life worth living.

"I am going for a walk," I announced as I got to my feet. "Who will accompany me?"

If I couldn't get outside for a little while, I feared I might even be inclined to do some needlework, and I didn't want to think I was that desperate. Ettu pursed her lips and Ahmose was already shaking her head. I went to the door and waited with my hand on the knob. Tall and Half hurried off to their bedchamber and I tossed Merytre the key to their door.

"I am going," I said, "and I will hear no arguments about it."

Ettu gave a great sigh.

"I suppose I shall come with you then," she said.

We didn't speak until we were out of the Palace. I took a deep breath of the night air. It was cool and fragrant. I suddenly felt lighter, as if the weight of my confinement had rolled off me by merely stepping outside. Ettu and I set off along one of the paths.

"Ettu." I kept my voice low, mindful of the guards who patrolled the grounds at all hours of the day and night. "I have been thinking about Tall and Half. We cannot continue to keep them in my chambers."

"I know."

We walked in silence for a few moments before she spoke again.

"They know it too," she said. "Half and I have discussed it, but he is determined not to leave you."

"What would they do if they left? Where would they go? How would they live?"

"I don't know, and I cannot say I think it is any safer for them to leave than to stay. Not after the attack on Half. Right now, nobody other than us, Khaemmalu and Gautseshen know he still lives. But as a pair, they are too distinctive. If word went around about two men like them in Thebes, the fellow who stabbed Half would know it is them. Whoever it is might come after him again, especially if they have reason to believe he knows something he shouldn't."

Her voice trembled a little as she spoke.

"I know you care for him," I said. "Half. Does he feel the same?"

She stopped to lean over and sniff a particular flower that had caught her eye. "Oh, that is lovely. I would like a perfume with that exact scent."

We walked a little further before she replied.

"I have not asked him," she said, "and nor have I told him of my feelings. There seems little point in it. Once I have fulfilled my service to you, I intend to make my own way in the world. There is no place in my plans for a husband."

It was no more than she had said the last time I asked.

"I suppose you don't necessarily need to marry him," I said.

"It's not quite that simple," she said. "I want to be free. To determine my own fate. I don't want a man, be he husband or not, to tell me what to do."

"Does it need to be like that, though?" I felt like I was stumbling in the dark. Ettu made me think about things I'd never considered before. Maybe it had something to do with her new attire. After all, dressing like a man surely gave a woman a different perspective. It almost made me wonder whether I should try wearing a *shendyt* myself. "Why couldn't your relationship be a partnership? Why does the man always get to make all the decisions?"

"Because they are men and we are women, and that is the world we live in," she said, a little tartly. "And it frustrates me no end. Why should a man decide my life for me? I am equally as intelligent as many of the men I have met. Why can I not make my own decisions?"

I wondered whether she was thinking of my father who had been the one to decide she would leave Babylon and everything she had ever known, and come with me to Egypt. Was it that event that made her so passionate about choosing her own fate, or was that merely one episode in a series of events that led her to these opinions? I didn't feel like I could ask.

"I don't know." I let my fingers trail along a bush as we passed it. Its leaves were soft and cool. "Like you said, it is the world we live in. I cannot imagine it being any other way."

"I like to think it will change one day. Maybe not in the time of our daughters or granddaughters, but maybe our great-granddaughters will have more freedom."

"It would be nice to think so." I didn't believe it, though. Women would never make their own decisions. Men would always control us.

Somewhere ahead of us, a bush rustled. It was only a slight movement, but it seemed loud in the night's silence.

"Hush," I said to Ettu. "Someone is there."

"It is just me, my lady." Khaemmalu stepped out from behind the bush and bowed. "I'm sorry if I startled you."

"Not at all," I said. "I knew it would be one of the guards."

"May I walk with you for a while?" he asked.

"Of course."

Ettu dropped back so Khaemmalu could walk beside me on the path.

"I heard you have been unwell," he said. "You and your sister both."

"We fell ill after dining with Pharaoh," I said. "Maybe the fish was bad."

"I see."

"What does that mean?"

"Nothing, my lady."

"You don't have to keep calling me that, especially in private."

"Nothing then, Lady Kassaya."

"Just Kassaya is fine," I said. "Really."

He made a small sound that might have been either a scoff or surprise. I was tempted to ask what that meant too, but held my tongue. I didn't want to sound argumentative.

"It is so nice out here at night," I said instead.

A light breeze had cooled the air pleasantly and whisked away the heaviest perfumes from the flower beds. Insects chirped and leaves rustled. The moon was high and almost full, and a multitude of stars blanketed the sky. Ahmose had told me the Egyptians believed their Pharaohs became stars when they died. It must be comforting to think of a favoured ruler spending eternity looking down on his people.

"I used to work the day shift and it was awful," Khaemmalu said. "I much prefer the nights when the air is cooler and there aren't so many people wandering around."

"Are we disturbing your peace then?"

"No, never."

"What does your family think of you working nights?" I asked. "Surely you must hardly see them if you sleep during the day and work all night."

"I have no family other than my sister."

"No wife or children?"

He cleared his throat and seemed a little uncomfortable at my question.

"You don't have to answer that," I said quickly. "I didn't mean to pry."

"No, it's fine. It's been three years, but I still have trouble finding the words to tell anyone."

I waited for him to continue. Our sandals whispered against the path and a lone owl hooted a few times before falling silent.

"I was married," Khaemmalu said eventually. "For almost two years. Then she… disappeared."

"She left you?" I didn't want to make assumptions, but his tone had turned ominous.

"If she did, I saw no sign it was about to happen. We were happy enough, or so I thought. We had been trying for a babe, but the gods hadn't seen fit to grant us one, and we were arguing about it. But I didn't think we were unhappy."

"What happened?" I asked.

"One day, we both went off to our jobs. I was still working the day shift then. I returned home shortly after sunset as usual, and she wasn't there. I thought she must have been held up. That maybe she had to work late for some reason, although it had never happened before. I waited all evening, but she never came back."

He stopped to clear his throat. I waited in silence. A feeling of dread had crept over me the moment he said his wife didn't come home.

"I went to her workplace and asked around," he said. "But nobody had seen her since earlier that day. I went to the homes of her parents and her brother, and each of her friends, but nobody had any news of her. In the morning, I went back and asked all of them again, and still nobody had seen her. She never came home again."

His voice was composed but tight, and it was obvious he still found it painful to remember. I didn't want to ask, but I had to know. I was pretty sure I already knew the answer.

"Where did she work?" I asked.

Khaemmalu sighed and looked away, out into the darkness.

"In Pharaoh's palace," he said.

CHAPTER 27

_I_ hardly knew how to respond. Khaemmalu's wife was yet another woman who had gone missing. Were they all connected? Could it be that the danger was actually in Pharaoh's palace, not here? We had privately speculated about the possibility of the queen's involvement. Could that really be true?

"I'm sorry," I said, having finally realised I still hadn't responded. "It must have brought up a lot of memories for you when Nebtu disappeared."

"Yes." He kept walking and I thought he wasn't going to elaborate, but at length, he sighed. "Every time I hear of another woman going missing, it reminds me all over again about those dark days after Tabiry didn't come home. I would rather think she left me. That one day, she simply got up and decided she couldn't bear to live with me any more, and she walked out the door and just kept walking. If it wasn't for the other women who have disappeared, I would think that. But it's happened too many times. I believe—"

His voice broke and I waited while he composed himself. We

kept walking, although the night air which previously felt cool and refreshing, now chilled me.

"I believe she has gone to the West," Khaemmalu said. "I suppose she might have been the one woman who was different. The one who left of her own accord, but I don't believe it to be so. We didn't have much, but she took nothing, not even any food. I truly believe she went to work that day with the intention of coming home again."

"But something happened to her," I said.

"Something happened."

We walked in silence for a few moments. I wondered whether I could push him any further. So far, he had seemed amenable to my questions.

"Do you have any idea what?" I asked. "Were there any clues?"

He gave me a sideways look, as if he took my measure, and seemed to hesitate.

"No," he said at last. "Nothing definite."

But his voice had changed. He knew more than he was saying. Despite the secrets he knew of mine, he wasn't yet ready to trust me with his own.

"Eventually, whoever it is, will make a mistake," I said. "They will take the wrong woman, or someone will see something. They will be caught one day."

"Maybe. But maybe it won't matter. Maybe the person responsible is too powerful."

So he, too, suspected the queen. I couldn't think who else it could possibly be. The only person more powerful than the queen was Pharaoh himself. It couldn't be him, though. He was above the law, as folk kept telling me. There was no reason for him to hide any crime he committed.

"It will all come out," I said. "The gods won't allow such things to remain hidden for ever. One day, the person responsible will be uncovered and they will be punished."

Khaemmalu tipped his head up to look at the stars. If I had

done that, I would surely have tripped over something, but he walked as sure-footedly as ever.

"I would like to believe that, Kassaya," he said. "I truly would. But for now, I should leave you to finish your walk while I continue my patrol."

He bowed and disappeared into the darkness without another word. Ettu caught up to me again. I had almost forgotten she followed us, she had been so quiet. She would have been listening to every word, though.

"Well," she said. "That was unexpected."

"How many missing women do we know of now? Nebtu, Kawit who disappeared from Pharaoh's palace, Khaemmalu's wife."

"Merytre said she knew of fifteen since she has been working here."

"There must be some connection between them," I said. "I'd like to know how many of those women had been to Pharaoh's palace in the days before they disappeared."

"Merytre won't know," Ettu said. "As I understand it, she didn't know any of them well."

"No, but others do. Every woman who disappears is somebody's daughter, somebody's sister or cousin or friend. They all have someone who cares about them. I wonder if anyone has asked those people what they know about the women's movements before they disappeared."

"It seems to me a dangerous course you're on." She darted a glance at me, and even in the darkness, I could see her concern.

"Nobody else is doing anything," I said. "Somebody has to find the truth. Why shouldn't it be me?"

"I still don't understand why this is so important to you. You are not responsible for any of those women."

I walked in silence for a while, trying to unravel my tangled thoughts.

"If it was me who went missing," I said at last, "I hope that somebody would care enough to find out what had happened. It seems so sad that all these women have disappeared and nobody is searching for them."

"I think folk have done what they can with the resources they have. But once you have exhausted that, what more can you do? That doesn't mean they have forgotten their loved ones, or that they have stopped missing them. It just means there is nothing else they can do."

"The more I hear, the more I suspect the queen is involved." We had been talking quietly, but I lowered my voice even more, not wanting to risk any nearby guard overhearing. Khaemmalu was not the only one who patrolled the grounds at night. "Some, at least, of these women disappeared from Pharaoh's palace."

"But what motive does she have?" Ettu asked. "I'm not saying I disagree with you. I'm just trying to think it through. She knows her husband has a whole palace of wives, and she surely knew it when she married him. And, let's be honest, the only thing he has going for him is his throne. So why would she care if he has other wives? The more time he spends with them, the less she has to interact with him herself."

"She certainly didn't seem terribly fond of him when I dined with them."

I hadn't paid much attention to it at the time, but Isis wasn't pleased that I helped save Pharaoh from drowning. If it was true the wind that tipped the boat over that day was the result of a spell, could Isis be responsible? Was it a scheme to put her son, Ramses, on the throne? And if so, were the missing women somehow connected?

"How did we come to suspect her in the first place?" Ettu asked.

"I don't remember. I think it came up when we were first talking about how Half said the queen wasn't happy about Ishtar being invited to the place where she lives."

"Maybe we are jumping to conclusions. The more I think

about it, the less likely it seems the queen could be involved. If I was in her position, I'd be encouraging Pharaoh to spend as much time with his other wives as I could."

"But if it's not her, who else could it be?" My nose tingled and I sneezed. The breeze had dropped and the heady scent of flowers had filled the air in its absence. "It has to be someone with resources."

"Someone in a position of power."

"And from what Half overheard, it's possible at least one of the administrators in Pharaoh's palace is helping to cover it up."

The path we were following had circled around, leading us back towards the Palace. I sneezed again and was grateful we would soon be back inside.

"I don't suppose…" I hesitated, thinking my idea too unlikely. But we had ruled out the queen, and although we hadn't discussed Pharaoh, it couldn't be him.

"What?" Ettu asked.

"I wonder if it is an administrator? We thought one of them must be involved, but what if it is an administrator who is responsible?"

"Pharaoh's most favoured servants." Ettu's voice was thoughtful.

"Who would suspect the men closest to Pharaoh? They are certainly in positions to cover up their crimes."

"And they are powerful. If they summoned a woman, she would go, likely thinking they had a message for her from Pharaoh."

"Or a gift even," I said. "Who would refuse such a summons with the possibility they might receive some expensive gift from Pharaoh?"

"The administrators are in the perfect position for such a thing."

"Ettu." I stopped walking as another thought occurred to me. We were almost within hearing distance of the guards at the front doors. "We are only thinking about the administrators in Pharaoh's palace. What if the administrators *here* are also involved?"

Her eyes widened.

"My lady," she whispered. "If that's true, then none of us are safe. What if they are colluding? Administrators at both palaces working together to steal away certain women."

"But for what purpose?" My horror turned to frustration. It didn't make any sense. "What is it that happens before a woman disappears? Does she see or hear something that someone would rather she didn't? Does she cause a problem for someone?"

"Does she ask too many questions?" Ettu's tone had turned grim again.

Amankhau was the one who said that. *You have already made a name for yourself as a trouble maker,* he told me. *Asking too many questions. Poking around in things that are none of your business. Women like you tend to get themselves into trouble.* Did he really mean that women like me tended to quietly disappear?

"Amankhau must be involved," I said. "He surely has a partner in Pharaoh's palace, but if anyone here is part of whatever this conspiracy is, it's him."

"But to what end? What or who decides on a particular woman? And if Amankhau is involved, does that mean Panouk is as well?"

"We need to talk with Merytre again."

"And maybe you could speak with Lady Tiye," Ettu said. "She has been here longer than anyone else I know of. She must know more than she has said."

Back in my chambers, we asked Merytre to again tell us everything she could remember about the women who had disappeared. Her knowledge, however, was frustratingly scant. She knew the names of some of the women, but not all. Some were Ornaments, some were servants in the Palace of the Ornaments, and some worked in Pharaoh's palace. She didn't know whether any of them knew each other, other than two Ornaments she had seen talking together in the hallway one time. She hadn't known about Khaemmalu's wife.

"So if you didn't know about Tabiry, there could be others as well," Ettu said.

"Yes, of course," Merytre said. "I never said I knew about all of them. This place is too big. If I know of fifteen, there could be many more I never heard about."

"And if there is any connection between the missing women, we don't know it yet," I said, sitting back with a groan.

"Maybe there is no connection," Merytre said. "Perhaps it is opportunistic. A woman is somewhere alone and can be snatched, so they do it."

"But why?" I asked. "It makes no sense."

Merytre and Ettu both looked as defeated as I felt. Ahmose's face was thoughtful. Half frowned. Tall jumped up from his seat and began pacing the chamber. He flapped his hands as he walked.

"Tall, what is it?" I asked. "Do you know something?"

"Danger!" he said. "Pharaoh!"

It was no more than he had said before and I still couldn't make any sense of it.

"I'm sorry," I said. "I just don't understand what you're saying."

"Danger!"

"There is danger, but we don't know enough to figure it out. Is there anything else you can tell us?"

"Danger! Pharaoh!"

"What is he saying?" Merytre asked.

"Sorry." I had become so used to slipping between Babylonian and Egyptian, I sometimes forgot Tall still only spoke in Babylonian. "He keeps saying danger and Pharaoh."

"Maybe he means Pharaoh knows something about it," she suggested.

"Could Pharaoh himself be covering up for whoever is responsible?" Ettu asked.

A very sick feeling slid through my body and I pushed away the thoughts I had barely let myself think. How could I tell them I wondered whether it was Pharaoh himself who was responsible for the disappearances? He had no reason to kill any woman, let alone cover up her death. He already held all the power in the world over us.

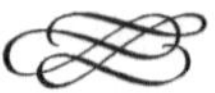

CHAPTER 28

Belet-ili appeared at my chambers the following morning. Ettu opened the door, but didn't invite her in.

"My lady asks if her sister would visit her today," Belet-ili said.

Ettu gave me a questioning look.

"I am going to sit with Tiye this morning," I said. "But I can go to Ishtar after that."

Belet-ili only nodded and hurried away. Ettu closed the door, then turned to me with a thoughtful expression.

"That was a little odd," she said.

"How do you mean?"

"I'm not sure. Just something about Belet-ili's manner."

"She seemed a little distracted."

"I suppose," she said. "I guess you'll find out soon enough what Lady Ishtar wants."

As my lady's maids bathed me a little while later, Abar pushed her way through them to confront me.

"Have you found my sister yet?" she demanded.

"Abar," Ettu said. "That is not how you speak to my lady."

"Have you found my sister yet, my lady?" Abar repeated, her tone mocking now.

I had completely forgotten. I could have asked Pharaoh again when Ishtar and I dined with him the other night, not that he was very helpful the last time I asked. I could hardly tell Abar that, though.

"Not yet," I said. "I am still looking."

"Tell me what you are doing to find her," Abar said.

"That is enough," Ettu said, more firmly. "Take my lady's nightgown to the laundry and ask after her clothes from two days ago. They should have been returned by now."

Abar didn't move, but continued to stare at me, waiting for my response.

"Go," Ettu said.

Abar left, although I didn't miss the sneer she gave Ettu on her way out.

"That girl is trouble," Khensa observed.

"She is also in a foreign land and not by her own choice," Ettu said.

I was pleased to hear her defend Abar after the way she rebuked the girl the last time she asked me about her sister.

"And she is separated from her sister," Sehener added. "That must be causing her some amount of distress."

"Very true." Ettu gave Sehener an approving nod.

I liked the way Sehener spoke up for Abar, even though the girl had given none of them any reason to do so. If I ever needed to invite another of my maids to live in my chambers, Sehener would be my first pick.

As I sat on Tiye's couch some time later, I was still mentally rehearsing what I wanted to say to her. We chatted and I waited for the right moment.

"Have you heard the news about Hydna?" she asked, her face animated. She seemed to be in a particularly good mood today.

"I don't think I know her, but no, I haven't heard anything."

"She is having an affair with one of the butlers." Tiye let out a hoot of laughter. "Isn't that the most ridiculous thing you have ever heard of?"

"Why is it ridiculous?"

"You know." She gave me a knowledgeable look, but I really didn't know what she meant.

"I don't."

"He is *modified*."

"Oh," I said. "Of course."

It was no secret that the men permitted inside the Palace were not only personally approved by Pharaoh, but they also had their male parts removed.

"How exactly do they get modified?" I asked.

Tiye raised her eyebrows at me, and I felt as if I had asked something ridiculous.

"I'm just curious," I said, maybe a little too defensively.

"By knife," she said. "A very, very sharp knife."

"Wouldn't there be a risk of them bleeding to death?" The memory of Half lying in his bed, blood spilling from his belly, rose in my mind. He had barely survived.

"Indeed. The risk is very high. Not all of those who are modified live long enough to even get inside the Palace."

"Why does Pharaoh think it necessary to do such a thing?" I asked.

"To ensure our loyalty, of course," she said, smoothing her skirt over her knees, although it looked to me like it was perfectly straight. "And he thinks other men can't be trusted. That if he allows men who are whole into the palace, they will sleep with all the Ornaments. And Pharaoh wants to know that any woman who belongs to him is touched by no other man."

"Wouldn't it be enough to have rules about it? Punishments for those who break them?"

"Oh, there are punishments," she said. "Severe ones. But there are still those who would risk it."

"Have you?"

She leaned back against the sofa and crossed her legs the other way.

"Me? No, and certainly not with a modified man."

"But there are Ornaments who do," I said. "Like Hydna. Maybe she cares enough for this butler, whoever he is, that the risk is worth it to her. Maybe she loves him."

"Some women say the modified men are able to pleasure them in a way no unmodified man ever has." Tiye's tone was more thoughtful now. "It still seems pointless to me, though. What does a few moments of pleasure matter against the fact that he will never be able to get her with child? What is the point of their affair?"

I shrugged, having too little experience with men to venture any suggestion. Khaemmalu's face appeared in my mind and I pushed it away. Not fast enough, though, as my ever-reliable cheeks heated.

"You are blushing," Tiye said. "That tells me you are thinking something you believe you shouldn't."

I shrugged and tried to appear unconcerned.

"I don't know what you're talking about," I said. "I blush all the time."

"Kassaya, you little minx. I do believe there's someone you're thinking about having an affair with."

"How do you know I'm just thinking about it?" I tried to sound brash, but failed miserably.

Tiye gave a hoot of laughter.

"You're not the type," she said. "Now your sister, on the other hand. If I heard she was having an affair, I'd believe it."

"I might have one." My cheeks flamed even hotter and I studiously avoided her eyes.

"No, there's someone you're tempted by, but you would never do it."

"You were the one who said Ishtar was a good little Ornament and I wasn't. So why do you think she would be the one to have an affair?"

"Why is this so important to you?" Tiye gave me that raised eyebrow look that always seem to imply she knew more than I did.

"It's not," I muttered and searched for a way to change the subject. Now was definitely not the moment to raise what I really wanted to talk to her about. "I don't think I told you I have a new lady's maid. From Kush."

"Yes, there have been a number of new Nubians around since the last campaign." Tiye clicked her fingers at Nammu and gestured for her to bring a drink. Nammu poured her some melon juice and offered the jug to me without being prompted. I pretended not to notice.

"Nubian?" I asked. "She told me she was from Kush."

Tiye shrugged. "The terms are interchangeable," she said. "The Nubians like to call themselves Kushites, but they are still Nubians."

Maybe I was reading too much into it, but it seemed Tiye thought there was something dirty or uncivilised about being a Nubian.

"She and her sister were captured and brought to Egypt as servants," I said.

Tiye shrugged. "It's not an uncommon fate, unfortunately."

"She asked me to help her find her sister."

Tiye gave me a steady look.

"And you, I assume, intend to help her."

"Of course I do. Why wouldn't I? She wants to know her sister is safe."

"She's just a servant. What she wants doesn't matter."

"How would I find out where her sister has been sent?"

Tiye sighed, as if there was something unreasonable about my question.

"I suppose if it was me, I would start with the administrators," she said. "They probably won't know, but they would have access to the right records. You, however, have made enemies of the administrators, so it's unlikely they would be inclined to help you."

"I haven't deliberately made any enemies."

"No. You were just being you. I know."

I bristled, but she laughed.

"I mean no offence, Kassaya," she said. "Only that you should be more cautious about who you offend. You never know when someone might become useful."

"So if I cannot ask the administrators for such a favour myself, what else can I do?"

"I suppose you could have someone ask them for you."

We eyed each other. She would make me say it, if only so it would be clear that I owed her.

"Would you ask them for me?" I asked.

"I suppose I could. What is it worth to you?"

What did I have that she would want? She already had everything. She told me once she had only to say she desired something and Pharaoh would get it for her. I had already offered her friendship, which seemed the only thing she couldn't request from Pharaoh.

"I have a hairbrush," I said. "It has an ivory handle which was made from the tusks of a beast the size of the Great Temple in Babylon. Would you like that?"

"Sounds intriguing. I accept. What is the girl's name?"

"My lady's maid is Abar and her sister is Atahar."

"From Nubia."

"Yes. Thank you, Tiye. Abar will be very appreciative if I can tell her where her sister is."

"Don't get your hopes up. The sister may not be anywhere they will meet again. She may not even still be alive."

"If that's what I have to tell her, I think she would rather know than always be wondering," I said. "But that reminds me of another thing I wanted to talk to you about."

She waited, studying me calmly. My heart beat a little faster as I tried to remember the words I rehearsed. We had discussed this in my chambers and came up with what we thought was a neutral way of raising the subject.

"I'm intrigued by the matter of the women who have gone missing," I said. *Intrigued* we had all agreed was a good word. Better than *interested* or *curious*. *Intrigued* suggested no particular intention to do anything. "Do you know much about them?"

Tiye's face immediately became shuttered. She made a show of crossing her legs again and stretched one arm along the back of the couch. I was sure she was only pretending to be so relaxed.

"Little," she said. "I'm not sure I ever spent much time with any of them other than Nebtu."

"Do you know whether they knew each other?"

"Kassaya, let it go." She looked away, off to the other side of the chamber, although when I followed her gaze, there seemed to be nothing there that would have called her attention.

"I'm merely intrigued."

"Then don't be. No good can come of it."

"You don't wonder what happened to them?"

She finally looked at me again and I was surprised at the blankness in her gaze.

"Of course I do," she said. "Nebtu was a friend of sorts. But they are gone and we are still here. Focus on that and stop poking around in matters that don't concern you."

CHAPTER 29

Ettu was waiting in the hallway when I left Tiye and we went straight to Ishtar's chambers. Belet-ili let us in, her face somber. She gestured towards Ishtar, who stood at the window, indicating I should go to her. She and Ettu went to the other side of the chamber, along with another maid I didn't recognise.

I went to stand beside Ishtar, wondering what had caught her attention. But there was nothing unusual in the grounds, not even a guard wandering around.

"You asked for me to visit," I said.

It was only when she didn't reply that I looked at her. Ishtar's face was pale with dark shadows under her eyes. Her cheeks seemed sunken and her hands resting on the windowsill were knotted together.

"Ishtar, are you still unwell?" I asked, somewhat alarmed at her appearance. She had always been slender, but she had lost weight in the week or so since I had seen her.

Tears came to her eyes and she drew in a shuddering breath.

"Ishtar?" I set my hand on her arm, increasingly alarmed. "What is it? Have you received news from home?"

Something had happened to one of our parents. That was the only thing I could think of. Something had happened and they had written to Ishtar but not to me.

"The babe," she whispered at last. "It is gone."

"Gone?"

My gaze went to her belly. She noticed and wrapped her hands protectively over herself.

"I lost the babe," she said.

"Again?"

It was a stupid thing to say. I wasn't thinking when I blurted it out, too stunned by her words. I had been so sure she was lying about being with child. Had I been wrong? Or had she lied, thinking she would be with child soon enough, and only realised the truth when she lost the babe?

Ishtar's face became shuttered at my question and she turned away from me, looking out the window again. My hand went to my own belly, still flat, although I imagined I could feel just the faintest hint of roundness. Did my babe still live? Ahmose's seeds hadn't sprouted yet, but it had only been a couple of days.

"Do you think it was because you were ill?" I asked.

She shrugged. "The healer couldn't say. She did say, though, there had been many sicknesses lately. Bad food, she thought."

"I wondered if it was the fish we ate that night."

"I didn't have any."

Of course she wouldn't have. She had been sick from bad fish as a child and could never bring herself to eat it again. So whatever caused our illness, it wasn't the fish.

"I'm sorry," I said, knowing the words were inadequate. "About the babe."

She shrugged a little and didn't look at me.

"Is there anything you need? Can I do something for you?"

"My lady's maids look after me well enough."

It was a curt dismissal and I supposed it was punishment for my careless words earlier.

"Why didn't you tell me?" she asked suddenly and I realised my hand still caressed my belly. I let my arm fall, but it was too late.

"I'm sorry," I said. "I wanted to be more certain before I told anyone. I wouldn't have even told Pharaoh just yet except…"

My voice trailed away. Except you told him about your babe was the only thing I could say.

"Perhaps Marduk will grant your child to live." Ishtar's tone was bitter. "He may favour you more than he favours me."

I had no reply for that. Who could say why one woman lost a babe and another didn't? Was it truly the whim of the gods?

"If you need something, please send for me," I said. "I will come immediately."

The only indication she had heard me was a slight nod. I wanted to ask if she had lied when she told Pharaoh, but couldn't bring myself to do it while she was so upset. I also needed to ask her about what Nammu had said. That Ishtar told her I asked for her three maids to be sent to Babylon with me. But this wasn't the time.

I left Ishtar standing at the window, her hands once again knotted on the windowsill. As we returned to my chambers, I could feel Ettu studying me.

"Did she tell you?" she asked.

"Yes. I assume Belet-ili told you." Thank Marduk I never told anyone I had thought Ishtar was lying about being with child. Maybe I misinterpreted her signals. Perhaps I didn't know her as well as I thought.

Ettu sighed. "Such a terrible thing. Belet-ili says Lady Ishtar is truly devastated."

"She will have to tell Pharaoh."

"I wonder how he will react?" she asked as we made our way up the stairs.

"I don't know. He has plenty of children as it is, and it's not like Ishtar's child would have had any chance of being heir."

Neither did mine, for that matter, no matter whether I pretended otherwise to myself. "It may be insignificant to him."

"Or it may not be."

She gave me a loaded look and I knew we were both remembering the bruises around Ishtar's neck after she had been with Pharaoh. If that was how he treated a woman who had done no wrong, what would he do if he blamed her for the loss of a potential son? My question about whether Pharaoh might be responsible for the missing women slid back through my mind. I took a deep breath and tried to find a way to ask Ettu what she thought. I couldn't do it.

"She is young enough that she could still bear him a child," I said instead.

"Some women never carry a child to full term. That she has lost two is not a good sign."

My hand went to my belly before I realised what I was doing. I quickly let my hand fall, but of course, Ettu had already noticed.

"We will take good care of you," she said. "You must rest and eat properly and avoid any unpleasantness."

I nodded and didn't object. She would probably lock me in my chambers until the child was born if she thought she would get away with it.

CHAPTER 30

"Something has arrived for you," Merytre said when she opened the door to my chambers for us. She slipped the bar into place as soon as Ettu and I were inside, then gestured towards the table where a linen package waited. It was the size of my fist and bound with a golden ribbon.

"What is it?" I asked.

"It is from Pharaoh," she said. "I didn't open it. Panouk brought it just a few minutes ago."

We must have only just missed him in the hallway. Ettu went off to unlock the door for Tall and Half. They came out quickly, followed by Ahmose who must have been in her own bedchamber. They all looked at me expectantly.

"Well, go on," Ettu said. "Aren't you going to open it? This must be the reward he promised."

Given I had requested information as my reward, I hadn't expected him to send me anything. Especially after the way he reacted when I asked about Nebtu. Had Ishtar's reward also been delivered? Would Pharaoh demand its return when he learned there would be no babe from her?

I untied the ribbon slowly. I didn't want to know what was

inside. It felt wrong to receive a reward for such a thing, especially when it hadn't been my choice to lie with him. He was not a man I would ever choose for myself, if there was any such thing as a world where a woman might make her own decisions about those matters.

The linen wrapping fell open. Nestled inside was a dark blue gem the size of a robin's egg. A silver setting contained the gem, with a cord threaded through a hole in the top, presumably to allow it to be worn around the neck.

"It's a sapphire," Ettu murmured. She stretched out one hand as if wanting to touch it but quickly withdrew.

"I have never seen one so big," Merytre said.

"Very fine indeed," Half said. "With the right buyer, you could support yourself in luxury for the rest of your life. Assuming you had reason to do so," he added quickly.

Neither Tall nor Ahmose commented. Tall's eyes were round. Ahmose didn't look either surprised or awed, but thoughtful as if, like Half, she was considering the value of such a gem.

"I should send a message of thanks," I said. "Merytre, would you send for Pentau?"

"Of course," she replied, and hurried out to find a runner boy.

I cradled the gem in my palm, still nestled in the linen. With one finger, I touched it, feeling its smoothness, and trying to imagine myself wearing it.

"You will need a new gown," Ettu said. "Perhaps blue linen to match, or white to accentuate it."

"There's no need for such a fuss," I replied.

"It really won't go with any of your gowns, and Pharaoh will expect to see you wearing it the next time he calls for you."

I had hoped there mightn't be a next time now he knew I was with child. There were plenty of other women he could spend time with. Forget my silly ideas of how I might position my child as heir if it was a boy. It was an impossible thought and Father surely never expected such a thing of me.

Pentau arrived and I dictated a brief message of thanks. He left as quickly as possible, perhaps before I could ask him to read it back to me. I felt restless after that. There were too many things on my mind. Ishtar's loss and my unworthy thoughts about whether she had lied about being with child. Tiye's strangeness and her insinuation that there were things better left unknown. When I went to bed, my mind still whirled and I couldn't get comfortable. After tossing and turning for some time, I rose and dressed.

Ahmose was the only one still up. A lamp turned down low lit the chamber, just enough for me to see she held something small. A little figurine perhaps. She seemed to be turning it around and around, although she stared off into the shadows and maybe didn't even realise what she was doing.

I cleared my throat, not wanting to startle her, but she jumped. The thing in her hand quickly disappeared.

"I need some air," I said. "Would you come for a walk with me?"

She got to her feet with a groan and I immediately regretted asking. She was too old to expect her to wander the gardens so late.

"Never mind," I said. "I will go by myself."

After all, if the queen was truly responsible for the missing women, I was safe enough here, and if it was the administrators, they could break down my door if they wanted to. Khaemmalu would be out there, anyway, keeping an eye on things. He wouldn't let anything happen to me. I didn't let myself linger on thoughts of him, not wanting to admit I hoped to see him.

"No, no," Ahmose said. "Just give me a moment to get my old bones moving."

We left, although I felt uneasy about leaving the door unbarred. But I didn't want to wake anyone to bar it and have them wait up for us to return.

Outside, I inhaled deeply, filling my lungs with cool, fresh air.

The evening was warm and the scent of flowers much too strong. It irritated my lungs and I coughed a little as I exhaled. I walked slowly, mindful of Ahmose's comment about her old bones. She said nothing and seemed content enough to wander with me. We left the torch-lined path and followed one that led into the dark.

The moon was no more than a sliver and I could see little once we were away from the torches. Insects chirped, an owl hooted, and something rustled the leaves of a nearby tree. I was disappointed there was no sign of Khaemmalu, although I wouldn't have admitted it to anyone. Nevertheless, the soft night noises soothed my restlessness and I began to feel quite weary. Maybe now I would be able to sleep.

As we turned back towards the Palace, a chill ran up my spine. I could neither see nor hear anyone nearby, but it felt like someone watched us. My nightmares of being stalked by lions returned and I focussed on keeping my breath steady. There were no lions in the gardens and it was a ridiculous thing to fear.

To my left, a bush rustled and a shadow stepped out.

"My lady," came Khaemmalu's voice.

I rested my hand over my heart, feeling how hard it pounded.

"I'm sorry if I startled you," he said. "There really isn't a gentle way to alert you to my presence."

"It felt like someone was there." I almost told him about my fear of the lions. I might have if Ahmose wasn't with me.

"May I walk with you?" Khaemmalu asked.

"Of course."

"Greetings, Old Mother," he said politely to Ahmose, who gave him a nod in return. He came to walk beside me and Ahmose dropped back to make room for him on the path.

"Couldn't sleep?" he asked as we set off.

"No." I couldn't decide what to tell him and I took so long about it that it seemed the moment had passed. "Has anyone else been out wandering tonight?" I asked instead, not wanting to seem unfriendly. He mightn't tell me he was there next time if I acted like I didn't want to speak with him.

"Only one," he said. "And it's better if I pretend I never saw her."

"Why is that?"

He cleared his throat and looked away.

"Oh," I said. "It's an Ornament who is having an affair."

"So you understand why it's better I forget seeing her."

"Do you know who she was meeting?"

"Of course. I would not be doing my job very well if I didn't know."

"Is it a guard?"

He shook his head. "Best you not know anything about it. The fewer people who know, the less chance of it coming out."

"I wouldn't tell anyone," I said, a little indignantly. "I'm not a gossip."

"I didn't think you would, but this place has many secrets and those who keep their own secrets would do best to avoid learning anyone else's. Too many secrets are not good for the mind."

"I suppose you know a lot of secrets," I said. "Given it is your job to sneak through the shadows and watch what everyone does."

He shot me a look I couldn't interpret.

"Yes," he said, "and discretion is an important part of my job. Those who wander the grounds at night can be assured I will hold my tongue if I can."

I got the feeling it wasn't what he had originally been going to say.

"If you can?" I asked.

"There are cases where I have to tell what I have seen. If someone's life is in danger, for example."

His words didn't seem to need a reply and we walked in silence for a little way.

"I was very sorry to learn about your wife," I said at last, feeling like I should mention her again. I didn't want him to think I had forgotten what he told me.

He sighed and looked up at the sky. He had also done that the last time we talked about her. Maybe he thought she was up there, looking down on him, like the Egyptians believed their dead pharaohs did.

"It is still difficult to talk about," he said at last.

"Did you love her?" I regretted it as soon as I asked. "I'm sorry. That is none of my business."

"It's all right," he said. "I did love her, in my own way. Maybe not as much as I should have, and not as much as she wanted, but I did."

We had circled around and now approached the torch-lined path that led back to the Palace.

"I should continue my rounds," Khaemmalu said. "Thank you for letting me walk with you."

He looked at me and I thought he was going to say more, but he only gave his head a slight shake, as if trying to dispel an unwanted thought. He stepped away back into the shadows. As he did, he took hold of my elbow for the briefest moment. His touch was gentle and fleeting, and once he was gone I wondered whether I had imagined it.

After all, Sutem had told me it could cost a guard his life if he touched an Ornament other than to save her life. I must have imagined Khaemmalu had touched me. Surely he wouldn't risk such a thing.

CHAPTER 31

"Abar, come here." I craned my neck to see the girl who stood behind the rest of my maids. They were fussing around with their scented lotions and perfumes, which they seemed to be applying even more liberally than usual. My head already pounded from the smell.

Abar pushed through the women and came to stand in front of me.

"Have you found her?" she demanded, her voice already filled with impatience.

"No, but I wanted to tell you I have someone else asking about her now."

"So you still don't know where my sister is?"

She gave me a sullen look and Ettu cleared her throat disapprovingly. As usual, Abar didn't seem to care. She thought nothing of the submissiveness expected of her position, as far as I could tell, and she made no effort to integrate herself with the rest of my maids. She came to my chambers every morning as required, but unless someone gave her a task to do, she merely stood off to the side and watched.

"The person who is looking for her is our best chance," I said. "If anyone can find out where your sister has been sent, she will."

"I only want to hear that you have found her, not that you are still *trying*." Her heavy emphasis of the final word told me she didn't believe me.

"Abar," Ettu said. "Go fetch more of this scented lotion. It will be in the chest closest to the door in the bathing chamber."

Abar slipped back through the crowd of women without another word.

"I'm trying," I said to Ettu. "She doesn't understand it takes time."

"You are doing more for her than most mistresses would," Ettu said. "She should be appreciative of that."

Would I in her situation, though? From her perspective, it probably looked like I had done nothing to find her sister and, in truth, I hadn't tried very hard. I would follow up with Tiye the very next time I saw her.

Later that day, a messenger brought an invitation to a gathering in Henutmire's chambers the following evening. I wondered whether it would be the same group of women who attended Ineni's party a few weeks ago. Ettu asked the messenger boy who else was invited, but apparently he gave her such a stricken look, that she said I would attend and sent him on his way.

"Will you ask if they know of any connections between the missing women?" Ettu asked as she and Merytre walked with me to Henutmire's the next evening. Her chambers were on the floor below mine, but not all that far away.

"It depends on who else is there."

I had told them of the way Tiye shut down my questions. If she was attending — and I presumed she would — I wouldn't say anything unless I had an opportunity to do so without her hearing. I couldn't ask Tiye about Abar's sister either. That was a conversation best held in private.

"I wonder if they will talk about whatever it was they weren't ready to let you hear last time," Ettu said.

"It sounded very mysterious," Merytre said.

"It did and I still have no idea what it was about." There was obviously a plot of some kind being hatched, but had I done enough to gain their trust?

Mindful of how uncomfortable I felt at being the first to arrive last time, I left it a little later to leave and arrived at the same time as Ineni. Henutmire greeted us with a raised goblet and a merry smile as if she had already been sampling the wine.

"Help yourselves." Henutmire gestured towards the table laden with pitchers and wine bottles. Someone knocked at the door and her attention was quickly diverted. I didn't get a chance to speak privately to her until some time later.

"Henutmire," I whispered to her while everyone else was occupied. "Have you heard anything about Nebtu?"

"Nothing." She studied my face. "Have you?"

"I heard a woman's body was found at the quarry. I don't know whether it was her."

Should I also tell her that Tiye heard a woman was found in the river? Surely Tiye would have told her if she thought there was any possibility it was Nebtu.

"Oh my." Henutmire reached for her mug, but found it empty. Her hand trembled and she fumbled as she picked up a wine bottle.

"Here, let me." I took the bottle from her, resolving not to mention the other woman. Henutmire was shocked enough as it was.

"Do you know what was being done with her?" Henutmire asked.

I couldn't tell her the body was being taken elsewhere, but that I didn't know where. Best to let her think the matter was being handled with respect.

"She was probably taken to the House of Life," I said. "On the other side of the city." The memory of the knife being thrust into the woman's belly flashed through my mind. That wasn't Nebtu, I reminded myself. There was no need to tell Henutmire.

"Yes, I know where it is." Henutmire accepted the refilled goblet from me and took a sip. She seemed to have regained her composure. "I suppose there is no way to know if it is her. The administrators will hardly tell us, even if they know."

I wanted to tell her I had snuck out to the House of Life. Just so she would know that someone else cared whether that was Nebtu's body. But I wasn't certain enough of her to trust her with such a secret and I couldn't give her the confirmation she wanted anyway.

"I will tell you if I hear something more," I said instead.

"Thank you." She looked me right in the eyes. "I won't ask how you came by such information. You must have taken some risk to get it and you have no reason to trust me, or indeed, any of us. But I would rather know Nebtu's fate, even if it is not what I wish it would be, and I thank you for telling me. You have my friendship, Kassaya."

"Thank you." I was oddly touched by her speech. The other women might not yet have decided whether they trusted me, but it seemed Henutmire had. This was my moment to ask about connections between the other missing women. She would surely tell me if she knew anything.

"That sounds very serious." I hadn't noticed Tiye come up behind us, but she pushed her way between us as she reached for the wine bottle. Neferu was right behind her. I swallowed my questions.

"Kassaya, I heard you have been ill," Neferu said. "Are you recovered now?"

I tried to avoid looking at her Eye of Horus pendant, which she wore on a chain around her neck as usual. Most of the other women carried their amulet bearing the stylised eye discreetly, but Neferu displayed hers proudly and it made me feel quite odd to see it. The pendant she had gifted me was in my pouch, wrapped in a piece of linen so I wouldn't accidentally touch it.

"Yes, I am quite well," I said. "I fell ill after dining with Pharaoh. So did Ishtar. I thought the fish might have been bad, but she didn't have any."

I was rambling and felt a little foolish for having gone so far as to say that Ishtar didn't eat the fish. Neferu frowned as she poured some wine, then passed the bottle to Gilukhipa. Henutmire urged us to eat and I had forgotten our conversation in the time it took me to fill a plate and find somewhere to sit. I had a mouthful of crunchy lettuce and cucumbers when Neferu spoke again.

"Kassaya's illness made me think," she said. "I have heard a few odd things lately."

"Oh, do tell," Tiye said, her tone light. I wondered whether it was intended as a warning to Neferu, but if it was, the woman paid no attention.

"Food spoiling unexpectedly," Neferu said. "Folk falling ill."

"It is *akhet*," Ineni said. "And the hottest time of the year. It's hardly unusual that food would spoil more quickly."

"I heard Dakini's cat died," Gilukhipa said.

"Oh," Ineni said. "She loved that cat. He wasn't much more than a kitten either."

"I heard the whole of the Palace's flock of hens died," Henutmire said. "All in one night."

My appetite fled as I looked down at the roasted leg on my plate.

"Well, it won't be these hens," Tiye said, making a show of taking a large bite from a leg.

I pushed mine towards the edge of the plate. After how sick I was following the meal with Pharaoh, I wouldn't risk it.

"My favourite brooch has disappeared," Ineni said slowly, as if she didn't want to admit it. "My lady's maids have searched my entire chambers."

"Has Kassaya been anywhere near your chambers?" Tiye asked, giving me a friendly look as if to ensure I knew she was joking.

"It could have been one of your maids who took it," Gilukhipa said. "Personally, I never trust mine with anything valuable. It is too much temptation for them. My jewels are locked in a chest and I carry the key in my pouch."

She patted the pouch at her waist.

"So what are we saying?" Ineni asked. "In a place this big, surely there are all sorts of things going missing. Folk fall ill all the time. None of this is unusual."

"There are a lot of odd things occurring all at once, though," Neferu said. "It makes me wonder…"

She stopped and stared down at her plate, as if lost in thought.

"What?" Ineni asked. "Don't keep us in suspense."

"We all know what happened to Kia." Neferu's gaze landed briefly on each of us, as if she searched for something, and the gravity on her face chilled me. "There has been no ceremony for her. Given how suddenly she went to the West, is it possible that…"

"You think her spirit lingers here?" Tiye asked, her voice still light as if it was all too much nonsense.

"It could explain some of the odd things that have happened lately," Henutmire said.

"I don't understand," Gilukhipa said, to my relief.

I was starting to feel like they were all speaking a language I couldn't decipher. She and I were the only ones who weren't born and raised in Egypt and I was grateful it wasn't just me who didn't grasp what everyone else seemed to.

"Some of the things that have been happening might be because of a mischievous spirit," Henutmire said. "Things disappearing. Food spoiling. Given how quickly Kia went to the West, she might not have accepted her fate yet."

"You think she is here somewhere, causing trouble?"

Gilukhipa glanced around as if she thought they meant Kia's spirit was right here with us in the chamber.

I resisted the urge to look over my shoulder myself. I knew little of what the people here believed about the afterlife, but I had had some very strange dreams lately. Could it be possible Kia was causing them? I was too embarrassed at my ignorance to ask.

"What does one do about a mischievous spirit then?" I took a sip of my wine and tried to look as unbothered as Tiye.

"We could hold a ceremony for her," Ineni said. "Something to encourage her spirit to move on to the afterlife."

Henutmire glanced at me and I wondered whether she was hoping I'd share what I told her about the body that was found. Maybe she thought we should hold a ceremony for Nebtu as well. But then, we had no certainty of her death. Again I saw the knife flashing down into the woman's belly. I tried to cover my shudder by taking a gulp of my wine.

"I suppose that could be a good idea." Gilukhipa sounded doubtful. "Tiye, what do you think?"

They all looked at Tiye. Clearly, it would be she who decided. Tiye fiddled with her goblet for a moment before nodding.

"Yes," she said. "I think we should. I doubt it is Kia causing these problems, but it can't hurt."

"Shall I make the arrangements then?" Ineni offered. "Perhaps we could have the ceremony in three days?"

"Was there anyone Kia was close to?" I asked. "Someone we should invite?"

I hadn't meant to say *we*, as if I thought myself to be part of their circle, but nobody reacted.

"What about Amanitore?" Henutmire suggested. "I saw them walking together in the gardens a couple of times. I don't know how close they were, though."

"I will speak with her," Ineni said. "Let's say sunset in three days at the chapel."

CHAPTER 32

That evening, I dreamed again about the priestess with the scaled face. We walked through the gardens together and she stopped to talk to some flowers. In my dream it seemed the flowers spoke back, but later I couldn't recall what they said. I couldn't remember what the priestess told me either, although I woke knowing she had shared some wisdom. Something important.

Urgency surged through me. It had felt like more than just a dream. I had to find the priestess. There was something she was trying to tell me. I rose from my bed and pulled on the first gown I found in my clothing chest. In the sitting chamber, Ahmose, Ettu and Half were already up and chatting quietly.

"I'm going for a walk," I said.

"Now?" Ettu asked. She was sitting next to Half with her feet tucked under her and looked like she hadn't quite woken up properly.

"I can go by myself," I said.

I couldn't tell anyone I hoped to find the priestess, and Ettu looked comfortable. Surely I'd be safe enough taking a quick walk through the grounds in the daylight. But Ettu was already on her feet.

"I will come," she said. "Are you sure you don't want to wait until after breakfast, though? Or at least until you are dressed?"

"I'm dressed." I wore a gown, a wig and sandals. It was no different to what my maids would have attired me in.

"But your face."

I waved away her objection. "Merytre can make up my face later if necessary. We likely won't even encounter anyone this early."

Ettu's mouth twisted in the way it did when she disapproved of something. She didn't make any further objection, though, only slipped her feet into her sandals and followed me to the door. Half hurried back down the hallway and I heard Ahmose slide the bar into place as soon as the door closed behind us.

It couldn't have been much past sunrise and the hallways were quiet this early, although not empty. We passed a number of servants and messenger boys, hurrying off to do whatever urgent task awaited them. No Ornaments, though. Not this early. Those who were awake were probably either breaking their fast or being readied to face the day by their maids. Relief filled me at having escaped the morning bathing ritual, for now at least. I wouldn't be surprised if Ettu and Merytre insisted on bathing me when I returned, even though I was already dressed.

Outside, the light was soft and the air cool. Birds chirped and the grass was damp from an overnight dew. Where had the priestess and I been walking in my dream? I could remember flower beds, but nothing specific, not even what kind of flowers they were.

"Let's go this way." I pointed and we set off along the path. I watched for any sign of the priestess or a spot that reminded me of my dream.

"Are you looking for something?" Ettu asked.

Of course she would notice. I should have brought Merytre

with me. She was less observant than Ettu. But Merytre had still been in bed.

"No, just wanted to stretch my legs," I said.

I felt bad about lying and even worse that she surely knew I was, but it was too ridiculous to admit I was looking for someone I thought might be trying to send me a message in a dream.

"I see," was all Ettu said.

We walked for quite a long way through the gardens, but I saw no sign of the priestess. It was a stupid idea anyway. How could a woman send a message through a dream, even if she was a priestess?

"Let's go back," I said at last. "I'm getting rather hungry."

I wasn't actually. The morning nausea continued to persist and usually lasted until well into the day. Ettu said nothing, only kept pace with me. I could feel the chill coming off her. She was unhappy, probably because she knew I had lied and she thought that meant I didn't trust her. I tried to think of a way I could reassure her without telling her how foolish I had been, but decided any attempt at an explanation would probably only make the situation worse. I'd find a way to make it up to her later.

We were almost back at the front doors when I spotted a flower bed off to my left. Something about that particular spot seemed familiar.

"Just a moment," I said to Ettu and hurried over. My sandals sank into the damp grass, leaving my toes cool and wet.

Yes, this was the spot from my dream. Now I saw it, I remembered more clearly. The flower bed with its earth disturbed as if it had been freshly weeded. The bright yellow flowers with their halo of petals, like the rays of a sun. Beside them, a dom palm with one branch browned and sagging a little too low. A gardener would remove that branch as soon as it was noticed. This was where the priestess had stopped to talk to the flowers in my dream. I closed my eyes and tried to remember. What had she said to them? Something about—

"My lady?"

Ettu's voice jarred me from my thoughts and the memory I had almost grasped slid away again. I hadn't noticed her following, but she was right behind me.

"Are you well?" she asked. "You are acting rather strange."

"I'm fine. I just was trying to remember what these flowers are called."

She gave me a sideways look, as if she knew I was lying again. We returned to the path.

"Narcissus," she said eventually.

"Hmm?"

"The flowers are narcissus."

Back in my chambers, Merytre was out of bed and had already sent my maids away, and the servants had brought breakfast. The smell of warm gruel made my stomach turn, but I took a small helping since I had told Ettu I was hungry. I managed one bite, but was sure my stomach would reject it if I ate any more, so I sat with my bowl in my lap for a while and hoped nobody would notice I wasn't eating.

When I thought I had spent enough time nursing the bowl, I set it aside and went to find the hairbrush I promised Tiye. The little chest I had packed myself before I left Babylon — the chest that contained the only things I chose to bring myself — wasn't where I remembered seeing it last. I searched my chamber, increasingly anxious about its disappearance.

"Do you need something, my lady?" Merytre asked from the doorway.

I jumped. I had been so focused on my search, I hadn't noticed her standing there.

"There is a chest," I said. "Much smaller than any of these. Have you seen it?"

"Sorry, no. What was in it? Perhaps it was discarded after being unpacked."

"Just some things I brought from home. A hairbrush, a few jewels."

"There is a hairbrush over there." She pointed to the tray with my makeup.

"Not that one. The one I want has an ivory handle."

"I haven't seen it," she said. "Shall I ask Ettu if she knows where it was put?"

"Yes," I said. "Please."

Ettu came in a few moments later.

"I know the chest you mean," she said. "I remember you asking for it to be taken to the boats. It was in that corner the last time I saw it."

"Where is it then?"

Frustration leaked into my voice and I wanted to cry, although I couldn't have said whether it was from exasperation or disappointment or sorrow. That chest held all my most precious items. The hairbrush. A shell my father brought me from Syria. The scarf Ishtar had embroidered for me when we were children. My favourite jewels. Everything I had brought from home — every thing I chose myself — was in it, and it was missing.

"I will go check the other chambers," Ettu said. "Perhaps it was moved for some reason."

She left and I continued my search, checking all my clothing chests again, even though I had already looked in each of them at least twice. Ettu returned just as I admitted it really wasn't anywhere in this chamber. She was empty handed, so I didn't need to ask if she had found it.

"It must be here somewhere," she said, casting her gaze around the chamber as if she hoped to spot the chest.

"Maybe it has been stolen," I said.

Too many people had access to my chambers. My lady's maids. The servants who brought our meals and the ones who came twice a week to clean. Any of them could have taken it. I wanted to cry for the loss of my special things, but restrained myself. Nobody else would think it important I had lost an old hairbrush and a scarf from my sister. They were special only to me.

"We would have noticed if someone left with it," Ettu said in the very reasonable tone she used when she thought I was being unreasonable. "It is not a large chest, but it is certainly not small enough to smuggle out. Nobody could have taken it without one of us seeing it, especially since there is almost always someone in the sitting chamber."

"Then where is it?" I asked.

"We will go through all the chambers again," she said. "You go sit down and I will get Merytre, Half and Tall. Between the four of us, we will search every last cubit of this place. We will find it, my lady."

I sighed and went out to the sitting chamber. Ettu was right when she said it wasn't something that could easily be taken without someone noticing, but there was no explanation for its disappearance other than theft. Perhaps one of the others had seen someone take it and hadn't realised what it was or that it belonged to me.

I dropped onto a chair with a frustrated groan. Merytre, Half and Tall had already gone to help Ettu, leaving only Ahmose with me. The old woman studied me, her face revealing nothing of her thoughts.

"It contains something precious, does it?" she asked.

"Nothing particularly valuable," I said. "Just some trinkets from home, but they are all I have from my old life."

"Then they are valuable indeed."

"I suppose so."

We lapsed into silence for a while. The others were working their way through all the chambers. They were being thorough, from what I could hear, and even moving the furniture.

"When will you teach me the things you promised?" My voice

was more strident than I intended it to be and I hoped Ahmose would understand it was because I was still upset about my missing chest.

"What kind of things do you wish to know?" she asked.

"I want…" I hadn't actually expected her to agree, given she had put me off every time I asked. At one time, I had considered asking for a spell to make Pharaoh lose interest in Ishtar. That hardly seemed fair now. Besides, I was the one who still carried a potential heir and not her. "I want to protect my babe. And if it is a son, I want to elevate him in Pharaoh's eyes so that he might one day have the chance to be heir."

"You wish to be queen?" As usual, her face gave no hint of what she thought.

"No," I said.

But the babe would be taken from me as soon as he or she was born. I didn't want to be like Tiye, living for the moment when I might catch a glimpse of my child. I wanted to be involved in his life. I wanted to see him grow up.

"I want to be near to my babe," I said. "If the only way to do that is to be queen, then yes, that is what I want."

Ahmose regarded me seriously, then nodded.

"Very well, then," she said.

CHAPTER 33

Several hours passed before Ettu and the others returned to the sitting chamber. They dropped into various chairs, seemingly thoroughly worn out, except for Merytre who went to stand at the window.

"We have looked everywhere at least twice," Ettu said. "I'm sorry, but we couldn't find your chest."

I nodded, too disappointed to answer without crying and not wanting them to think me ridiculous for being upset about a box of old things. Had it been stolen or was this another of Kia's tricks? If it was Kia, was there a way I could assuage her so she would return it? I would ask Ahmose when I could speak with her privately, not wanting the others to hear such a foolish question.

"Oh, your seeds," Merytre said suddenly. She stopped on her way from the window to a chair and peered down into the tray. "Something has sprouted."

I got up too quickly and my head spun for a moment. Tall was quick to grab my arm.

"Fall!" he said.

"Yes," I said. "Thank you. I feel quite well now."

Ahmose and Ettu were on their way over to the tray as well and we all crowded around to stare down at the seeds. Merytre was right. It was no more than the merest hint of green, but something was definitely growing. My legs felt weak at the relief that filled me. My child would live. If we had indeed been poisoned, the babe had survived.

"Which is it?" I asked, barely able to breathe for anticipation. This was it. The moment when I would learn whether my babe was a son. A possible heir to the throne of Egypt.

Ahmose leaned down to study them more closely. "I can't be certain, but I think it might be the barley."

"And barley was for…" Ettu's voice trailed away, the question unsaid.

"A boy," I said. "If it's barley, the babe is a boy."

"Oh, congratulations, my lady," Merytre said. "How wonderful."

"A boy." Ettu gazed down at the seeds with a funny little smile. I wondered if she was picturing the day she might be waiting for seeds to sprout to confirm whether a babe of her own would be a boy or a girl.

Shortly before sunset on the day of Kia's ceremony, I went to the chapel. I had been here only once before, for the ceremony of Isis and Nephthys. I hoped this wouldn't be like that, where we all wore animal masks and stood in a circle while the lioness prowled around us. I still dreamed of lions stalking me through the gardens, although the terror had faded somewhat. Ettu and Merytre walked with me, leaving Ahmose to bar the door behind us and ensure nobody got in to find Tall and Half.

I wondered whether I should take an offering of some sort, so I stopped to pick some flowers on the way. Not knowing what Kia had liked, I chose an assortment of colours and sizes. In the centre of my posy were some of the narcissus I had dreamed of. Maybe there was nothing significant in the dream, but if I was to make an offering of flowers, it felt right to include them.

Lamplight shone around the edges of the shutters as we approached the chapel. A number of other lady's maids waited nearby, chatting and seemingly at ease. Ettu and Merytre hurried off to join them, leaving me to walk the last few paces alone.

As I drew near to the open door, my footsteps faltered a little. Memories of the last ceremony loomed before me. The shifting shadows, the pounding of the drum, and the mismatched harmony of harp and tambourine. The drink that made everything seem strange and distorted. The lioness who stalked our circle. I shook my head, trying to dislodge the memories. Tonight would be nothing like that. This was a ceremony to farewell Kia and encourage her spirit to move on.

"Kassaya."

I hadn't even noticed Ineni appear in the doorway. Her gaze went to the flowers in my hand.

"Hold onto your offering for now. There will be a point in the ceremony where we each present our gifts to Kia."

Thank Marduk I had thought to bring something. It would have been embarrassing to be the only one who had nothing to offer. I took a deep breath and went inside. This would be nothing like the last ceremony.

Henutmire and Gilukhipa had already arrived. Henutmire gave me a small smile, while Gilukhipa arranged candles and incense on a little table and didn't seem to notice me. I didn't know what to do with myself, or whether it would be appropriate to go and talk with Henutmire, so I waited alone near a window.

Neferu arrived soon after, and then a woman I assumed was Amanitore, the one who was friendly with Kia. I hadn't recognised her name when Henutmire said it, but I did know her face. She was there the day Pharaoh summoned us all to the courtyard to regale us with a speech about his own greatness. I remembered wondering who she was. Amanitore was tall and black-skinned, with a face that seemed fixed in an expression of haughtiness.

Her gaze flicked around the room, landing briefly on me but apparently dismissing me as nobody of importance.

Tiye arrived and Ineni closed the door behind her, signalling she was the last. I felt a little nervous now with not knowing what to expect and realised I was clutching the flowers too tightly, crushing their stems. Their heady fragrances assaulted my nose, making it tingle, and I wished I could set them down somewhere until I needed them.

"Come," Ineni said to us. "Gather around. We will begin our ceremony."

We moved in closer, standing in a ragged circle around the little table with the candles and incense. Gilukhipa passed candles to each of us, set in small clay holders so the wax wouldn't drip on our hands. Ineni lit her own candle, then used it to light that of Tiye who stood on her left. Tiye lit the candle of Neferu beside her. Around the circle we went, each woman lighting the candle of the next. Henutmire lit mine and I felt myself blushing as I turned to Amanitore. She studied me cooly as I held my flame to her candle and I prayed she couldn't see my flushing cheeks.

"Sisters, we gather to honour our departed sister, Kia, daughter of Djau," Ineni said. "Kia departed for the West under tragic and unexpected circumstances, and we grieve her loss even as we rejoice that she may now partake of the afterlife. She will relax under shady trees and enjoy fragrant breezes. She will walk on soft grass under a sun which never burns her skin. She will spend her days feasting and drinking and relaxing. One day, she will be reunited with everyone she has ever loved."

"May you have eternal life," the women murmured together. They obviously all knew when to say it. Caught off guard, I fixed the phrase in my mind and hoped I would be quick enough to join in next time.

"One by one, we now share with Kia our most beloved memory of her," Ineni continued. "We do this to show her she is not forgotten. Kia, I remember the day I first met you. I had only just arrived and I felt lost and alone. You showed me kindness that day when you invited me to dine with you. You were the first Ornament who spoke to me and I will never forget that. But now it is time for you to go to your rest."

Ineni blew out her candle, then set her offering for Kia — a small wooden figurine of a lioness — on the table in the centre of our circle. She nodded to Tiye on her left.

"Kia, I remember the way you challenged me when I told you to clean my bathing chamber," Tiye said. "You drew yourself up and told me you were not a servant. You did it anyway, of course, but I remember your fire and I admired you for it. But now it is time for you to go to your rest."

She blew out her candle and set a golden finger ring on the table. Around the circle we went. Neferu spoke of a picnic she and Kia had shared in the gardens one summer day and Henutmire told us about an evening when she and Kia both dined with Pharaoh.

"It was my first time meeting him," she said, "but not yours. I was so nervous as we arrived and you reached out to take my hand. You told me I shouldn't be nervous because I was too plain for Pharaoh to notice." She laughed a little. "It was the only time I had ever been grateful to be considered plain. But now it is time for you to go to your rest."

She blew out her candle and then it was my turn. My mouth was dry and I still didn't know what I could say.

"Kia, I never had the opportunity to get to know you well." Despite my uncertainty, my voice sounded confident. "We only met for the first time on the day you died, but I remember watching you that afternoon as we sailed with Pharaoh. You were so beautiful and elegant, and I envied your poise. I looked for you afterwards. After the boat had turned over. I'm so sorry I didn't find you soon enough. I would have saved you if I could have. But now it is time for you to go to your rest."

I blew out my candle and hoped I had said enough to satisfy Kia's spirit. I lay my flowers on the table, careful to ensure they didn't cover any of the other offerings.

Amanitore was the last to speak and she told us about Kia's kindness to her when she received a letter about her mother's death. The memories each woman shared were poignant and I was truly sorry I never got the chance to get to know Kia. She had obviously been a kind and compassionate woman. Perhaps we might have been friends.

"Kia," Ineni said after Amanitore blew out her candle. "We have shown that you are not forgotten. Now is the time for you to go to your reward. So go, face Osiris in his Hall of Judgement. Allow your heart to be weighed against the Feather of Truth, and then make your way to the Field of Reeds, where we will all meet again one day, if the gods allow it."

"May you have eternal life," the women said and this time I managed to join in halfway through.

Ineni bowed her head as if praying and it seemed the ceremony was over. I waited, unsure of the etiquette, but the others started to wander away.

"It was a beautiful ceremony," I told Ineni. "If Kia was listening, I'm sure she was very touched by it."

"I believe she was here," Ineni said. "I felt her spirit, but she is gone now. I think we will find her mischievous acts will stop."

"What will happen to the offerings?"

"I will take them down to the pleasure lake and throw them in. Since it is where Kia departed for the West, our offerings might soothe her pain about that place."

I only nodded, unsure of how to respond or whether it would be appropriate to offer to help her. I reached out to clasp her hand briefly, then left.

CHAPTER 34

The sun had well and truly set by the time I left the chapel, and the grounds were in darkness as Ettu, Merytre and I made our way back to the Palace. I was lost in thought, remembering the ceremony and Ineni's comments about feeling Kia's presence, when Khaemmalu suddenly appeared beside me.

"My lady," he said with a bow.

"Khaemmalu." I felt a rush of pleasure at seeing him, and probably greeted him a little too enthusiastically.

"May I join you?" he asked.

"Of course."

We walked in silence for a few moments.

"Are you coming from the ceremony for Lady Kia?" he asked.

"I am."

"How did you find it?"

"I have never attended something like that before so I didn't know what to expect, but it was… nice. I think Kia would have been pleased."

Had he held such a ceremony for his wife after she disappeared? Or had he waited, still hoping she would come back?

"I hear some of the women think her spirit has been causing mischief," he said.

"I don't know what to think about that. They say she is responsible for things going missing, food going off. It is rather strange."

I didn't mention my missing chest, not wanting him to think me foolish if he didn't share the belief that a lingering spirit might cause trouble.

"It makes sense to me," he said. "Her death was abrupt. It's different when one is old or has been unwell. Death is a gentler transition. But for Kia, a woman in her prime, it would have been the last thing on her mind that day."

"As it was for all of us."

"You are fortunate you could swim. You and your sister both."

"We were taught as children. I thought it was all a game really. Never thought it would save my life one day."

"Should the gods ever bless me with a child," Khaemmalu said, "I will be sure to teach him to swim."

My hand went to my belly. He didn't know, of course. Nobody did other than Pharaoh, Ishtar, and those who shared my chambers, plus Henutmire who had guessed.

"And if it is a girl?" I asked.

"Him or her."

Would I ever have the chance to teach my son to swim? Perhaps the best I could do would be to send a message to Pharaoh asking for him to be taught. Surely after the way I had helped save his life, Pharaoh would see the benefit in it. Maybe all his children were taught to swim anyway. Maybe Pharaoh himself was even learning now. The thought amused me and I tried to restrain my grin, feeling that mirth was inappropriate given the ceremony I had just attended.

"Why do you smile?" Khaemmalu asked.

"Just wondering whether Pharaoh has been learning to swim since that day," I confessed.

He made a small noise that sounded suspiciously like a chuckle.

"If he has, I have heard nothing of it," he said.

"Would you be likely to hear?"

"Perhaps," he said with a shrug. "It is the sort of thing that would certainly be talked about."

We were close to the Palace entrance by this point and Khaemmalu stepped off the path, his intention to leave clear. The disappointment that filled me took me by surprise.

"Good night," he said to me. "I hope the gods send you pleasant dreams."

"Good night."

He disappeared into the shadows.

Back at my suite, Ahmose let us in and Half emerged from the men's bedchamber. He climbed up onto a couch using the little stool we left out for him.

"Where's Tall?" I asked as I sat down.

Merytre brought me some melon juice and I sipped it gratefully, surprised at how parched my throat was. Ettu came to sit next to Half and Merytre claimed another chair. Ahmose didn't return and I assumed she had gone off to bed. She was an old woman, after all, and needed more sleep than the rest of us.

"He's already asleep." Half frowned. "To be honest, my lady, I am a little worried for him."

"What is it?"

He seemed to think carefully before he replied.

"Something burdens him," he said. "He has always been an anxious sort, and he is not much of a talker, but of late he has said even less than usual and he constantly flaps his hands.

"He does that when he is worried about something," I said.

"I know, but he's doing it a lot more than usual. I have asked what the problem is, but he won't tell me."

"Maybe he is unhappy at being here. I have been thinking it

isn't fair on either of you. That maybe we should smuggle you back out of the Palace and let you get on with living your lives."

He seemed to consider this carefully, swinging his legs a little as he thought.

"It is true this is not the life I expected to have here," he said at last. "But we have food and shelter, and we are safe enough, for now at least. Here within your chambers, nobody mocks us or treats us as if we are fools."

"But are you not bored? Don't you feel frustrated at never being able to so much as go out for a walk? I see Tall standing by the window all the time and think he must be longing to be outside."

"I try not to think about it," Half said with a shrug. "It serves no purpose. This is the situation I have and I must make of it what I can. For me, I am pleased to have Teacher's company. She is very knowledgeable and I enjoy my conversations with her."

He glanced towards Ettu as if wondering whether to say he was also pleased to be near her, but whatever he was thinking went unsaid.

"I don't think this is good for you," I said. "Or for Tall. I think we should consider finding a way to get you out of here."

"We serve you at your pleasure, my lady," Half said. "We will do whatever you ask."

"It wouldn't be fair of me to ask you to spend the rest of your lives confined to my chambers," I said. "Scurrying off down the hallway to be locked in every time we need to open the door. Living in fear of someone coming to search the chambers. They would execute you if they found you."

"It is indeed a risk," he said.

"Too much of a risk," I said. "I won't turn you out, but I ask that you consider whether it's time for you to leave. Tall too. I will release you from my service if you want to go, and if we can find my chest, I have some jewels I can give you. Enough to fund your travels to wherever you want to go. Maybe you could return to Babylon."

I avoided looking at Ettu, not wanting to know her reaction. The last time she and I discussed her eventual departure, she was adamant she wouldn't take Half with her. However, my son would be born in a few months, and maybe she would change her mind. Perhaps by then, Tall and Half would be ready to leave, and surely Ettu would want to go with them, whether she wanted a husband or not.

CHAPTER 35

"You won't believe what I found," Ettu said to me the day after the ceremony for Kia.

Merytre and I were standing at the window, both of us trying to pretend we weren't hoping to spot anyone in particular. There was little chance I would see Khaemmalu since he only worked nights, but she might see Sutem. Half was busy working on his little woodcarving, while Tall was apparently taking a nap. It was only once Half mentioned his concern that I noticed how much Tall seemed to sleep lately.

"Go on," I said.

"Your chest. The one from Babylon."

"You found it? Show me. Where was it?" I hurried out of the sitting chamber, leaving Merytre alone at the window.

"Right where it was supposed to be." Ettu followed me into my bedchamber. "Look."

Indeed, it was in the corner where it should have been.

"I looked there," I said. "How could I have missed it?"

"We all looked. It wasn't there."

"So where was it? And who returned it?"

"Maybe it was Kia after all," she said with a shrug.

"You're suggesting she took my chest and has now returned it?" Despite the unexpected return of the chest, I still found it difficult to believe.

"You said the other Ornaments thought she was responsible for the odd things that have been happening."

Ettu reached out to touch the chest, gently running one finger over the top, as if to convince herself it was really there.

"But why my chest?" I asked. "It would mean nothing to her."

She shrugged. "Maybe she knew it was important to you. Or maybe it was just small enough for her to move. I don't know. All I can tell you is that it was nowhere in your chambers when we were looking for it the other day."

Ineni did say she felt Kia's presence during our farewell ceremony. Maybe Ettu was right and the ceremony had somehow appeased Kia. Perhaps she was trying to make up for the mischief she had caused.

"Well, if that was you, Kia, thank you for returning it," I said.

If Kia was in the chamber with us, I felt no sign of her.

I lifted the lid and was relief to see everything looked as I had left it. I lifted the items out one by one. Ishtar's scarf, carefully folded across the top. The shell from Syria. The hairbrush I had promised Tiye. My jewels. My fingers lingered on a pendant that had always been my favourite: a yellow gem in a wooden heart-shaped setting threaded on a black cord. Compared to the jewels I had now, it was mediocre, but I had always thought it beautiful. I should wear it some time.

I set the hairbrush and the scarf aside and packed everything else back into the chest. The scarf I would give to Khaemmalu to pass onto Gautseshen. I had meant to send her a gift for saving Half and this would do as well as anything. I would be sorry to lose the scarf, but it was one of the few things I owned myself.

"Do you want me to put the chest somewhere else?" Ettu asked. "Perhaps under your bed where it will be out of sight?"

"If it was Kia who took it, I doubt putting it under the bed would make much difference."

"But if it was someone else, at least the chest won't be there if they go looking for it again. We could lock it in the men's bedchamber with your jewels."

I studied the hairbrush as I considered her suggestion. It was made of wood with soft bristles and an ivory handle. It too was something I had always thought a fine item, but it had obviously been well used and it looked a little shabby. I found myself embarrassed to have offered it to Tiye. Perhaps I should say I had lost it.

"No," I said. "Now that it's been returned, I don't think we will have the same problem again."

Whether it was Kia or someone else, nothing had been stolen.

"Remind me to take this tomorrow when I go to see Tiye." I set the hairbrush on top of the chest.

Ettu nodded and left. As I followed her, I stopped to poke my head into the men's bedchamber. Tall lay on his side with his back to the door.

"Tall?" I whispered. "Are you awake?"

He didn't reply, so either he was asleep or he didn't want to talk. I let him be.

CHAPTER 36

"I heard Weren suspects someone in the Palace is using magic," Tiye said when I visited her the following day. Her tone was so casual that at first I missed the significance of her comments.

"Who?" I asked, before I realised what she had said. "Magic?"

My heart pounded. None of us had snuck out since the night Ettu, Merytre, Tall and I went to the House of Life. Why would it only be now that someone became suspicious?

"One of the butlers. Apparently the odd things that were happening have aroused his interest," Tiye said.

"The things some folk thought were because of Kia?" I didn't look at her as I spoke, not wanting her to see my guilt about sneaking out. My cheeks heated and I knew there was no way she would miss that.

But Tiye only nodded and if she noticed my blush, for once she didn't comment.

"Have there been any more strange incidents?" I asked.

"I haven't heard of anything since the ceremony, but apparently there were so many odd things before that Weren has been sniffing around."

"If it really was Kia and it's all stopped now, he won't find anything," I said.

"No." She gave me that cool look that always seemed to suggest she knew more than she said. "If anyone did happen to be using magic, it would be prudent of them to stop, for a while at least."

I looked her in the eyes, hoping it would make me seem more at ease with the conversation than I felt.

"I can't imagine what anyone would use magic for in the first place," I said.

"Hmm, I suppose you wouldn't."

I didn't know how to interpret that and I didn't want to ask. Appearing too interested in what she meant might well signal my guilt.

"Have you had a chance to ask the administrators about Abar's sister?" I asked in an attempt to change the subject.

"Not yet," Tiye said. "I will ask Panouk the next time I see him. I would rather not ask anything of Amankhau."

"I can hardly blame you," I said. "Amankhau is odious."

"He has certainly taken a dislike to you." She gave me a look that almost seemed worried. "You should take more care around men like him."

Was it a hint that she too thought Amankhau was involved in the matter of the missing women? I couldn't find a way to ask without telling her my own suspicion and I didn't want to look foolish if she considered him to be nothing more than a horrid man.

"I almost forgot," I said instead. "I brought you this."

I handed her the little linen bag with my hairbrush inside. When she took the hairbrush out and studied it, I felt a rush of embarrassment at how shabby it looked. I should have pretended I couldn't find it.

"I have had it since I was a girl," I said. "The handle is made from the tusk of a beast that is supposed to be the size of the

Great Temple in Babylon."

"An elephant?" Tiye asked.

"Maybe. I can't remember what the creature was called. I was very young and it's name was of less importance to me at the time than its size."

"I saw an elephant once. They are big, but not the size of a temple. Not unless it is a very small temple."

Now I felt even more foolish.

"You don't have to keep it," I said. "It's just I said I would give it to you and I wanted to keep my word."

"No, I will take it," she said to my dismay. "The handle is impressive. Perhaps I will have it reset."

I nodded and tried not to show my disappointment. That hairbrush was one of my childhood treasures and she intended to pull it apart.

I didn't stay for much longer, making an excuse about a gown fitting and fleeing before I said more than I should. Tiye seemed absorbed in her thoughts and I wasn't sure she even noticed my departure. As Ettu and I turned down the hallway that led to my chambers, I spotted a familiar figure approaching.

"Marduk, not today," I muttered.

Other than when Amankhau interrogated me about the letter from my father, I hadn't spoken with him since the incident with Tiye's stolen jewels. That ended in me securing Ettu's release by threatening to tell all the Ornaments Amankhau was stealing their treasures and plotting against them. I had made an enemy of him that day and had no doubt he intended to get his revenge. It was just a matter of time.

Unfortunately there was no way to avoid him so I took a deep breath and focused my gaze straight ahead. I would walk right past. There was no need to speak, or even to acknowledge him. But it seemed Amankhau didn't have the same thought. He stopped in front of me, in the middle of the hallway, forcing me to either halt or amend my course to walk around him. I stopped.

I was an Ornament and I carried Pharaoh's son. I refused to be intimidated by a servant.

He sneered at me. Taking a lesson from Tiye, I raised my eyebrows and gave him a cool stare.

"Is there a problem, Administrator?" I asked.

"I don't suppose you know anything about the items that have gone missing lately," he said.

He gave me a hard look and I restrained a sigh. Was he really going to try accusing me of being a thief again?

"The only thing I know that's gone missing is from my own chambers," I said. "And the item in question was returned a few days later."

His gaze went from me to Ettu, probably remembering the confession that was coerced out of her after he found one of Tiye's stolen jewels in her pouch.

"Oh? And what might that be?" His tone was snide.

"As I said, it has been returned, so it hardly matters. Now, if you don't mind, Administrator, I have somewhere I need to be."

I pretended I was Tiye as I swept past him with my head held high. Thankfully, I didn't trip over my hem and I didn't even blush. Ettu waited until Amankhau was out of hearing before she spoke.

"He still bears a grudge," she said.

"As do I."

"He is a dangerous man. There is something about him that gives me chills."

"He makes me feel like I need to bathe after I have spoken with him."

"I wonder why he's even here this late," Ettu said. "He is supposed to be a creature of the night, but it's not the first time we have found him skulking in the hallways during the day."

Her words made me smile. A creature of the night seemed like a perfect description for such a vile man.

Back in my chambers, I told the others what Tiye said about

the butler, Weren, looking for evidence of magic being used. Ahmose frowned a little, but didn't seem particularly disturbed.

"Do you think he has found out about the potions?" Merytre asked.

"Not from what Tiye said," I replied. "She only spoke about the things that some of the Ornaments thought might be because of Kia."

"The things that have stopped happening," Ettu said.

I nodded. "So maybe he will lose interest once he can't find any evidence."

"I am running low on some of my herbs," Ahmose said, "including the one I use for the invisibility potion, but perhaps now is not the time to restock them."

"Wait until the attention dies down," I said. "Besides, we won't need that potion again any time soon."

My gaze went to Half before I realised. He was looking down at his hands and didn't notice. We hadn't spoken again about my suggestion that he and Tall should leave, and I wondered how seriously he was considering it.

CHAPTER 37

"*M*y lady."

Merytre had just returned from fetching me some flowers from the gardens, an errand I sent her on to stop her from standing at the window and sighing at the lack of sightings of Sutem. But she had returned with empty hands.

"Were there no flowers in bloom today?" I asked, trying to conceal my grin. She had likely found Sutem and been so distracted that she forgot my flowers.

Merytre looked down at her hands as if surprised to find them empty.

"Oh," she said.

"Never mind. You know I didn't really want any flowers."

It was bad enough having to smell them every time I went outside. I didn't need their stench through my chambers as well, competing with the oils and lotions my maids applied liberally to my skin every morning.

"I spoke with Sutem," she said.

"I guessed as much."

I glanced around the sitting chamber, wondering if anyone else was as amused as I was. We were all there. Ahmose perched in her favourite chair, the one she had used when her arm was broken. Tall, who was actually out of bed and seemed reasonably cheerful today, stood to the side of a window, where he could peer out without risking someone seeing him. Half and Ettu sat on a couch, their heads together as they spoke quietly, although they had stopped as soon as Merytre returned.

"Sutem said Lady Ishtar went to dine with Pharaoh at his palace two nights ago," Merytre said.

My cheerfulness dissipated. Had Ishtar told Pharaoh she lost the babe? Was he angry with her?

"Maybe I should go see her today," I said. "If she told him—"

"She hasn't come back." The words burst out of Merytre as if she couldn't hold them in any longer.

"What do you mean?" My breath caught in my chest and the chamber seemed to wobble and tilt. "You said she went two nights ago."

"Sutem heard it from Khaemmalu, who saw her leave," Merytre said. "Pharaoh sent a palanquin for her. When she didn't return by dawn, Khaemmalu asked Sutem to watch for her. She never came back."

"She went alone?" I could hardly get the words out. My chest was tight and my heart hurt. Maybe there was something wrong with me. Maybe my heart was about to burst.

Merytre nodded, but before she could say anything else, someone knocked on the door. Ettu waited until Tall and Half were safely in their bedchamber before she opened the door. It was Belet-ili and she pushed right past Ettu to drop to her knees at my feet. Her face was streaked with tears.

"My lady," she said with a sob. "Lady Ishtar has not returned and I don't know what to do."

"She has been gone for two nights?" Faced with Belet-ili's distress, I somehow found calmness within myself. I might fall apart in front of my closest companions, but not in front of my sister's maid.

"She went to dine with Pharaoh," she said. I could hardly make out Belet-ili's words through her sobs. "When she didn't return by dawn, I wasn't very worried. But she didn't come back by evening, so I went to the administrator."

"Which one?" I asked.

"Amankhau. I asked for Panouk, but he had already left for the night. Amankhau said Lady Ishtar had probably returned to her father. It isn't true, though, my lady. She would never leave and not tell me. She wouldn't leave me here without her."

Everything around me faded. Nothing else was important. Another woman was missing and once again the administrators said she had gone home. Another woman who disappeared from Pharaoh's palace, or maybe on the way there. But this time, it was my sister.

"Belet-ili, here, drink this." Ettu pressed a mug into Belet-ili's hands and wrapped her fingers around it so she wouldn't drop it. "You need to calm down so you can tell us everything you know."

"That is everything," Belet-ili said with a sob. She sat back on her heels and took a sip of the wine. It seemed to steady her a little and she scrubbed the tears from her face.

Ahmose came to hand me a mug, which I absently sipped. The wine was bitter, signalling she had added something to it. A herb to soothe me, perhaps. That must be why Belet-ili was calming so quickly.

"Why didn't you come sooner?" I asked.

"I'm sorry." Belet-ili burst into sobs again. "I didn't know how long I should wait. I was sure she would come back and then I got scared. I didn't want to come and tell you because..." She hiccupped and her voice trailed away.

"Because that would make it real," Ettu guessed.

Belet-ili nodded. Merytre brought her a linen cloth and Belet-ili wiped her face, then scrunched the cloth in her hand as if she wanted to throw it at somebody.

I felt very calm. There was no fear. No anger. No emotion at all, just the knowledge that Ishtar was missing, and I needed to find her.

"Fetch Panouk," I said. "Not Amankhau. I want Panouk in my chambers immediately. Ettu, go to him yourself and make him come. Do not come back without him."

Ettu left without a word. Merytre helped Belet-ili to her feet and led her to a couch. The woman still sniffled and let out the occasional sob, but whatever Ahmose had put in the wine had steadied her.

Panouk arrived in a remarkably short time. Ettu must have been very insistent about the urgency of my summons. He gave me a brief bow and waited, a quizzical look on his face. I guessed Ettu hadn't told him why I wanted to see him.

"My sister is missing," I said without introduction. There was no point wasting time on niceties. "I want every person you can mobilise out searching for her. Here, in the town, Pharaoh's palace. Everywhere."

"My lady, that is really not necessary," Panouk said. "We know where Lady Ishtar is."

"You do?" Hope rose. She was safe. She had already been found. "Where is she? I want to see her."

"She has returned home," he said. "Amankhau investigated as soon as her maid reported her missing and discovered she was on her way north to the coast. Arrangements were made for her to sail to Babylon."

"That can't be true. She wouldn't leave without telling me and she can't go home. Our father sent her here. He won't accept her back."

Panouk shrugged. "Amankhau reported that she asked Pharaoh to allow her to go home and one of his administrators arranged immediate transport for her. I believe she left directly from Pharaoh's palace. I suppose there was no time for her to return here to make her goodbyes. Perhaps she will write to you once she arrives in Babylon."

"You don't find it strange that every woman who disappears has supposedly returned home?" I asked. "And without farewelling anyone she was close to?"

"I can hardly stop a woman who has made her decision to leave," Panouk said. "As to why they usually depart without farewells, I cannot say. I suppose they find it too difficult, or they don't want to answer any questions."

"If what you say is true, why didn't Amankhau come to tell me Ishtar had left?" I asked.

"Why would he?" Panouk countered. "How was he to know she hadn't already told you of her intention? It is hardly his responsibility to ensure she informed anyone who might wish to know. Even I, when your maid insisted I leave my duties and come to you at once, never for a moment thought it might be about this."

I frowned as I studied him. As much as I didn't believe him, neither his face nor his voice suggested he was lying. Whatever the truth was, Panouk seemed to believe his own words.

"Send for Amankhau," I said. "I want to hear it from his mouth."

A flicker of annoyance crossed Panouk's face.

"My lady, I understand you are upset," he said. "And you want answers. But I have faithfully told you everything Amankhau told me. What reason do you have to mistrust my word?"

"Maybe there is something you have forgotten," I said. "Something that will prove to be significant."

"But what other information do you need?" He gestured, palms up, around the chamber, as if indicating the answer was right there in front of me. "Your sister is perfectly safe. She has simply made the decision to return to your father."

"Like every other woman who disappears from this place."

"You are hardly a prisoner here. If you wanted to leave, nobody would stop you. I would personally arrange transport for you."

Anger welled within me, but I pushed it down so I could stay calm. I would not lose my temper in front of Panouk.

"If every woman who disappears has returned to her father, how do you explain the bodies that were found recently?" I asked.

He looked at me blankly. "Bodies?"

"Surely you have heard. Two women were found. Dead. One of them was Nebtu."

I must have sounded confident enough for him to believe me, because his eyes widened and he frowned.

"That can't be correct," he said. "Lady Nebtu returned to her father's house. We received confirmation from a messenger."

"A boy of about ten years old who appeared to be reciting a memorised script."

"No." He shook his head. "Amankhau sent the messenger himself, at your insistence I believe."

"Amankhau *told* you he sent a messenger."

Panouk seemed to go very still and gave me a hard look.

"My lady, what exactly are you accusing Amankhau of?" he asked.

"Have you yourself ever sent a messenger to the family of one of the missing women and received confirmation of her safe arrival? Have you ever heard of anyone receiving a message from one of the women at some later time? Have you ever spoken to any of these women before they left?"

"Well, no." He stammered a little, seemingly flustered now. "They always seem to leave at night. I typically work during the day and Amankhau looks after the Palace at night."

"You don't find that suspicious? That every missing woman leaves at night?"

"Of course not." He cast his gaze around the chamber, as if looking for an explanation. "What reason would I have to not believe Amankhau? He is very trustworthy. Pharaoh himself appointed him to his position."

Ettu and I had speculated that perhaps an administrator was

responsible, and this conversation was doing nothing to change my mind, although I didn't think it was Panouk. I couldn't yet rule out the possibility of the queen's involvement — perhaps she ordered the removal of women she was jealous of, or disliked, or who took too much of her husband's attention — but it seemed likely that Amankhau was one of those who caused the women to disappear. Whatever was happening, and whether the queen was involved or not, all I could be sure of was that Amankhau had something to do with it.

"Too many women have disappeared," I said. "And Amankhau seems to be right there in the middle of it each time."

"My lady Kassaya." Panouk's voice was overly conciliatory now. "I realise you and Amankhau have had your disagreements. He was, I concede, a little too heavy-handed in the matter of the missing jewels. Perhaps we both were. And I realise Lady Ishtar's departure has caused you some measure of distress, but these accusations against Amankhau are unfounded."

"Then fetch him," I said. "Call him here to account for himself in front of both you and I. If he is innocent, let me hear it from his own mouth."

"This has gone far enough." Panouk straightened himself and stood a little taller, making it seem like he was looking down his nose at me. "I realise your distress is probably causing a momentary lack of judgement, but I really cannot tolerate baseless accusations being made against a senior Palace official. If you have some definitive evidence of Amankhau's involvement in whatever it is you are suggesting he is involved with, then bring it to me. But if all you have is coincidence and speculation, then I really must return to my duties."

He hurried out without giving me any further chance to speak. It was clear that if I actually had evidence against Amankhau, Panouk didn't want to hear it.

CHAPTER 38

There was silence in the chamber for a few moments after Panouk's departure.

"Well," Ettu said at last. "I hardly know what to think."

My calmness was gone and now I felt numb. Belet-ili let out a muffled sob. I had forgotten she was there.

"Belet-ili, I will come to you myself as soon as there is any news," Ettu said.

She took the woman by her shoulders and led her to the door. Belet-ili shot me a look that seemed to beg me to let her stay, but I said nothing. Tall and Half would have to remain hidden away for as long as she was here. As soon as the door was barred again, Ettu went to let the men out, although some time passed before the three of them returned. I guessed she must have been filling them in on Panouk's visit.

Ahmose, Merytre and I sat in silence while we waited. My mind whirled and I couldn't think of anything to say. I had too many questions, too many suspicions, and I couldn't tell which of them were reasonable or plausible. Tall came to sit beside me.

"Danger!" he said, very earnestly. "Sister!"

"Yes, I fear my sister is in danger." I felt very distant, as if I was in another place and it was someone else who sat here on the couch and replied so calmly to Tall.

"Danger!" he said again.

"What is he saying?" Merytre whispered to someone.

Ahmose replied quietly.

"Sister!" Tall flapped his hands.

Through my numb fog, I remember the time Tall tried to tell me I wouldn't be queen. Queen, he kept saying, sounding first frustrated, then sorrowful, when I didn't understand.

"Tall, do you know what might have happened to Ishtar?" I asked.

He looked down at the floor, still flapping his hands. I reached out to take one hand, meaning to hold it. I thought it might help to focus his attention, but he squawked and pulled his hand out of my grip. I had forgotten he didn't like to be touched like that.

"Tall, what else can you tell me?" I asked.

"Sister!"

"What do you know about Sister?"

"Danger!"

"Yes, I think she's in terrible danger."

If she was even still alive. It had been two nights. A full day and a half. I might be too late to save her, even if I could find her. No, don't think like that. Just focus on finding her. Finding her safe.

"Careful! Pharaoh! Danger!"

It was the same three words he had said to me before. Ahmose quietly translated for Merytre. Careful, Pharaoh, danger. It was a clear message, but what? I had originally thought he meant Pharaoh was in danger, but maybe he was trying to say Pharaoh was somehow involved? If the queen was removing competition, that might make it seem to Tall like Pharaoh had something to do with it. Or was the thought I had hardly let myself think the correct answer all along: that Pharaoh himself was responsible for the missing women?

"Merytre, are you sure you can't think of any connection between the women who have disappeared?" Ettu asked. "Someone they were friendly with, some habit or interest they had? Anything at all they might have had in common? I know we have asked before, but think again. Maybe there is something you have forgotten."

Merytre frowned and shook her head.

"I'm sorry," she said. "I don't know enough about most of them to know. There's nothing I haven't already told you. Some disappeared from here, some from Pharaoh's palace. Some were Ornaments, some servants. I think I have told you folk speak of men who come in the night to steal women away from their chambers."

"Do we actually know that any of them went missing from their own chambers?" I asked. "Ishtar certainly didn't."

Merytre only shrugged. I didn't push her. She knew only as much as she had heard.

"We know she definitely left the Palace," Ettu said.

"What we don't know is whether she ever arrived at Pharaoh's palace," Merytre added.

She and Ettu looked at each other.

"Or if something happened to her on the way," Ettu finished.

"We need to find out," I said. "I'm going to speak with Tiye. If anyone here has a reliable informant within Pharaoh's palace, it will be her."

"Panouk would have contacts there," Ahmose pointed out. "But I suppose you don't trust him."

"I, too, know folk there," Half said. Beside him, Ettu was already shaking her head. "I could go back and see what I can find out."

"No." Ettu and I spoke at the same time.

"It's too dangerous," I said.

"You barely got out alive last time." Ettu rested her hand on his. "You cannot go back."

"Me!" Tall said.

"No," I said. "You cannot go either, with Half or without him. I won't risk either of you. I'm going to see Tiye."

When I arrived at Tiye's chambers, her maid hesitated before letting me in, and I wondered whether I was interrupting something. However, Tiye was standing at a window, watching something in the gardens, and didn't seem to be at all busy.

"Kassaya." Her voice sounded friendly enough, although she didn't turn away from the window. I hoped she was in a good mood. "It is much later than you usually visit. I didn't expect to see you today."

"Ishtar is missing," I said.

Tiye seemed to freeze and it took a long time for her to turn to face me.

"Oh dear," she said.

"She went to visit Pharaoh," I said. "I need to know whether she ever made it to his palace."

"How do you propose to find that out?"

"You must have a contact there. I know someone warns you before Pharaoh visits here. Can you get a message to that person about Ishtar?"

She studied me for a moment.

"Kassaya, I'm sure I have told you this before, but you play a dangerous game."

"My sister is missing. I'm not playing any games."

"How long has she been gone?"

"Two nights."

"Then she has already either gone to the West or is on her way home." Tiye's voice was casual, but it sounded forced.

"I don't believe she left. I cannot. She wouldn't leave without telling me."

"My understanding is your relationship has been strained since she arrived. That you recently argued."

"That doesn't mean she would just leave. We are sisters. Blood."

"She is jealous of you." Tiye's voice was cool, giving me no indication of what she thought of this. "You have made a life here for yourself. Companions. Friends, even. You have your secrets and you don't share them with anyone outside your circle, not even your sister."

"I don't have any secrets." I gave her a hard look, trying to figure out whether she was bluffing. For once, my cheeks didn't give away my lie.

"We all have secrets, especially in a place like this."

"Not me."

"As you wish." Tiye moved to sit on a couch. She crossed her legs and draped one arm along the back. I stayed where I was standing. There was no time to sit down and chat.

"Please," I said. "I thought we were friends. I need to know whether Ishtar ever reached Pharaoh's palace."

"And what do you intend to do with that information? If she didn't arrive, or if she did?"

"I don't know, but it's a start. If I can discover where she disappeared from, then maybe I still have a chance to find her."

"You might not like what you learn." She looked away and tapped her fingers on the back of the couch. Her demeanour puzzled me, but there was no room in my mind today for trying to understand Tiye. Ishtar had to be my only focus.

"I'd rather know than not," I said. "Maybe I can save her."

Like Abar. She wanted to know her sister's fate, whatever it was, and Tiye had said she would ask Panouk. I couldn't ask now, though. Didn't want to remind her she was already doing me one favour.

Tiye studied me for a while longer. I held my breath, expecting she would refuse.

"Give me a few hours," she said at last. "I can't promise anything, but I will see what I can find out."

CHAPTER 39

It was Nammu who brought the message from Tiye. I had spent the entire afternoon pacing the sitting chamber and wondering why Tiye was taking so long. I had resolved to go ask her several times, but there was always someone to talk me out of it. Ettu urged me to patience. Merytre said I should wait. Half pointed out it was quite a long way to Pharaoh's palace, and Tiye's messenger, whoever it was, had to walk there and back. Ahmose said the news would come no faster if I badgered Tiye than if I left her to do as she said she would. Tall only flapped his hands and muttered about danger.

With the men safely locked away, Merytre let Nammu in.

"My lady." Nammu's voice was as sullen as it always was on the occasions she had to speak with me.

"What is it?" I asked, too worried about Ishtar to care about the sharpness of my tone.

"My lady Tiye said to tell you her contact has confirmed Lady Ishtar's arrival at Pharaoh's palace two nights ago."

The world seemed to go still for a moment and I even forgot to breathe. I only remembered when my chest started hurting. I took a deep breath and fought for composure. Tears burned, but I wouldn't cry in front of Nammu.

"What else did she find out?" I asked when I was sure I could speak without bursting into tears.

"That is all," Nammu said.

"That's all? There must be more to the message." I eyed her, wondering if she might deliberately forget to pass on some of whatever she knew.

"That is all she told me to tell you. That her contact said Lady Ishtar arrived the night before last."

"And does anyone know what happened after that? Did anyone see her leave?"

"I don't know."

My fingers itched to grab her shoulders and shake her. I clenched my fists and tried to keep myself under control.

"Nammu, you know she is missing, don't you?" I asked. "Do you care nothing about that?"

"I know she is missing." Nammu drew herself up taller and glared at me. "And I was sorry to hear it. She was a good mistress to me."

I could hear her unspoken words: better than you ever were.

"But it is not Lady Ishtar I serve now, and that is the whole message I was sent to give you," she finished.

"Go then," I said. "Tell your mistress to send word to me immediately if she hears anything more."

Nammu left without saying anything else. The door closed behind her and Ettu slipped away to let the men out.

"What do we do now?" I asked, once they had all returned.

I looked around the chamber, meeting the eyes of each of my companions. Ettu, who served Ishtar before she served me. Ahmose, Half and Tall, all people who had made their lives on the fringes of society. Merytre, the newest of my companions, and probably the one who best understood this world we had been thrust into. "What is my next move?"

"So we know she arrived at Pharaoh's palace," Half said. "We need to determine what happened after that. Did she ever reach Pharaoh or did she go missing before then?"

"Did they eat or drink?" Ahmose added. "If they didn't, we can probably rule out any possibility she was drugged."

"Why would she be drugged?" I hadn't even considered such a thing.

"A woman is more easily stolen away if she is quiet," Ahmose said. "If Lady Ishtar was kicking and screaming, as surely she would have if someone attacked her, there is a greater chance of drawing unwanted attention."

"Once we know whether she actually got to Pharaoh, we then need to know what happened when she left," Ettu said. "Someone would have seen her. A guard who escorted her to her transport. The slave master or the slaves who carried her palanquin. We need to know whether she ever left the Palace."

"If she did, then we work on determining what happened on the way back here," Half said. "We take it step by step. Each stage of her journey. This palace to that one. Arrival to Pharaoh. Pharaoh to transport. The journey back. She disappeared some-where in between."

It sounded so simple when he broke it down like that, although I knew it would be anything but. Determining Ishtar's movements would require us to have different contacts for each stage of the evening. But we already had the first piece of infor-mation we needed. We knew she had arrived at Pharaoh's palace. Now we needed to work on finding out whether she ever made it from her transport to Pharaoh.

"Maybe one of the guards can help," Merytre suggested. "Sutem has friends in Pharaoh's palace. He will be off duty for the night now, though."

"Khaemmalu then." I couldn't bear to wait until morning before I did anything else. I needed to be working on the next stage of Ishtar's journey. The longer I waited, the more likely it was that whoever had seen her would forget or misremember.

"I will come with you." Ettu was already on her feet.

We hurried down the three flights of stairs and out to the grounds.

"Slow down a little," Ettu said, puffing from somewhere behind me, as I strode along the path. "I already have a pain in my side from trying to keep up."

"Sorry." I hadn't realised how fast I was moving. I slowed to a more moderate pace and Ettu caught up, coming to walk beside me.

"Where is he?" I muttered, peering into the shadows. I never found Khaemmalu when I went looking for him. He always found me.

"We have only been out here a few moments. He might be in a different part of the grounds."

"Khaemmalu," I called.

"Shh." Ettu gave me a startled look. "My lady, you don't want everyone to know you are looking for him."

"Why? It's not like I am planning some illicit encounter."

I prayed the darkness would hide my blush. It was hard to think about Khaemmalu without remembering how he must have thought I was flirting with him the night I arrived.

"Lady Kassaya." Khaemmalu's voice was low and came from the shadows to my left.

"I need to speak with you urgently."

"I gathered that." His voice was dry and I wondered whether I had embarrassed him by calling out for him. There was no time to worry about such things right now, though. "Come back here. Leave your maid to keep watch."

I nodded at Ettu and slipped away into the shadows. Away from the torch-lit path, I could see nothing. I hesitated, waiting for my eyes to adjust.

"Here." Khaemmalu's fingers grazed my elbow. "Come further back."

I followed his voice and we huddled together in a small space in the middle of some bushes. We stood barely a hand's width apart, so close I could feel his breath on my face.

"My sister is missing," I said, before remembering he already knew. He was the one who told Sutem to watch for her. "We have confirmed she arrived at Pharaoh's palace that night. Do you have any friends there who might be able to tell us about her movements after that?"

The words came out in a rush and for a moment I wasn't even sure they were intelligible. I took a breath, ready to repeat myself, but Khaemmalu nodded.

"I have a friend in Pharaoh's personal squad," he said. "If she did indeed meet with Pharaoh that evening, he will know of it. But Kassaya" — his fingers grazed my arm again and I tried not to notice how my heart beat faster at his touch — "are you sure you want to know?"

"Of course I do. I might be able to find her before…"

My voice trailed away. I couldn't make myself say it.

"Kassaya, I'm sorry." His voice was gentle. "It's been three nights now. She has already gone to the West."

Three nights. I hadn't thought of it like that. But, of course, when I first found out earlier today, it was only two nights. A whole day had passed since then. Three nights sounded so… final.

"Don't say that," I said. "You don't know that."

"I have worked here long enough to know that once a woman is missing for more than a few hours, she won't be found alive."

I concentrated on breathing in and out, and tried not to listen to his words ringing in my head. *She won't be found alive.*

"No," I said. "I can save her. I just have to find her."

CHAPTER 40

Khaemmalu said for me to come back midmorning. I understood he wasn't supposed to leave during his shift, but he did the night Half was stabbed, and Ishtar might be in no less danger. She could be injured. Lying somewhere waiting for help. But I already owed Khaemmalu a debt several times over and I couldn't ask that he risk his job for me any more than he already had.

Ettu and I were waiting for him long before midmorning. We sat on a bench beneath a shady tree and made a show of admiring the gardens around us.

"Those flowers over there are particularly pretty," Ettu said. "Do you know what they are?"

I had barely noticed the bright red flowers she pointed at. The bush had an unusual swollen trunk and small, green leaves.

"I have no idea." I scanned the depths of the greenery around us for any sign of Khaemmalu.

"He will let us know when he arrives," Ettu whispered. "It might be best if you don't appear so obviously to be looking for someone."

She was right. I made an effort to look engaged with our conversation.

"Oh, look at those ones." I pointed to some cheerful daisies. "They are my favourite, I think."

"I find them rather boring," Ettu said. "I prefer brighter flowers with more scent."

"I like that they don't have much of a smell. I have a constant headache from all the perfumes and lotions and flowers."

"I didn't realise it was that bad." Ettu shot me an apologetic glance. "I will see about getting you some lotions with a milder scent and will speak to your other maids about being a little less liberal with the perfumes."

"I have already asked them, but they ignore me."

"The folk here are very fond of scents, but if I tell them this is what you want, they will have to comply."

"Very good."

We lapsed into silence for a while. My legs were restless and I longed to walk around, but it would be easier for Khaemmalu to find us if we stayed in the one spot. Still, I tapped my feet and picked at a thread on my skirt, until I realised what I was doing. It would be obvious to anyone watching that I was anxious about something. I tucked my hands beneath my thighs and tried to keep my feet still.

"I think Khaemmalu is here," Ettu whispered.

She glanced briefly off to the side to show me which direction he was in.

"I will stay here and keep watch," she said.

"I'm going to pick some flowers for my bedchamber," I said as I rose from the bench.

Trying to look casual, I sauntered around the area and plucked a few blossoms before ducking in behind the shrubbery. Khaemmalu's face gave me no hint of what he had learned.

"What is it?" I whispered. "Tell me, quickly."

"My friend confirmed she made it to Pharaoh," he said. "But he couldn't say what happened after that."

"What do you mean? Did she leave the palace that night or not?"

"She stayed until very late. My friend's squad was dismissed before she left."

"Dismissed?"

"Sent off duty. Normally they would stay until Pharaoh goes to bed, but that night they were sent away sometime after midnight."

"No guards stayed?"

"Only two." His face was grim now. "Pharaoh's captain and his second-in-command. It was his captain who told them to go."

"Is that unusual?" My mind whirled and I couldn't think. I couldn't even figure out what I should be asking. What did Khaemmalu's news mean?

"Somewhat, but it is not unprecedented. They are sometimes sent away if he is up late. Pharaoh's captain and second always stay with him, though."

"So they are the only ones who would be able to confirm whether Ishtar left the palace that night?"

Khaemmalu's mouth tightened and he glanced away for a moment. He shook his head.

"We cannot ask them," he said.

"Why not?"

"My friend has… suspicions about them. Has for some time now."

"I don't understand."

"About what kind of tasks they might do for Pharaoh that the rest of the squad doesn't know about."

I looked at him blankly.

"Khaemmalu, you need to speak plainly. I don't know what you mean."

"My friend believes that Pharaoh sometimes mistreats his women, and that his captain and second cover for him."

My chest tightened and for a moment I couldn't breathe.

"Lady Kassaya?" Khaemmalu's voice finally pierced the fog surrounding me and I realised he was holding my arm. "Do you need to sit down? You suddenly went very white and I thought you were going to faint."

"No, no, I am fine. Tell me what else your friend knows."

"I need you to understand something first." He peered at me intently. "There are… particular requirements of Pharaoh's personal squad. One of them is absolute discretion. No matter what they see or hear, they are expected to tell nobody. My friend is loyal to Pharaoh and his job, and he told me only because we are like brothers. We have known each other since we were boys. There is nobody else in the world he would share such a thing with and I would die before I betrayed his trust in me."

"I understand," I said faintly. He was about to tell me something terrible. Something I didn't want to hear. And once I knew it, I would never be able to forget. But I had to know.

"My friend believes that sometimes the women who spend time with Pharaoh… don't survive the encounter."

He paused and looked at me hard, as if waiting to see whether I would faint. I could only nod for him to continue.

"His captain and second… My friend believes they dispose of the bodies. Of the women Pharaoh has mistreated. Do you understand what I am saying?"

The answer had been right in front of me all this time and I hadn't let myself see it. I had thought it, once or twice, and always dismissed the idea. Why would Pharaoh do such a thing? We were entirely within his power. He controlled every aspect of our lives. There must be something wrong with him to do such a thing, and not just once, but over and over. Something dark and disturbing and evil. When I finally managed to make my mouth work, my voice was surprisingly strong.

"You are telling me that Ishtar is dead, and that Pharaoh killed her."

"I cannot say for certain." Khaemmalu's voice was gentle and I finally realised he was still holding my arm. "But it seems like a strong possibility."

CHAPTER 41

$\mathcal{I}$ left Khaemmalu in the bushes and returned to Ettu on unsteady legs.

"Did you find enough flowers?" she asked brightly as I sat beside her. She reached over to squeeze my hand, perhaps telling me she had noticed my paleness.

I glanced down at the few I had picked. They would make a sorry bunch, hardly enough to bother with a vase.

"This will be enough," I managed to say. "I couldn't find the ones I particularly wanted."

"He had news?" she whispered.

I swallowed hard, preparing myself for the words I had to say. I couldn't afford to fall apart.

"His friend believes it is Pharaoh," I said. "Pharaoh is responsible for the missing women."

She shot me a look of horror.

"I thought it was the queen," she whispered.

"We all did."

"Or maybe Amankhau. He is a snake and I wouldn't have been surprised if he was involved. But if it is Pharaoh…"

Her voice trailed away, but I knew what it was she couldn't

bring herself to say. If it was Pharaoh, there was no recourse. No police chief would arrest him, no magistrate would try him. Pharaoh was above any law. He *was* the law.

"Tiye tried to tell me," I said. "She said if I knew anything about Nebtu, I should keep it to myself. That it would be dangerous for anyone to think I knew something."

"She could have said it more plainly to be sure you understood."

"I don't think she could, not without knowing whether she could trust me. What if I told other people what she said? What if I reported her to the administrators for spreading lies about Pharaoh? She tried to warn me in the only way she could, but she was protecting herself at the same time."

"There must be other Ornaments who know."

A memory of Ishtar's bruised neck rose in my mind. She knew Pharaoh might hurt her again. She was probably afraid of him, and she never told me. She went to him when he called for her. And the night she and I were summoned to dine with him — the night I asked him about Nebtu — she told me I shouldn't try to talk to him about things like that. *You don't just endanger your-self when you anger him,* she said to me. *You endanger all of us.* Was Ishtar's fate partly my fault? Was he still angry I asked about Nebtu and took it out on Ishtar? Maybe he couldn't remember which sister it was who had angered him.

The image of Ishtar's bruises faded, replaced by one of her broken body as it might have been after Pharaoh was finished with her. I closed my eyes and shook my head, trying to dispel the image. I couldn't let myself think about how he might have done it. Not yet.

"Is there any possibility Khaemmalu's informant is wrong?" Ettu asked.

I shook my head. "He doesn't seem to think so. I just..."

My voice broke and I swallowed hard. It was a little while before I could speak again.

"He has all the power," I said at last. "Why would he do such a thing? Is he truly so evil?"

"I have never really thought before about what evil would look like," Ettu said. "I suppose I didn't expect it to wear a crown."

"There must be something wrong with him. Deep down in his soul."

"What are we going to do?" Ettu whispered. She squeezed my hand again.

"I don't know," I said. "But if Pharaoh is responsible, I will make sure he is held to account."

"I think we should return to your chambers," she said. "The longer we stay here, the more we risk drawing attention. You are quite pale and it will be clear to anyone who sees you that something has alarmed you."

I barely noticed our journey back. I walked in a daze, not thinking or making plans, just concentrating on putting one foot in front of the other. Merytre let us in when we reached my chambers.

"You learnt something?" she asked.

Her gaze went from me to Ettu, and it was only now I realised Ettu was rather pale. I probably looked no better.

I sank down onto a couch. Now that I didn't have to worry about who was watching me, I burst into tears. I could hear Ettu's voice as I cried, but not her words. She must be telling them what Khaemmalu said.

Someone pressed a cloth into my hands and a mug of wine appeared on the table beside me. My tears continued unabated. My nose was running and I couldn't breathe and my eyes were so swollen, I wasn't even sure I could open them properly. When the tears finally slowed, the chamber was empty except for Tall, who sat beside me. I hadn't noticed him arrive. He patted my arm.

"Pharaoh!" he said. "Danger!"

The tears came again. Tall had known. He tried to tell me, but I didn't listen, just like I didn't listen when he told me I wouldn't be queen. I should have tried harder to understand what he was saying. Ishtar might still be alive if I had. I could have warned her. Could have sent her away from this place before it was too late.

"I'm sorry," I said between sobs. "I'm sorry I didn't listen properly."

Some time later, the others returned. They came one by one, Ettu first, then Ahmose. Half, then Merytre.

"We need to know for certain," Ettu said. "Half will take Ahmose's potion and see what he can discover."

My tears started again, less violent this time. I should tell Half not to go. That it wasn't safe for him since we didn't know who had stabbed him. But I needed certainty about Ishtar.

"Go," I said to Half. "But be careful."

"I will prepare the potion," Ahmose said, getting to her feet with a soft groan. "I have just enough left of my herbs to make two final doses. There will be no more, though, after that. Not until it is safe to restock."

She hobbled out, one hand on her lower back as if it pained her.

As we waited for sunset and the chance for Half to slip out through the gates, my mind was busy. If Ishtar was indeed dead, she deserved justice. That meant I needed evidence — lots of it — and someone who was willing to hold a god to account for his actions.

There was a time, not all that long ago, when I thought I might be able to be happy with this kind of life. But not anymore. Now that I knew about the abuses being covered up, I could never accept a life like this. Pharaoh was rich and powerful, and I was just one of hundreds of women he considered his own. Women whose lives he controlled in every way. Women he discarded when he was finished with them, as if they were no more than dirty rags.

I didn't have much of a plan yet, but I knew that whatever it was, my son would be part of it. It seemed clear there were others here who knew about, or at least suspected, Pharaoh's crimes, but they wouldn't stand up to him. Not to a god who held the power of life and death over them.

If Ishtar was to be avenged, it would have to be by me, and there was only one way I could hold Pharaoh accountable for his actions.

I needed to become powerful.

Someone to be feared.

Someone even Pharaoh would fear.

***

Kassaya's journey continues in
Book Four: A Game of Senet

ABOUT THE AUTHOR

Kylie writes about women who defy society's expectations. Her novels are for readers who like fantasy with a basis in history or mythology. Her interests include Dr Who, jellyfish and cocktails. She needs to get fit before the zombies come.

Swan – the epilogue to the Tales of Silver Downs series – is available exclusively to her newsletter subscribers. Sign up at kyliequillinan.com.